Death at Sunset

by
Don Rizzo

Death At Sunset

by Don Rizzo

Beverly Hills, FL - USA

ISBN   **978-1-937067-16-8**

For information or publicity,
Locksmithing Education, LLC,
12 South Lee Street
Beverly Hills, FL - 34465

donrizzo@donrizzo.com

ISBN 978-1-937067-17-5   31.95 USD

First Edition
10 9 8 7 6 5 4 3 2 1
Printed in the United States of America

Death At Sunset
by **Don Rizzo**
Beverly Hills, FL - USA

Chapter 1

Being a dispatcher in Sunset Cove was not without its visual rewards. Jim Sullivan returned the phone to its cradle, and went to the radio. He glanced out the window at the late afternoon Sun in the warm Florida sky and watched the palm trees sway gently in the breeze. It made him wish he was out fishing on the Gulf in his small boat instead of spending his retirement days working as a dispatcher where he had once commanded respect.

He glanced at the large analog clock on the wall and saw he had only thirty minutes till Sue Bennet replaced him on dispatch. He smiled, looking forward to the end of shift. When the phone rang his smile turned to a frown. Something told him that this was not going to be something small. He was right.

The caller was a Hispanic male named Jose Ramos, who stated he had just returned home from a short trip to find his condo burglarized and his girlfriend murdered. Jim shuddered a little, looking in the Chief's direction. But he knew what the Chief would say when he finally had to face him, and figured he might as well just do what needs done.

"827", he called into the microphone.

"827", Officer Kevin Wolf responded.

"827, see the man at Playa Del Sol condo number 206. Possible 1-8-7. Code Three."

"10-4", Officer Wolf responded, already reaching for the lights and siren indicated by code three.

When he arrived on the scene, he was disappointed to see that there were already news media vans and reporters crowding the parking lot.

"This cannot be good", he commented to himself as he exited the vehicle. He made his way through the crowd of reporters, ignoring everything they said or did. He ascended the stairs to the second floor and knocked on the door at 206 where he was greeted by an obviously distraught Hispanic male, about thirty years of age, possibly high. Kevin Wolf wondered about that, but concluded it probably was not important to discern if it was shock or drugs, at least at this point.

If the guy turned into a viable suspect, there was plenty of time to have him tested. "She's in the bedroom", the male stated. "She's dead."

"Slow down", Kevin said, "and tell me what happened."

"I flew to Fort Lauderdale this morning on business. I was not gone very long. When I got back she was supposed to pick me up in my car. But she wasn't at the airport and didn't answer my calls. So I took a freaking cab all the way here, and found her like that. Dead. And I called you guys and the Channel 10 news line."

'Why the news line?", Officer Wolf asked.

"I'm no dummy", the man responded. "I know you guys will try to pin it on me because I'm not white. I want the world to know I am innocent."

"In case you did not notice, I am not white either. I am of the Lenape tribe." "Whatever. You're still a cop."

"OK, well, what is done is done. You cannot un-call them now anyway. But let's go the rest of the way inside to finish our talk. OK?"

The male paused a moment, then stepped back and said "OK." Officer Wolf stepped inside and shut the door.

"That is better', he stated. "Now let's start again. I am Officer Wolf of the Sunset Cove Police Department. And you are?"

"Jose Ramos. I live here. Rebeccah is my girlfriend and she lives - lived - here too."

"OK. I am going to ask you to wait right here while I go take a look at her. Is that okay with you?"

"Yeah. I guess."

Kevin walked over to the bedroom, carefully noting everything around him as he did, and alert for any sudden movements on the part of Mr. Ramos. He passed a table that was perfectly clear except for a napkin rack, and appeared, from the pattern of dried streaks, to have been wiped clean fairly recently. The rest of the room showed no signs of disarray, either. A small travel bag sat next to the couch. The bedroom door was open, and he could see inside as he approached it.

"Was this door already open when you got here?", he asked. "Yes", replied Ramos.

"Did you touch anything inside?"

"No. When I got to the door, I could tell she was dead, so I didn't go any farther."

Officer Wolf nodded his head in approval. "That is very good", he stated.

He stepped into the room, careful not to step anywhere too close to the body or in any blood spatter. The girl was lying naked on her stomach with her head showing a large deep gash and the rest of her body showing many deep cuts. Blood had seeped from under her as well, so Kevin surmised the cuts were not limited to the back of her body. Her legs were spread fairly widely, possibly indicating sexual contact. The Medical Examiner would decide her cause of death, but it was obviously not accidental or a suicide.

The room was in a fair amount of disarray, and some of the blood spatter near the end of the bed had been stepped upon.

He clicked the radio on, and asked dispatch to send an ambulance and call the Medical Examiner. He then photographed the scene and exited the room, approaching Ramos.

"Take off your shoes", he commanded.

'My shoes?", Ramos asked.

"Your shoes. I need to examine them."

3

Ramos complied, and Kevin observed a small spot of spatter on one sole. "Want to tell me again whether you entered the room?", he asked.

"OK. I went into the room, but I didn't go anywhere near the body. I just wanted to see what was missing. I could tell from the doorway that the jewelry that we normally keep on the nightstand was gone, and I wanted to know what else, so I looked in the closet."

"The closet." Officer Wolf stated.

Responding as though it were a question, Ramos replied "We had some paintings and stuff in there. It's all still there."

Officer Wolf thought about it a moment. The blood on the shoe was minimal, not as though Ramos had been the killer, at least in Kevin's opinion. The forensic guys had the final determination regarding the evidence, but he felt confident he knew what their response would be.

"You say you took a flight to and from Fort Lauderdale and took a cab here from the airport?"

"Yes. I have receipts", Ramos said, reaching into his pockets. He pulled out an airline ticket stub and a cab receipt. The cab receipt had a date on it and nothing more.

"That cab receipt is blank", Officer Wolf stated.

"I guess he left it for me to fill out, thinking it would get him a bigger tip", Ramos answered. Officer Wolf knew that was typical of local cabbies. He nodded his head.

"We will have to confirm your alibi, of course, but if you are telling the truth that should be easy. On the other hand, if you are not, that will also be easy, but it will go hard on you."

"It's true", Ramos said. "You'll see."

"So you say some jewelry was stolen?"

4

"Yes, a lot of it. Her father was a jeweler in New York and he gave her lots of stuff, and she bought me lots of stuff with the old man's money. Lots of gold for me, and she liked to wear diamonds."

"If it is insured, there will be pictures of it."

"I don't know anything about that. If it was insured it would have been through her father, and he doesn't seem the type. But I have pictures of us wearing a lot of it."

"Are they on your phone?"

"I have some that are, but she liked to print them out. They're in the drawer in the living room area."

"I will need your phone for evidence", Officer Wolf stated, "as well as those pictures."

"Is that really necessary? I need my phone for business."

"If you don't want to go to jail, I need to be able to prove you called her from the airport, and I need pictures of the jewelry. Your phone is evidence."

Ramos reluctantly handed over the phone and went to the drawer he had indicated earlier and pulled out a stack of glossy printouts. He handed them to Officer Wolf.

"OK, I am going to ask you to sit at the table here until the Medical Examiner arrives and does his thing", Officer Wolf stated. "Touch nothing."

Ramos said nothing but sat down as Wolf placed a call directly to the Medical Examiner's office to be certain dispatch had contacted them and they understood the priority. Kevin's face lit up slightly when Joanie answered. He told her the situation and she stated the M.E. was already on his way. He arrived sixteen minutes later.

When the M.E. had finished, and the body had been removed, Kevin pulled the door closed and prepared to put yellow tape across the opening.

"Do you have somewhere else you could sleep tonight, until I can get the County forensics guys in? You can probably return tomorrow, though the bedroom itself will be off limits for a few days."

"Yeah. I can stay with friends."

"You DO understand that if you go back into the bedroom again prior to being Permitted, you can be arrested, right?"

"Got it. Can I take my travel bag with me, and is it okay to leave now, as soon as I put on some boat shoes from the bag?"

"Once you give me your keys, you can leave. I will need to look inside the bag before I can let you take it. Contact our dispatcher with a number and address where you can be reached, and stay in the area."

Ramos handed the officer the keys, picked up the small bag he had placed next to the couch earlier, watched as Officer Wolf inspected it, and left.

A few moments later, Officer Wolf closed the outer door and locked the deadbolt. He noted that the camera crews and reporters had left the scene. He completed applying the yellow tape and posted a sign on the door prohibiting entry and providing a contact number.

"Probably followed Ramos for a quote", he said aloud to himself in regard to the lack of news vans. "Hope he is smart enough not to give them one."

In his cruiser, he contacted dispatch, where Jim had been replaced for the evening three to eleven shift by Sue, and asked her to contact the crime scene forensic guys from the county, also giving her the details on the flight and cab to check out.

He had driven only a few blocks back toward the station when Sue's voice on the radio confirmed that the Crime Scene unit would be there in less than an hour, and that the flight and cab ride had been confirmed.

Kevin thought about it a moment, then turned back toward the condo to await the arrival of the forensic team. He waited while they worked, and when they had completed their examination of the area, he once again locked up the condo and started back to the station, this time uninterrupted. The sun was just beginning to set. His shift, which was in overtime now, would end once he returned to the station and filed his paperwork, and he could get some well- earned sleep.

Chapter 2

Five days earlier

At about 1 am in Sunset Cove, Florida, on the opposite side of town from the beach, the killer awoke as he almost always did at that hour.

The dark motel room was cheap and stank of alcohol and cigarettes that were not his. Through the window he had opened to let the air in and the stench out, the light from the neon sign, and its accompanying LED sign, stretched across the room and lit it with a red and pink hue like something out of a horror movie. The noisy clinks and clangs of the cheap air conditioner below the window fought against the sounds of tree frogs and the occasional sound of a passing motorist.

He quickly showered in the pale pink and black tiled bathroom with the white tub surround kit poorly fitted in place, always feeling like it might crack and send him to whatever lay beneath, but he had become accustomed to it over the past few days, and although it took his notice, it caused him no alarm.

He pulled his clothing on after the briefest of toweling, the dampness offering a resistance to the cloth of each piece. He had chosen a thick charcoal grey tee shirt and a pair of stretch denim trousers, along with grey socks and dark boat shoes.

He would take no identification or credit cards with him and only the least cash he thought he might need. If he were discovered and arrested he had no intention of making it easy for them to track him. Besides, once he located his victims he would soon have plenty of identification to use.

He quietly grouped the tools of his trade into various pockets for quick retrieval, with the garrote in his back left pocket and his knife in the right, its hilt covered by the tee shirt. He felt so much stronger and more complete with the two weapons in ready reach behind his back.

As he left the cheap motel room, he stopped briefly by the pool to read the papers left by the day's visitors as he usually did. In them he always learned much that would affect him, as well as learning about what competition he might have on the beaches.

This was his favorite time of the day, because he felt so free. In spite of the tree frogs, he could hear cars approaching from as far as six Florida blocks away and even footsteps were typically heard echoing from more than a block or two. With his habit of walking toe to heel and his soft boat shoes, his own steps would be nearly inaudible in the night winds.

He had a car, but he mostly just drove it from killing to killing, preferring to walk once he was in the right neighborhood. The proliferation of cheap motels in Florida made it easy for him to find housing close to his planned kills, and he had been covering much of the state for the last few months, trying to keep his profile low. It only took a few hours to get anywhere in the state and there were always cheap motel rooms to be found.

But so far, there was no one who suspected him, so the killer had finally felt safe carrying out business in his home area. As far as he could tell, no one anywhere had linked any of his killings across the state together, so he had pretty much free reign. Even though his most recent jobs had all been very rewarding and there was no financial need to continue, his own need persisted.

He always had several jobs in the planning. When each job was finished, he would move to the next one, funded by what he would gain financially from his victims as they shared their last moments with him. He did not collect trophies as many killers do. He took only things of value that could be quickly turned over, and identification that could be used and later sold.

Unfortunately, due to an increased activity involving some sort of group of kids burglarizing homes and causing increased police activity in this area, turning the proceeds and identification over had become a bit more risky and difficult, but that was all part of what you had to expect along the way.

Although he had been involved with the drug trade, and occasionally carried out a few kills related to that, it was his personally chosen kills that meant the most to him. His personally chosen targets were always chosen from days to weeks before being carried out, and he had watched them and recorded their habits until he almost felt like they were a part of him. And soon after the selection, each would be. Victims and killer would become one in the process of the killing. He knew that and it inspired him even more to feel free. He was literally taking their lives, making their lives his as they should have been. What had happened to his family was not right. It should have been him who was born into wealth. But he was taking his life back by taking theirs.

And he truly enjoyed punishing the ladies. They would fill his every wish and command. He was in total control of their bodies. And when he punished them he often thought of the night he had covered up his first murder. He always smiled when he remembered the intense scene and felt again the warmth it had brought him on an already hot and humid night. He thought of how she had last looked, strangled and stabbed and her throat cut, before he left and her world collapsed on her. She had made the fatal mistake of calling him a loser.

"Who's the loser, now", he thought to himself. He thought how she had looked with blood all over her body before he had disposed of it, and smiled widely.

As he walked, he passed a convenience store and was tempted to enter and buy refreshments of some sort, but he knew they would have a camera, and he did not want to be recorded on this trip. His tall, thin, ropy body and long legs would make him too easy to spot and remember.

He thought with joy about his soon-to-be victims. One of the benefits of his 'day job' was that its hours varied, allowing him a freedom to do things that many others would not have. He had followed them for three days, and knew them and their habits as though they were a part of him. Once again they were wealthy with no common sense. He regretted that lack of common sense in his victims a little, because it meant they were flawed and he hated making that flaw a part of himself. But they were young and beautiful to go along with their wealth, and that would make up for it. They were his fountain of youth. In their dying he would be reborn, and so would his finances.

Not that his finances were all that much in need of a rebirth, of course. From every kill he kept the best pieces and half of whatever cash he had acquired to save for a rainy day. He had been killing all over central Florida, and it could rain like Hell before it would make a dent in his savings. The cash alone accounted for many tens of thousands, much of it hidden carefully in places where no one was likely to ever find it except him. He even had a gym bag full of emergency cash in the trunk of the car. And he did not waste any of his acquisitions on fancy sleeping rooms or a shiny car. There would be a time for fancy things. But this was the time to collect his life.

He knew that with the release of their blood and life would come his own release, and the two experiences would become one, giving him back his youth, and making him once again feel like a successful and rich man who could do anything, as his family should have been when he was growing up.

That was important to him. He needed the frequent rebirth in order to exist. The hot Florida sun had begun to wither and leather his skin, making his image in the mirror appear old long before his time, and he was often no longer seen as a young rising possible winner.

People had really never been talking of his great potential or how successful he was. The duties of his job had remained essentially the same over the years. But when he had the rebirthings, he took on the vigor of life and people could tell that he still had his youth and now was a success. He could see the recognition in their eyes, feel it in their interactions with him. The killings were a necessary and vital part of his life. People could tell he was different after each of them. They saw him as he once had seen himself in the mirrors of his youth. Not that he was really all that old. But he wasn't young anymore, either. He no longer felt comfortable with the college crowd, and that told him he was getting older.

He finally arrived at the bar. Like most Florida bars, it was open until 2 am on Thursday through Saturday nights. And like many of them, when it closed, it only closed the front doors and turned off the lighted sign. The back and side doors, opening into a small unlit alcove, remained unlocked for the patrons who wished a little more of the Florida life than 2 am allowed.

11

He entered the alcove and then the main barroom, and chose a table near the rest rooms where he was certain he would see most of the patrons. He quickly spotted his next victims across the room, buying drinks wantonly for anyone who sat near them. Their excitement and life were so obvious to him he could taste it from across the room.

The jukebox played loudly enough that he could not hear most of what was said by them. In fact, he could barely hear what was said at the next table over. He did not particularly like this kind of music, but at the same time he knew it was the music of youth so he should at least seem to appreciate it. The room was large, with just the finest of clouds of smoke and dust hanging high close to the ceiling. He had been at many of the other bars in the neighborhood, and despite occasional signs prohibiting it, some were so stale with cigarette smoke you could barely see the bartender. But this place had high ceilings and large ceiling fans which drew the small amount of smoke in the room up quickly and held it there.

The two bartenders kept the four waitresses busy, filling tray after tray with the exotically colored drinks favored by the majority of this crowd. The waitresses wore plastic smiles that could actually have been made of plastic but were not. There was no emotion in the smile and the rest of their faces did not reflect the smile at all.

What conversations he could make out at all were injected with words like 'scooter' and 'Hobie Cat' said with a seriousness that hid the lack of content in the actual conversations of the widely smiling patrons.

But the killer was not interested in overhearing bits of conversation. He was focused on the couple in the center of the room and who were trying desperately to be the center of attention. He knew from his many nights of watching that soon they would leave the bar and go home and make love. Soon after that he would strike and they would become one with him. It was difficult to wait, but it heightened his sense of awareness of them and would make the completion far more intense.

In the corner opposite where he sat, a huge, muscled man in blue jeans and a white golf shirt pushed his table away with a grating, scraping sound and stood up. He ambled across the room, bumping into other customers and spilling their drinks. Several irate customers yelled at him and others yelled to their waitress for replacements.

One young customer jumped in front of him and threatened to take him on if he didn't replace the spilt drinks, but a quick undercut to the jaw sent the young loudmouth flying and he didn't get up from the floor where he landed. His friends and date quickly ran to his side and began sympathizing with him and praising him for his courage.

The mountainous man continued across the room ignoring everyone and everything in his way. The killer barely noticed him, assuming him to be on a bathroom mission. Usually in a place like this, when someone heads straight in a direction ignoring patrons and tables, making it to the bathroom is their clear goal. The killer continued to focus on the young couple in the center of the room, never realizing they were directly in the trajectory of the mass of flesh and muscle parting the tables and spilling drinks.

When they clashed it was horrific. The mountainous beast lifted the young man like a kite in the wind with a single hand, and threw him against the bar, his huge hand grasping the throat beneath the pale yellow shirt and squeezing tightly.

"You think you have all the answers, don't you, punk?", he ranted. "You think you are all that matters. You got more money than brains and you want to show it off to everyone. You don't care about the people who worked hard to get where they are. You just got to be in the center of it all. The whole world has to worship at your feet. You think you're better than everybody else. You think you're better than ME?"

Even though that probably would have described more than half the patrons that night, all of his anger was directed at the young man he had singled out, though the reason was patently unclear.

He hit the young man, the target of the killer's plan, crushing his nose and spraying blood over the woman with him. Then he released his hold on the man's neck and hit him with his other fist.

His rant and attack would probably have continued, even though what remained unbloodied of the young man's face was showing serious signs of turning purple, and in spite of various customers attempting to pull the big guy back, but the bar bouncer showed up with a breaker bar intended for the nuts on a truck engine. He seated it firmly on the back of the mountainous head, and the huge body went down without a gasp or a word. It also worked well on nuts like this one.

The bar manager's voice came over the sound system.

 "Bar's closed, people. We have to call the cops and an ambulance, and you don't want to be here when they arrive. You don't have to go home, but you can't stay here. Everybody out."

The killer knew that what the manager was saying was right, but he also knew this meant he could no longer follow the couple tonight. The young man would be waiting for the police and transported by ambulance, and his girlfriend would wait with him. In fact, they would probably be unreachable for several days. Fortunately he had other couples in the planning stage, so he could wait, but it meant no satisfaction tonight.

Tonight's incident would be described to police as a parking lot attack broken up by some unknown third party who struck with the breaker bar and then ran from the scene. The police would know who had wielded the breaker bar, but they would play along and even do a quick search of the area. The killer could not afford to draw attention to himself by hanging around during the interrogations.

His night was ruined. He was upset at the idea that his planning and execution would be worthless for at least another night. He felt betrayed. The couple would indeed pay for treating him this way, he thought, wondering for a moment if he had said it aloud. He was feeling helpless and he hated the emotions it exposed. But his anger would do him no good tonight, and he knew it. Slowly he walked back to the hotel.

As he walked across the parking lot, he was aware of the odors along the way. He could smell spots where other bar patrons had stopped to relieve themselves on the path to their expensive cars, and it seemed to degrade him even more. It was not only disgusting. It was an insult to him personally. They would pay for it someday, he muttered to himself, this time aloud, though not very. Someday every one of them would pay like the young couple would. But that day was not tonight.

Tonight he would simply return to the motel room and wait. Just outside the room door he encountered a large yellow and black Banana Spider, almost two inches in diameter, which dared him and challenged him, moving back and forth across the sidewalk in front of him like a wrestler. He took no pleasure in doing so, but he quickly and quietly stomped it to death, its large body flattened and its legs writhing independently with no clear direction. By morning the ants would carry away every trace of it. Even that thought brought him no change in feeling.

Once in his room, he stripped quickly, dropping his clothing to the floor, and laid on top of the bed staring at the ceiling and remembering and waiting. Eventually he would drift off to sleep and arise again in the light of day. The killer decided to take a day or two off from killing to reflect on tonight's events, and then perhaps do a late afternoon hit.

He had just the couple in mind. It was an excellent choice from several standpoints, not the least of which was that they were predictable. He had watched them for several days and their patterns rarely varied. Best of all, he could hit them right in their own residence in the middle of the day, so no one else could interfere, and their lifestyle promised to reward him enough to more than compensate for tonight's losses. But even that lovely thought did little to allay his mood.

Someone must have caused him to fail, he thought. In his mind he knew his plans do not go wrong, so if they did, there must be someone else to blame. But who could cause him to fail?

Who would? There had to be someone behind it. He knew with complete and absolute certainty that tonight could not be his own fault. Someone must be to blame, and he found it difficult to believe it could be the stupid loud-mouthed muscle man or the money and lust centered patrons of the bar. They could not outwit him and leave him feeling so small. They were all incapable of it. There MUST be someone else who somehow set it all in motion against him. And he WOULD find them.

But it was far too much to think about tonight. Finally, he went back to simply staring at the ceiling and waiting. Eventually he drifted off to sleep.

Chapter 3

That same night, in New York City

Even in the night, New York City streets have the ability to be both noisy and silent at the same time. As Michael approached the building which was his destination he was very aware of both aspects.

Sirens had to be distant, and the silence could not become absolute. Any change in either sound level bode poorly for his carefully established plan, putting an end to his painstaking efforts.

But there were none, and though it had taken nearly a hundred visits past the door over the months gone by to carefully transform an uncut key into a properly operating key for the lock, the key Michael had fashioned turned smoothly, and he was in.

The silence inside was almost deafening as he crossed the small lobby to the painting that he had fondly come to know as 'Speckles of Red mixed with Stripes of Blue and Yellow.'

No doubt the artist, if one actually had anything to do with its creation, had a different name in mind for it.

The bright colors and the smooth modern look of it clashed with the brown wood hues and the functional traditional design of the rest of the room. No doubt it had been selected not by the owner of the space but by the same alarm installer who had so carefully mortised the control box into the wall behind it and painstakingly hand-fed the alarm wires through the walls and joists so as to keep its location perfectly hidden.

Perfectly except to a person with some sense of design, that is. Still, Michael had very nearly missed it. It had taken three visits to the premises in three different disguises to locate and identify the alarm's control panel.

Credit should be given to its installer, whoever he was. Most alarm control boxes are merely slapped onto a wall, often visible from the entrance door or, at best, put into a closet or the cubbyhole under a flight of steps, and most wiring can be easily traced and bypassed.

This one had nearly thrown him. In fact, had Michael not found it on his third and last visit, the hit would have been cancelled.

But it hadn't been, and the painting swung out on invisible hinges to expose the control panel. He had already ascertained that it was on the standard factory key, and had studied its wiring diagram until he knew it inside out, forward and backward.

Once opened with the key, it took only twenty seconds for Michael to reset the wiring as well as could have been done with the remote keypad just inside the entrance door.

But nothing in the jewelry district is typical, and Michael knew from his studies of the place that already a guard was counting down the seconds before going to a full alarm condition at the central alarm station.

Learning the Alarm Company Central Stations' secret phone number for preferred subscribers and the code word to correct an after-hours opening of which the central station had not been properly notified had taken Michael a full two weeks of wiretaps.

No common thief could or would do that, no matter how many cops called him a pro. The average cop usually calls anyone above the rank of amateur a pro. When they talk about a professional thief they usually use the term quite loosely to describe a repeat offender who has graduated from the common smash and enter techniques to something a little less noisy.

Why not? Contrary to what crime prevention officers would have you believe, most police, even detectives, investigators and crime prevention officers, know very little about locks, safes, alarms, or burglary.

Ask them about the crimes against person - assault, armed robbery, rape, etc., and they know what they're talking about. They've seen and heard it all, more than anyone should ever have to.

But burglary is, by its very nature, a crime of secrecy, done without witnesses whenever possible. And the locks and alarm systems don't tell their story except to an expert.

And while expert forensic locksmiths and burglary specialists exist, they are usually called in by the insurance companies, not the city.

Michael picked up the phone and dialed the alarm company's secret number. When it was answered, he said: "Rainbow 4527."

True to form, the person at the other end said "What?" and Michael repeated, "Rainbow 4527. Sorry I forgot to let you know again."

"No problem. Have a nice night."

The other end clicked off and Michael was all alone.

Nevertheless, he tred across the room as quietly as possible in a room intended to prevent quiet travel.

His soft soles clicked and slapped the hard surfaces and echoed against the sloped ceilings. No one could cross it by day without being heard by its occupants.

But this was not day, and there were no occupants to hear him.

Michael passed a one-way glass acting as a mirror for the customers by day. He took a moment to confirm his appearance. The picture it returned seemed strange to him, but was exactly as he had practiced it. With the exception of his loose-fitting white cotton long sleeved shirt, he was dressed in black from head to toe. He had black shoes, black trousers, a black Jacket and a black hat. Two long strands of black hair curled down the sides of his face from the carefully trimmed black wig he wore, and his eyebrows had been darkened using water soluble mascara.

The last thing anyone would take him for was Michael O'Shea, the grandson of an Irish coal miner (on his father's side) and a Scotch-Irish thief (his mother's dear old dad).

Instead, if he were seen coming or going, he would be seen as a New York common sight, and later be interpreted as belonging in the diamond district, despite the hour.

On the other side of the room stood the next to last barrier to his target, a massive door secured only by an inexpensive cylinder in an otherwise sturdy mortise lock. It yielded quickly to the gentle strokes of his quality hand-made picks.

A lesser thief might have just used force on the door, or "bumped" open the lock using techniques shown in great detail on the evening news on slow nights, but these were techniques that increased the likelihood of being caught, and such was not a part of Michael's plan for the evening.

No amount of money could buy a pick set like these, made of precisely the best steel for it, formed in exactly the right shape at just the correct temperature. These were his Grandfather's task of manhood, and had proved his worthiness to learn the last of the family secrets.

The picks had been handed to Michael's father, and passed on to Michael, even as he would one day pass them on to his son, if he ever got married or otherwise acquired one, which was not looking very likely given his present circumstances.

Michael rarely dated, almost never the same person twice, and probably spent as much or more time with doctors checking to make sure he was still healthy as he did in the brief encounters that encouraged him to go to the doctors.

He enjoyed each of the women's company, and they had all been beautiful and intelligent and very sexy, but it always seemed to be lacking something.

Without that something, it did not seem real or to have any true potential. Michael wished he knew what that something was. It was a lonely life, but it was the life he had chosen, and one which rewarded him in many other ways. He took great pride in being a professional thief.

Inside the room stood several safes of varying sizes. The largest was one of the new European imports that are protected on all six sides against attack. Michael sincerely hoped not to have to tackle that one, but at the same time felt confident that he wouldn't have to.

The gems he was looking for were likely to be the least valuable items in the room. It was unlikely, therefore, although still possible, that they would be protected in a thirty thousand dollar safe.

In fact, as Michael had that thought, an odd idea struck him, and his eyes lighted on a four drawer file cabinet to his right.

He had it open in seconds. The top drawer was a disappointment. It contained only files, as did the second. But the third held a small cashbox with about $500 in assorted bills and change, which would help to cover his expenses.

However, it was the bottom drawer that rewarded his efforts. A small cloth bag full of tiny chips that could pass for cracked ice lay next to a tray with about a dozen gold rings.

Michael already had a buyer lined up for the diamonds. He wasn't there for the gold, and the last thing he needed on a caper this sweet was any sort of complications.

Nevertheless, he admitted to himself that he would be a liar if he said he wasn't tempted. There is something about gold that has caused the downfall of many a man and many a civilization.

Yet we are still attracted to it like moths to the flame. It blinds us. It can be, and often is, a fatal attraction, a deadly diversion.

But it would not be for him this time. Removing the stones he had come for, Michael quickly closed the drawer and relocked the file cabinet.

A forty inch tall stepped square door record safe next to the file cabinet was his next temptation.

Michael knew it offered little, if any, resistance to attack, and he could have it open in minutes, perhaps even by touch alone.

Who knew what wonders it might hold.

But his mind recalled the story of the Monkey Trap.

It claimed that monkeys are caught by filling a coconut attached to a chain with sweet sugar candy. A hole is made in the coconut just large enough for the monkey's hand and a couple of pieces of candy to pass through.

The monkey gets greedy, though, and grabs a handful, refusing to give it up, even when his hand is trapped in the coconut and his captor approaches.

Michael didn't remember where he first heard it, a book from his childhood perhaps, and he didn't even know if it was true, but the moral of the story was quite clear. And Michael wasn't ready to be caught.

He left the room and relocked its inexpensive cylinder.

One might wonder at such a considerate move when time was so precious, but actually it was to extend the time before his visit, and the theft, were noticed.

It was unlikely that anyone would be in before morning, but if they happened to be, Michael wanted as little to tip them to the burglary as possible. The longer it took to be discovered, the farther from the site he would be with the stolen items, and the less chance of being caught.

He crossed the room to the alarm panel, reset it to "alarm on" position, swung the painting back into place and quickly moved to the front door.

If Michael was not out within fifteen seconds, the alarm company's central station would again be notified, and this time a visit by their armed guards would be inevitable, possibly before he could get out of the neighborhood.

But he was out within ten seconds, the small cloth bag hidden in his loose clothing and his walk as careful, unhurried, and yet measured as it had been on the way in.

His footsteps had to be measured "just so", and must appear sure of themselves as though directed by habit. He was just another merchant, taking care of business late at night in the middle of the week

It is this sort of attention to detail that marks the true professional - detail and, of course, patience.

Twenty thousand dollars' worth of extremely small, basically meaningless, stones were now in his grasp and on their way to a Gypsy in Queens who would use them to authenticate the solid gold antique jewelry he would create from reclaimed brass melted down in his small travel trailer.

These family heirlooms would be greedily grabbed up for a fraction of their perceived value all across the country.

Some of his customers would never learn the truth, and they would be passed down through the generations as authentic, perhaps with the quaint story of how good old Gramps really put one over on the strange down-on-his-luck foreigner.

Because the stones were so small and of so little resale value through legitimate channels, they would barely be missed, and no real furor would be raised to trace them, which would have been nearly impossible, anyway.

"A nice clean hit", he reflected.

Of course, it's not twenty grand to Michael. His end of the take was 40 cents on the dollar. So that was only eight thousand, but it was still double what it would have been if he had to use a traditional fence.

And eight thousand for a month of part time work is not a bad wage in today's economy, especially because this was not his only job of the month.

Michael had set up the hit himself without a hitch, and told no one about it except the Gypsy, who he knew from past experience forgets how to speak English at the first sign of trouble, and never brags about his work.

The Gypsy's culture prevented him from learning to write, so there would never be a paper trail to trace, never a scribble found on a napkin.

"Nearly Risk-Free", Michael mused contentedly. At that point he had no idea of the events he had set into motion.

As Michael walked back toward the Port Authority bus terminal from the jewelry district, he suffered no feelings of guilt.

Guilt occurs when you do something that violates your sense of morality, ethics, and fair play.

He was playing by all the rules of the game as he had learned them. They may not be the officially published rules of the game as society claims to play it, but he was very aware that most of the players use house rules instead of the official rules, just to speed up the game and make it more interesting.

Nixon truly believed it when he said, "I am not a crook." and he was right. He played by the rules he had learned well, beginning in college.

In the U.S. Senate, he was a close associate of JFK and the two shared many illicit "dirty tricks" at the expense of those who opposed or threatened them.

Today one is a hero no one could believe capable of dirty tricks and the other a villain, even though both had played by exactly the same set of house rules.

Michael's rules, truly house rules in every sense of the word, were a family tradition. The males in his mother's family had been professional thieves since the family was stripped of its land centuries ago.

Michael had been raised to believe this was strictly "man's work". In fact, that is why his grandfather taught Michael's father instead of Michael's mother, even though she was the grandfather's own daughter.

As Michael walked down Tenth, he passed one of his favorite New York City spots – an eatery and bar owned by the wife of a fireman who died in the line of duty saving a kid long before 9-11 made NYFD popular.

Between the insurance and the monies collected by firemen all over the city, she had paid off their house in Queens and bought the restaurant and bar where he used to go to relax sometimes.

It was almost always packed, and most of her clientele were firemen.

She had a walnut pie that was generally considered without equal. Michael had spent many an evening there, but he was confident no one looking out tonight would recognize him.

A young couple sat at one of the outdoor tables, completely engrossed in each other's company, enjoying a piece of that pie as he walked by.

Michael envied them. Being a burglar did not lend itself to finding that special someone to spend your life with, and he always wondered how his Grandfather had accomplished it.

Finally he arrived at the Port Authority. A faint ammonia smell disrupted his thoughts and directed his attention to an old lady, wrinkled and shriveled to about 65 pounds, who was dragging about 40 pounds of garbage in plastic bags as she approached.

She was trying to be patient with her sister who was being foolish, but it was plain that before long she wouldn't be able to hold the anger in.

For a brief moment he wondered where her sister was, or if she ever actually had a sister.

He even wondered fleetingly if she was wearing a cellular phone and he was mis-judging her.

But before he could get too far with that train of thought, her patience finally reached its limits and the two sisters began an argument that could at best be described as a shouting match.

Although Michael couldn't hear the sister's side of the argument, it was plain that she didn't like being told what to do.

He couldn't blame her for that. He really didn't either. Maybe no one does.

But carelessly focusing on her had brought Michael very close to a Mutt and Jeff team of two cops who were thankfully too engrossed in conversation with a long-legged black hooker to notice him.

Mutt and Jeff were a comedy team from the Sunday papers of the fifties and sixties, Mutt tall and lanky and Jeff short and pudgy, but there was nothing funny about these guys.

The tall one had the look of a stone cold killer and the short one with the wiry moustache looked like he would enjoy giving real pain.

Two of New York's finest. In a city with as many cops as New York, it was inevitable that there would be some like these, but that didn't make it a good thing.

Michael never cared for crooked cops. Sure, a family man a little behind on his bills or wanting to give his family something nice for a change might look the other way.

That's human nature, but truly crooked cops like these were a crime against nature. They weren't cops with a weak spot. They were crooks with a uniform, and they were dangerous to everyone, especially guys like him.

The hooker was obviously nervous. She hadn't made her quota that night, and they thought she was trying to hold out on them. They were evidently right, because when Jeff reached into her low-cut red stretch blouse, he came out with one rather well-shaped breast with a mole at the base of it and a small fistful of money.

She made no attempt to replace the breast, but instead braced herself for the slap she knew was coming.

And when it came, she seemed almost relieved, even though it knocked her half way to the floor. Mutt told her to go back on the street until she earned as much more as she had tried to hold out.

When she asked for some dope, Jeff slapped her again. "No dope, sweetlips. Not 'til you earn it."

"But I did honey, I really did. I was only teasing about the money. I was gonna' give it to you. Honest I was. Please, just a little dope. I don't mind goin' back to work, honey. I just need a little dope is all."

Michael would have liked to stay around until he found out if she won or not, but he was still a little too close to the scene, and soon one of them could have noticed him, which was the last thing a professional thief needs.

The fact that no one else seemed to notice or care bothered Michael a little. But he supposed the betrayal of trust and the presence of violence were simply signs of the state of civilization.

Shakespeare's Macbeth said it so long ago.

"I have supped full with horror. Direness familiar to my slaughterous thoughts cannot now give me start."

There isn't a reason, or if there is, it's MacGregor's Rat.

MacGregor was a scientist who found that rats multiply at a faster rate when the food supply is good, but when their multiplication reaches a certain point, super-rats are born that are larger and more aggressive.

As each fights for his share of the pie, the rat population begins to dwindle.

And when the population dwindles, no new super-rats are created.

An interesting phenomenon that might explain the random factor.

Call it the balance of nature. When scientists developed better and stronger antibiotics to fight disease, they often found that the antibiotics also kill the so-called "friendly microbes", creating newer and more deadly diseases that couldn't be controlled by the antibiotics. Nature always finds a way.

Michael casually but quickly turned up the short stairs toward the Eternal Commuters, their white plaster features frozen in the act of waiting for a bus that would never come, to take them from Nowhere to Nowhere.

Somehow those statues seemed to say everything there was to say about that place. He increased his pace and moved to the gate where the clock on the wall told him that his bus would soon take him to Secaucus, New Jersey, where his van was parked, and after a brief meeting with the Gypsy in an abandoned lot there, he would drive home to the Lehigh Valley in Pennsylvania.

As he crossed into Pennsylvania on old Route 22. Michael once again found himself leaning into the familiar turns in Cemetery Hill Curve, as though his weight could balance his light van against overturning.

No matter how many times he traveled it, his body's reaction was always the same.   As he rode it out, he felt the pangs of sorrow for the truckers who had helped it to justify its name over the years.

It was originally named for the fact that the curves were necessary to wind around and between the cemetery, but its name had proved to show great foresight as well.

Soon it was well behind him and he was turning onto the narrow road that would lead to a narrower road, and eventually to his home nestled in the tall trees that shaded it against the summer sun and the winter snows.

The small stones comprising the little-used road rumbled under the weight of the tires, but he barely noticed.

Actually, it was not officially his home, or at least not Michael's. It belongs to one Brian Stonewell, who never existed. Nonetheless, he owns a few local businesses and does reasonably well for himself.

Unlike Michael O'Shea, a somewhat down on his luck consultant in New York City with an office on the second floor of an off-Broadway converted loft building, Brian was a pillar of the local community, donating to charities, helping with fund-raiser dinners, and giving speeches to local youth groups.

Thanks to his grandfather's insistence, Michael was lucky enough to get two Social Security cards at a young age, back before they started computerizing and beefing up the identification system.

He had been a cautious taxpayer ever since his teenage years, preferring to overpay rather than underpay, in both his roles.

Many investment counselors had tried to convince Brian to protect his money by investing in tax shelters, and were astounded that such a successful businessman wouldn't use the advantages the tax system would give him on these.

He never used the term "low profile" to them, or perhaps they might have understood, which was far from the top of his priority list of things to hope for.

Michael rested in his home that night, and well into the next morning, to recover from the previous night's vigilance.

When he arose, he followed his usual morning routine and then dressed to make the deposits.

Breakfast was taken at a small diner on Hamilton Street that was frequented by a wide cross section of the population. He had a bagel with cream cheese, toast and two cups of coffee with French Vanilla flavoring to sweeten it.

As Brian, he deposited $1,000 Brian had allegedly earned in consultant fees into his account at his local bank.

Then Michael drove to Philadelphia, where he deposited $7,000 in proceeds allegedly from Brian's other businesses with the teller who greeted him with a warm smile, bright eyes, and a cheery "Good Morning, Brian."

She was quite attractive, and he found himself wishing he could find a soulmate to open up to and share his life. But it probably wouldn't be her.

Still, it's always nice to be recognized.

Or maybe it's not.

Chapter 4

Four days before the murder, in New York City

Once the deposit was made, Michael drove to Secaucus and took the bus back into the city, where he walked the short distance from the Port Authority to his office.

The office was on the second floor of a loft building on the corner of Forty-second street and Broadway, just off Times Square, and above a small store. There is a small door in the alcove by the store entry, and inside is a corridor.

At the end of the corridor is an elevator which would never meet code in any city other than New York. The elevator operator (no automatic controls here) is the first line of defense against the dregs of the city who might otherwise try to sleep in the hallways, and after hours both the first floor corridor and the elevator were locked up tightly.

The place is a remnant of the time when Forty-second Street was littered with porn stores and girlie joints. Guys had once stood out front, saying "Girls. Girls. Girls. Just one flight up." But those days were long gone.

Basically now, unless you know who or what you are looking for, you don't see anything on any of the upper floors. The fourth floor people get even more security. The main elevator only goes to the third floor, and there is a second elevator that goes only between the third and fourth floors, and a third from the fourth floor up to the top levels. Michael had never asked, nor particularly wished to wonder, what goes on up there, or why anyone would have designed such a system.

Michael was sitting at his desk in the small New York office of Michael O'Shea, General Consultant, updating the books and records to reflect the money he had so recently earned by doing whatever it is that general consultants do. The majority of his time in the office was usually spent reading the magazines and newspapers, including online newspapers, watching for clues pointing to a worthwhile target.

He was in the middle of a newspaper article about a new set of paintings on display at the Museum of Modern Art. Art theft had always fascinated Michael, but tended to be sort of a specialty. You have to know exactly what you are looking for and where to sell it. Michael had handled a couple of pre-assigned art hits over the years, but would never want to do a job like that on speculation. He turned the page finally, looking for anything else of interest.

The knock at the door startled him. He got very few visitors at that door. And fewer yet turn out to be Hasidic Jews when he answered it. Considering his activities the previous night, this was not a welcome sight by any means.

The two younger ones both stood well over six feet tall, and looked as if they might spread lox on Jeeps for a midnight snack. Their faces were almost as long as their beards, and their skin had a craggy, beaten look that said they didn't spend a lot of time smiling. Their clothes bound in spots, showing a lot of hidden muscle beneath their baggy appearance. And their eyes had the look of death in them – cold, hard and ever calculating. A vision of rattlesnakes quickly entered Michael's head and then was gone.

The older one who stood between them looked frail and withered in contrast. But if you looked closely, you could see he was far from either. Looking closely, Michael could see the visitor was something else also. He was Shemuel "Sam" Levine, the victim of a recent burglary in the Jewelry district that Michael knew a bit too well. It was Sam who spoke.

"Michael O'Shea? Yes, I see that you are. I may step in?" It was really more of a quiet order than a question.

But literate son-of-a-gun that he could be, Michael wittily replied, "Uh, Yes", and stepped back to allow Shemuel to do so. While Michael's mind raced down a thousand alleyways, he quickly pulled his face back into shape and began the practiced routines that his mind would not have been able to create just then.

Michael smiled and said, "I'm sorry if I appear startled. Most of my customers are referrals from other customers and contact me by phone." Proudly, his face held its newly gained composure when the visitor replied.

"Most of your customers never see you, which is just the way a burglar such as yourself prefers it. Is it not?"

"My sons can wait in the hall", Shemuel continued, not waiting for a reply. Nodding slightly as if to confirm it, he repeated, "They will wait in the hall and see that we are not disturbed."

"It's impossible that I gave myself away", Michael thought, reviewing everything in his mind, and yet, standing in front of him was clear and indisputable proof that somehow he must have. Frustration didn't even come close to describing what he felt at that moment. This was recognition he could well have done without.

Moving toward the window, Michael sat down behind his dark wooden desk in what executives sometimes refer to as the seat of power. It was carefully arranged to take advantage of Feng Shui and grant power to the man behind the desk. But Michael felt powerless as the small man who sat in the uncomfortable chair across from him continued to speak.

"I tell you what I am about to for the purpose of saving us both wasted time. It is safe to assume that you have already disposed of the stones. If you did not already have a buyer for them, you would have taken the gold rings also, would you not?

"Further, it would be an unconventional market where you could get perhaps thirty cents on the dollar rather than the more usual twenty. If you were using a standard fence, he would have bought the rings as well."

This guy was asking all the questions, but he didn't have to wait for Michael to answer because he had most of the answers too, even if his monologue was not totally correct. Michael wondered, almost aloud, "What gives?"

"The money will already have been secreted into quiet, legitimate outlets of one sort or another where they will remain relatively liquid, and yet would be quite difficult for an outsider such as myself to locate", Shemuel continued.

"I see that you are shocked, Mr. O'Shea. Your face and eyes say that you are innocent, but twice as I spoke your mouth wanted to reply or question me, and did not dare to. And now you are calculating how much I know and how to best handle it, are you not?"

As before, the question required no answer. But even so, Michael was not expecting what followed it.

"That is good. Your Grandfather would be happy to see how well you have learned."

The air came out of Michael's lungs in one massive sigh of shock and relief as the muscles of his body relaxed from their state of panic. The crisis was over. Whatever the situation was, there would be a livable solution.

"You knew him?", Michael asked, almost timidly.

"He was a business acquaintance of my father. You bear a strong resemblance to him. That is why I noticed you when you entered my store, no doubt surveying it. I met him many times when I was younger.

Those were not good times for the Jew, you know, and many things that rightfully belonged to the Jewish people instead rested in evil hands.

"Sometimes your grandfather would, how did he put it? . . . Yes, 'liberate' such pieces. He needed a buyer for them. What more logical choice than to return them to their rightful owners for a small fee, which we were more than willing to pay. Your grandfather selected my father as his contact. Only my father knew who was slowly returning the objects to us."

"I never met your father, though my own father pointed him out to me one time as a good person to know and remember, who could be very useful.", he continued.

"And now here we are."

Michael was speechless for a moment, acutely reflecting that the man had just stolen his best line. But he doggedly continued on, trying to form a response.

"So, assuming that what you have told me is true", Michael began, "What's the point? If you're so sure that I stole something from you, which I'm not admitting, already sold it and buried the money, what are you after? Why are you here?"

"A fair return on my investment", Shemuel replied. "Stones that small would have been difficult to sell. I might have ended up with thirty cents on the dollar myself. They were part of a purchase, however, of enough value to justify their price as a part of the package.

"Still, a man should get something for his money, should he not? What I would like is your services, for one time only. I will pay your expenses, and you will in turn locate a particular piece of my property and see that it gets safely back to me, no questions asked, and no finder's fee, although I will cover your expenses.

"If you find something else there that you like, that is not my concern. Take it if it pleases you. The object is all I care about. Are we agreed?"

To which Michael could only reply, "No."

It was Sam Levine's turn to be shocked, and he didn't hide it well. If his jaw had dropped any lower it would have dribbled on the floor like a bounced and forgotten basketball. His eyes were wide with questions and disbelief, and his mouth could only utter a quiet, almost whining, "What?"

"Look, pal", Michael said in his best Leo Gorcey voice (practiced after many late nights watching black and white movies from the past), "I think it's just fine and dandy that my grand-dad and your dad was pals. Don't get me wrong. But it's a long trip from there to the slammer, and it's a visit I ain't especially overanxiously perspirin' to make. See?

"I try not to even work for fences because they know too many people and tend to talk too much. But a guy like you, with a grudge on your shoulders about whose this 'object' rightfully is, has probably been blabbing it all over town, which this town really ain't so small, y'know?

"Further, if the guy what's got it knows you think it's yours and that you want it back, it won't be hard for him to figure out where it is when it goes missing. First thing you know, he's at your door, you're pointing the finger, and I'm on the lam. No dice, pal."

Michael then shut up, smug and assured that he had firmly closed the subject and gained the upper hand.

Quietly Shemuel spoke again, "You are wrong, Mr. O'Shea. No one, including my sons out there, know of this. Had my daughter Rebeccah known of it, I might not be in this position. And fortunately, the man who has it knows nothing of its real nature or value."

"So just what exactly is its real nature and value?", Michael asked.

"I can only say that it is of significance to the Jewish people. It is a vital part of our heritage that was entrusted to me for safekeeping many years ago. Recently I hid it on the back of a small and ugly painting, one of a set of three that came with my alarm system. You've already seen one of them, have you not?"

Michael didn't answer him. Instead, he asked, "So what happened?"

"My daughter is now a young lady, or so I should call her, with a streak of wildness in her. Young people today don't understand the value of tradition. So she wears too much make-up, all the wrong kinds and colors of clothing, and makes all the wrong decisions.

"Most recently she moved out of the house into a condominium in Florida with a young man who lives too well and too quickly. Knowing that I don't like the paintings, they had become her favorite, and, along with some other items, she took two of the three with her, the third being attached to the burglar alarm box. So, you see the position I am in? I would send my sons to collect it but I believe they would be rather noticeable near the beaches in Florida."

Michael thought about it. If everything was as Shemuel claimed, the job should be a breeze. But where, as the actors say, was the motivation? Getting something back for Shemuel was just great, but what's in it for Michael? Michael was not primarily in the business of helping others, after all, and this wouldn't be tax deductible, even under the Brian identity.

"Tell me a little about the guy", Michael said.

"You'll take it then?"

A little too anxious, Pops. Now Michael knew for sure that Shemuel had no hard evidence that Michael had pulled the job with the diamonds. In fact, Shemuel was probably beginning to wonder if he was even right about it.

"I didn't say that. I said to tell me a little about the guy."

"I'm sorry", Shemuel said, and Michael found himself believing he really was. "His name is Jose Ramos. He's slightly older than her, tall, thin, and dark. His clothes are tailor-made and he drives a new sports car. But neither the clothes nor the car fit him quite right. One can sense a wrongness about him. His lips smile, but not his face.

"I don't know where he's from, but he sometimes speaks a kind of gutter Spanish - not clean, but as if he were spitting instead of talking. You can hear the radio in his car for a great distance as he drives away. His condominium in Sunset Cove is one of the more expensive in the area. This is all that I know about him. This, and that my daughter is with him, and they have the painting."

"It's enough", Michael heard himself saying before he fully realized that he had decided to take the job. "He's trying to buy respectability. That's why the clothes, the car, and maybe even your daughter. His money came too quickly, probably from drugs. His type has a tendency to collect things of value and leave them in plain sight, so I should be able to come out of this at a profit. Can I depend on you to handle any jewelry I grab while I'm there?"

Shemuel obviously hadn't thought in that direction, and the decision didn't come easy to him, but he said "Yes". If he hadn't, the deal would have been off then and he knew it.

They discussed expenses, and Michael got the rest of the details from Shemuel, including all his contact information. Michael arranged to see a picture of Sam's daughter before he ended the conversation. It was easy for Shemuel to describe the exact painting he wanted. It was speckles of yellow mixed with stripes of red and blue. The third in the set, which Shemuel didn't care about, was, of course, speckles of blue mixed with stripes of red and yellow. The artist had a vivid imagination.

Michael went to his desktop computer and arranged a coach seat on a discount airline. He was surprised the penalty for last minute sign-up, though quite annoying, was not as bad as he expected. Surprisingly, he got a flight with only one stopover.

Chapter 5

That same morning

In Sunset Cove, Florida, the morning sun shined brightly in Margaret Hoover's large, well-appointed kitchen. Margaret bent over the oven and smelled the rich aroma of the soft mincemeat cookies she was baking. Her grandsons were visiting this weekend and she looked forward to their excitement when they saw the cookies, which were their favorite. The cookies were not quite done yet, so she closed the oven door and returned to the table in her large eat-in kitchen.

The house was a two story wooden structure, which was rare in this part of Florida, but it was still solid. Jack had always taken good care of it, treating the area for termites regularly even though they never saw any. She took a moment to remember him and appreciate their many years together before he had passed.

Now the home was a bit too much for her. Five bedrooms, a Florida room, a game room complete with pool table and plenty of room to play, a large eat-in kitchen, a huge dining room, a traditional Southern library, complete with walls of dark wooden bookshelves full of books, a screened porch larger than some homes she had seen, and two full bathrooms is a lot for one person alone.

When her six children had lived there, it had been a marvelously appropriate home, and when the family got together, with all the grandchildren, it still was.

But that was now just two times a year - Christmas and Thanksgiving. And the time each family spent there grew less each year as competing priorities surfaced. She knew that soon it would truly be only her in the huge home, its walls echoing in the absence of other sounds.

But the neighborhood was a nice one, with houses just far enough apart to provide privacy yet within comfortable distance to permit gossip visits, which Pearl, her neighbor on the left, truly enjoyed.

Margaret liked Pearl, though she always wondered if Pearl gossiped about her to the other neighbors.

Margaret's musings were interrupted by the ringing of the door chime, a baritone clanging of a short riff from a familiar tune.

Looking through the screen she saw three young boys, somewhere between seven and twelve years of age. The tallest was red-haired and freckled and for a moment she was reminded of Howdy Doody from her childhood television. The shortest had straw colored hair and a sort of bashful yet egregious look that reminded her of Opie from the television series she remembered as Andy of Mayberry. The third was a black child, skin the color of rich chocolate, which was rare in her area where most "non-whites" tended more toward a dark tan. He had the friendliest face of the three, and it was he who spoke.

"Is Dickie Peterson here?", he asked.

"No", Margaret answered, "I think you have the wrong house. I don't even know him."

She wished the cookies had been finished so she could offer them to the boys. They seemed like such fine children and Margaret really loved children and missed having them around more often. It was ten-thirty in the morning on a school day, and she wondered for a moment why they were not in school, but realized it was probably a "teacher's in-service" or one of the other excuses schools have these days for not taking the time to actually teach. Margaret was very critical of modern education, especially the amount of time spent on standardized testing and presentations rather than teaching. Her grandchildren were brilliant in her mind, but much of their homework seemed to her to be less than they were capable of handling, and focused more on art and projects than real learning.

"Sorry", the tall red-haired boy said, interrupting her thoughts, "I think it might be the next street over."

The boys turned and walked away.

"Such nice kids", she thought, as she closed her door.

She did not follow their path or she would have wondered why they stopped at Pearl's house next. And at the house to Pearl's left, and the one after that, until they finally came to an empty home where the occupants were at work.

They then smashed a window near the door, reached in and unlocked the door, and began to ransack it looking for valuables to fill their backpacks with.

When the homeowners returned for lunch a short while later, they phoned in the incident to the Sunset Cove Police department, where Jim Sullivan was still on duty and took the call.

"Anyone on the West Side?" he broadcast.

"833",

Jim smiled. 833 was Mickey Clements, the youngest member of the force. Mickey was probably on the West Side delivering bags of peanuts to the stores and bars and eateries there. Mickey thought it was a secret that he did it on police time, but even though Sunset Cove was the fourth largest city in the county, it was still basically a small town in many ways, and too many people were involved to keep an item like his side business very secret.

"833, go to 1243 Primrose. See the lady. Report of a burglary."

"Roger that. 10-4."

Jim paused a moment, staring at the Chief's office, then went to the door and knocked. When invited, he entered.

John Lawson sat behind his large wooden desk, a throwback to an earlier time. The rest of the offices had all been modernized years ago, with smooth operating metal desks, but Lawson liked the feel of being behind a wooden desk. It reassured him when times were tough, comforted him during times when things were sad, and seemed to share the joys of his successes. He was not sure exactly how an inanimate object like a desk could do that, but it did, at least for him.

Lawson was a big man, everyone said. But he knew he was not that much taller than others and not all that big boned or muscular, so he wondered where it came from. But constantly people would say to him things like "That's easy for you because you're a big guy. I'm a lot smaller. It isn't as easy for me."

Jim looked at Chief Lawson. He could see the Chief was having a good day, had finished his coffee and bagel, and was relaxed. Most people had a hard time reading the Chief, because his features were kind of stony most of the time - rigid and unmoving. But Jim had worked with him long enough to be able to read him fairly well.

"Got another burglary in the West end. Looks like the three kids again."

"Wonder what they will look like today", the Chief said, "Who do we have on it?"

"833.", Jim replied.

"Smart kid. He will know to interview all the neighbors and get a few descriptions. Was he already working the West end when the call came in?"

"I think he was visiting local businesses", Jim answered.

Lawson said nothing to that. He did not want to publicly acknowledge what they all knew, but at the same time did not want to seem out of the loop by implying he thought Mickey was just visiting businesses for the good will of the Police department.

"This case should have been closed long ago. Well over eight months of this already, and what do we have so far?", he asked.

Although the Chief had intended it a rhetorical question, Jim responded. His eagerness to do so reminded the Chief that Jim had once been a ranking officer.

"Burglars seen by many witnesses, with totally different descriptions. Not really much to go on.", Jim replied.

Chief Lawson pondered that a few moments before continuing. In the silence the tall cherrywood 'grandfather clock' in the office ticked away audibly. He moved some papers around on the desk without much concentration on the task, and focused on his thoughts.

"That is what bothers me the most about this case, the descriptions varying so much. These kids have been seen by many people, so we should have a clear picture of them, but instead we have dozens of different descriptions.

Makes no sense. People are not all that reliable as witnesses in general, but this takes it to a whole new level."

"No argument there", Jim muttered, "and it makes us look bad."

How the force was perceived was important to him. Jim had been a patrolman many years earlier, and after twenty successful and reasonably happy years on the force had "retired" from the streets and begun as dispatcher.

When he started dispatching, computers were in their infancy and he had a dumb terminal attached by phone line to the County Sheriff's office where a room-sized computer ran huge reels of tape to access the new NCIC database and the Florida DMV records.

He was known for constantly reminiscing how it was in those days. It was still sharp in his mind. To run a computer search for a vehicle with a 1971 Florida tag of FHY341 that had been stopped back then, he had to type:

QT. TGS/FL. TGY/71. TAG/FHY341.

Then he would wait and a couple minutes later, out would come the description of the registry. To also find out if it was wanted (a 10-29 request) he had to type:

QW. TGS/FL. TGY/71. TAG/FHY341.

And if he got the name of the individual to whom it was registered he would have to do a 10-28/10-29 (warrants and history) check on the person, which meant for the history on a Thomas Butters, he would have had to type:

QH. NAM/Butters,Thomas. DOB/10-28,49. SEX/M.

And after each search, the same few minutes wait for an answer.

Worse yet, the computers at the Sheriff's office, the phone lines, and the dumb terminals back then all had really unreliable connections and were constantly malfunctioning and going down, sometimes for days at a time. It was not uncommon to get a 'want' back on a stopped vehicle three days after it had been stopped and released.

Today the entire process took less than five seconds, with no complicated syntax to remember. Yet, back then the public thought the Police were practically gods. Today people generally had no faith in the department at all. It made no sense to him.

"Council brought up switching to FDLE or Sheriff's office and shutting us down to save costs again at last night's meeting", Chief Lawson commented. "A break in this case would really help us right now. It got voted down again, but they keep bringing it up every few months, it seems."

"I'm sure Mickey will do his best today. He's a good officer, and people like to answer his questions. I think it's his boyish charm", Jim responded.

"I'm sure he will."

The Chief went back to reading the folder in front of him, and Jim took it as a sign of dismissal, turned and left the office. He returned to the dispatch desk to await Sue's arrival at 3 pm to replace him. It was a few hours away yet, but he would watch the clock until she arrived unless something new came in.

Chapter 6

Three days before the murder

It was the kind of day Larry Evanston enjoyed. There was enough sun to keep it warm, but sufficient breeze to offset it and keep it from being considered hot. He and his partner, the rookie Don Falcone, were in a Sunset Cove city cruiser on their way to the Saint Petersburg Sheriff's Office. The day permitted them to drive with the windows open and the air conditioner off, which was a blessing. Cruisers tend to pick up a lot of backseat odors that creep into the air conditioning system, making it annoying on hot days.

As Larry drove, Don continued making phone calls to the local taxi companies, bus lines, and other forms of mass transportation, trying in vain to figure out how the stolen goods moved from Sunset Cove to the considerably distant St Petersburg pawn shops. He had his notepad open and was taking down statements, as well as the phone numbers and contacts of drivers who might be more knowledgeable about who had ridden the conveyances. Then he phoned each of them also. A lot of people preferred digital recording devices, but Larry had trained Don to do it old school, where you could more easily review the notes and make comparisons that might be missed in a sequential digital recording.

Larry, noticing the frustration on his partner's face, waited till Don was between calls, and then asked, "No good news, I guess?"

"Less than none", Don responded. "These kids HAVE to have an adult driving them. That was the last of the drivers of the last of the three taxicab companies. Just as with the drivers for the bus line, no kids rode any major distances."

"Well, disappointing as that may be, it is still a clue."

"Yeah, but one that doesn't enlighten us any."

"It is what it is. Let's just hope Ted has some better news for us."

They took the exit ramp onto Seminole Boulevard, then took the right that led them downtown. The Sheriff's office was in a three story brick building with a set of prestigious statues adjoining its doors. It was a leftover from a time when the offices were considered an important part of the city architecture. Larry smiled, noting to himself the difference between that and the sleek modern offices of his own department. But as impressive as it looked, a towering jail with tiny windows stood behind the building, and dwarfed it. The presence of the jail took away the office structure's illusion of historic significance.

An elevator took them to the second floor, its gears whining the whole time. They entered the office marked 'Detectives" and moved quickly to the small office in the back right corner, occupied by Ted Whiting. Unlike the desks in the outer office area, Ted's desk was clutter-free. His shelves were neatly organized and the file cabinets labeled clearly. Ted was shorter than Larry, but taller than Don. He had a slight paunch around the waistline, a military style haircut, and wore black plastic framed glasses. He remained seated as they entered his office.

"Have a seat, gents", he stated flatly. "How are y'all doing today?"

"Not bad, all things considered", Larry answered. " How by you?"

"I made a little progress with the list you Faxed over, so I guess it goes well enough", he responded, "but the news may not be what you are hoping to hear."

"How so?", Larry asked.

"Most of the items on your list that are traceable did appear in the local pawn shops. But none of them were pawned by the same individuals, and no one remembers the person pawning any of them being accompanied by a minor."

"So it is a dead end."

"Not entirely. Some were pawned by recognized vagrants, and most of the others were by servicemen either here on leave or stationed nearby."

"How does that help us any?", Larry asked, missing the connection between that and good news. Don remained silent. This was Larry's part of the show.

"It forms a pattern. I interviewed the ones I could locate, and all of them were approached by kids who claimed their mother was sick, and they needed to get food and medicine for her, so they were trying to sell some household things. But, they claimed, the mean guy in the pawn shop would not do business with them because they were just kids. So they were having to do without food, and their mother could not get the medicine she needs. With the kids practically in tears, the military people they approached felt they were doing a good thing by pawning the items for them."

"And the vagrants? Same thing?", Larry asked, beginning to see the picture more clearly.

"Almost. The kids offered to split the proceeds with the vagrants, giving them a third of whatever they claimed they got. But even some of them felt obligated to not take it."

"Smart little bastards", Larry muttered, almost under his breath. "They have to have an adult laying all this out."

"Seems that way to me, also" Ted answered.

"But it still doesn't help very much."

"Not so far", Ted answered, "but there is hope on the horizon. The last list you sent us, there are some rare collectible coins on it. We have put every pawn shop, coin and jewelry store in the area on alert. If anyone tries to sell them, the managers will call me immediately and try to stall them till deputies can get on the scene. Hopefully, the kids will still be waiting outside. And if not, at least we will have a fresh witness."

"A fresh witness won't do us much good, in all likelihood. These kids have been seen by many people and for some reason, the descriptions are all over the place."

"Well, then, let's hope they are still waiting when we get there."

"Sounds like a good plan to me", Larry said, his voice hopeful. "I really appreciate all your help."

"It's what we are here for", Ted answered modestly.

"Yeah, but you are really good at what you do. You run a tight ship in a loose world."

"Flattery will get you everywhere", Ted joked.

"I mean it sincerely", Larry stated. "You're a professional and that is a rare commodity anymore." He rose from his seat, and Don did the same.

"Nice to have met you", Don said.

"Oh, Ted, I forgot you two aren't acquainted", Larry said awkwardly. "This is my partner, Don Falcone."

Don secretly felt a moment of pride and relief that Larry had not mentioned he was still a rookie.

"Nice to meet you, too, Officer Falcone", Ted responded. Don nodded acknowledgement. The pair then turned and left the office, Larry saying "Thanks again" as they did

Chapter 7

The day before the murder

Michael's flight to Florida was a memorable one. Not that it was an enjoyable one, of course, just memorable, much like lasagna in a cheap restaurant. But having scheduled it with only two days advance, he was given few choices.

He flew out of Pennsylvania on a mid-morning flight in a British Aerospace B131, which very much resembled an antique Volkswagen Microbus that someone had fitted with wings and a pair of wobbly propellers. The seats were half the standard width, and the aisle could only be walked sideways. Needless to say, a businessman with a fifty inch waist found it nearly impossible to traverse it sideways as well, and after several feeble attempts, finally settled into the two twenty inch wide seats across the aisle from Michael.

Michael longed for a non-stop flight on a wide body 1011, but without that possibility, he was pleased as punch to land at Washington Dulles Airport and change planes to a jet aircraft, any jet aircraft.

The shuttle across the airport was packed as usual, so Michael anticipated the likelihood of the loss of his luggage, at least for a few days. Before they started searching checked luggage it had been worse, though. At least now, the last person to have checked it would leave their identification in it, leading to questions from above if it turned up missing or if anything from it disappeared.

But his pleasure wasn't over yet. The jet turned out to be a 727 model 100. Most of the respectable airlines use the series 200 as their bottom of the line aircraft and the better ones use a 747. From the 200 up, they are comfortable, functional, and relatively economical to fly. Some of the discount airlines even have a considerable amount of legroom. Michael would normally have preferred to fly on at least a 737 on Southwest or True Blue and get the legroom, but to get where he wanted to go, from where and when he wanted to leave, that had not been an option.

This plane had seen better days. The seats were nearly threadbare. The armrests, if lifted upright for more seating space, would pivot backward into the lap of the person sitting behind you. And something on the plane rattled like an old bus on a pebble road. Periodically one of the overhead compartments would pop open of its own will, and it became a sort of game for Michael to guess which compartment would be next.

As he deplaned at the Tampa/Saint Petersburg airport, he vowed, for at least the fortieth time in as many trips over the years, never to fly on that airline again. The money saved on its lower fares just wasn't worth it, and there were others like Jet Blue and Southwest that offered a nice flight for only a little more expense. And with Southwest, the bags would have flown without a surcharge, so it might even be cheaper some of the time..

Michael grabbed a cab outside and rode across the bay to Clearwater in air conditioned luxury. He could have enjoyed it more if the driver had rolled up his window, but what can you do? It wasn't worth the effort of complaining. It was the best ride he had that day.

In Clearwater Michael rented a standard size car from one of the many agencies that offer unlimited mileage within the state. He knew he could have rented it at the airport but this was less easily traced. Then he began the short trek down the coastline to the city where his target awaited him. As long as he was cautious about parking and traffic tickets, there would be nothing to link Michael O'Shea with anything farther South in the state, which was very important to him.

Michael had gotten this far along life's trail without acquiring a police record, except one gambling charge during his stint in Military Intelligence. (Who knew the young Lieutenant would have no sense of humor about losing his uniform trying to regain his losses?)

Michael had no intention of changing such a nice habit now.

The speedometer needle never budged above the speed limit, even though traffic was constantly passing. He could have made better time on the Interstates, but he was in no hurry. As a matter of fact, Michael had a little time to kill.

Toward dark he saw a beat up 1964 Studebaker station wagon full of fish nets, wash tubs, and similar devices turn off the highway onto a small dirt road that wound through the moss covered trees, and followed it. Even in Florida there are far fewer vehicles like that around. The "Cash for Clunkers" program had erased most of them, to the delight of the auto makers. The older cars did not have as much planned obsolescence built into them.

Michael found himself reminiscing about his grandfather who had grown up with the cars of that era, and who had taught him to identify them at antique shows. Each was fully identifiable, down to make, model and year in most cases. He thought for a moment of the unique looks of the Renault Dauphine, the VW Beetle and Kharman Ghia, the early Thunderbirds, the various years of Chevrolet and Oldsmobile… The list was almost limitless and he had appreciated learning each one.

Not many opportunities arose to use that knowledge any more. The automotive market had been undergoing a huge growth potential market in those years, and each manufacturer wanted their product to be recognizable as number one. And they had made them to last.

Today's autos were all so similar It was tough to tell a cheap one from a luxury model, and neither was built to last. The magazines had made him aware the rental he was driving was prone to having to replace the pistons and rods if the serpentine belt broke due to not being replaced when it 'should' every 50,000 miles or so. The manufacturer had cut it too closely on headspace in the valve area in order to save costs, collapsing them in the common failure of the belt.

Cars of the previous era had used a chain instead of a composite belt, and had plenty of room in the valve area. Running hundreds of thousands of miles with minimal maintenance had been typical.

This particular Studebaker was a Lark in a pale turquoise color. Thanks to his grandfather's interest, he had seen a lot of sales brochure pictures of Larks as well as seeing restored Larks at auto shows, but never had seen one that color, though an earlier bullet nose style from 1949 had used the color.

Nevertheless, it was probably original, and the car had probably been passed down as a 'work car' for a few generations. It surely did not look much like a restored antique.

Its driver was most likely going night fishing in the Gulf, and would park the car where it wouldn't be bothered by vandals or police. There would be an abundance of cars there, and one car more or less would go unnoticed, even an old one like that.

It made it a perfect place for Michael to catch up on his rest until morning. He listened to the radio until just after midnight, then turned it off and went to sleep.

Michael had kept the engine running while he listened to the radio so that he needn't fear the battery running down. The gas tank indicator read a little above a half tank when he .turned the radio off.

Michael awakened at daybreak, and continued down the coastline. At 6:59, he pulled into a convenience store to fill the car's small gas tank. Because it was so early, he had to wait while the manager turned the pumps on. He wanted no record of the transaction so he paid cash, with a crisp fifty dollar bill.

The young manager glanced at the fifty, and without looking up at him, she said, "I ain't opened the safe yet to get change out. Can you wait a minute while I do?"

A faint aroma of pot and alcohol hung in the air, clinging to her words. He assured her he could most certainly wait, and she stepped into the back room. Ten seconds later he heard the safe's lid clang back into place and she returned with a small cloth bag.

She carefully separated its contents into her tray, then counted out his change and handed it to him, dropping the fifty under the tray in the register. By his quick count she now had three hundred forty six dollars in bills in the drawer, plus the assorted small change. As he re-entered the highway he took special notice of the precise location of the store for future reference, using the rental car's GPS.

It was only about a half hour's drive North of Sunset Cove, which was his intended destination where Shemuel had told him the Playa del Sol condominiums were located.

Michael had been somewhat familiar with Sunset Cove from an earlier visit, and recalled it was not all beach. Although it included an oval peninsula running parallel to the mainland, almost half the town was actually on the mainland.

There were two bridges that connected the beach section to the mainland portion. One was a large drawbridge over the St. John river and the other a simple arched concrete bridge over the same river, closer to where it dumped into the bay. His destination had taken him over the concrete bridge.

A short while later, before the sun had reached its peak at noon, Michael reached the city limits and was welcomed to his 'final' destination.

As he crossed the concrete bridge, he noticed the speed limit dropped quickly on the other side. Being accustomed to paying careful attention to such things, Michael slowed and began to search for a nearby patrol car. It didn't take him long to spot it, though very little was visible until it was in his rear view mirror. It was hidden behind a billboard officially welcoming you to Sunset Cove.

"Some welcome", Michael thought. "Probably to trap tourists."

Although he had not programmed his destination into the GPS provided by the rental company, he had no problem in finding the Playa Del Sol Condominiums that his temporary employer, Shemuel Levine, had told him about. They were visible from the highway, looming large and ugly stark white between the small beach motels and the water. One motel still had the sign up offering its guests the pleasure of enjoying a "Room on the Beach", but somehow Michael suspected that no one would take it very seriously, since it was now nearly surrounded by the condos.

Michael had quickly located the door he wanted on the second floor by reading the list by the doorbells and simply walking down the halls. The doorbells were for convenience only, because the hallways were unlocked. Some condos fronted on the ground floor, while others, like the Ramos and Levine one, opened to the second level and used a staircase. Still others required the use of the glass-windowed elevator, which probably had video cameras. There were none in the stairwell or hallways, however.

Returning to the car, he had watched the condo entrance, and waited until he saw Rebeccah Levine depart. She looked exactly like the photo her father had shown him, except for the outfit. His photo had been of a conservative daughter. She was dressed as a fun-loving beach girl and wealthy tourist when she left the condo.

Quite fortunate for Michael, she had been accompanied, arm in arm, by a tall, thin Hispanic male slightly older than her. He was wearing a white shirt and trousers, five gold chains and an eagle medallion around his neck, a gold watch band, and gold rings on both hands.

Michael had a pretty good hunch that her companion was Jose Ramos. He almost perfectly fit the description Shemuel had given of him. They got into a red sports car, turned on the radio, and drove off into the afternoon sun, the radio sounds trailing long after they had passed out of clear view.

Michael gave them five minutes to remember anything they might have forgotten, and then entered the building. The Ramos condo, being on the second floor, provided a little extra cover for him to work. Nevertheless, he knocked, just to be certain the place was empty.

The lock was an excellent model featuring a full one inch deadbolt and a free-spinning outer knob. The cylinder, as he had quickly noticed, was one known for a complex keyway and tight tolerances, which can make picking very close to impossible.

Nevertheless, the only way to be certain is to try. And when he did, it popped open more quickly than a person could probably have selected a proper key from their key ring if they were the legitimate tenant. Some days things just go that way. Michael had taken it as a good sign.

Michael put the small tip of a tooth pick into the keyway. He always broke off a small piece of a tooth pick during meals and carried them in his pocket. While no one could be arrested for their being burglary tools, they certainly were a burglar's best friend. If another keyholder came while he was inside, it would cause a few moments delay while the lock cylinder caused the key to "stick".

Yet, when Michael would later rotate the keyway back to lock it on exit, it would not affect him because he was not using a key. He also had left the keyway turned just slightly so he would not have to pick it to relock it.

Michael had known he might not be so lucky the second time.

Inside the condominium was a veritable thieves' paradise. Ramos was quite evidently very confident of himself. He feared neither thief nor police, because scattered around the apartment was almost anything you could imagine.

On the dining table was about a half ounce of cocaine loosely spilling from what appeared to be a sandwich wrap baggie.

The bedroom dressing table had enough diamond jewelry to outfit an entire wedding party in style, and they were good stones in excellent settings. The nightstand next to the bed was littered with men's gold chains and medallions, one of them huge. And the list of goodies could continue.

In the freezer, next to two ice buckets full of cracked ice that told Michael that either Jose or Rebeccah was probably a Marguerita fan, were two aluminum foil pouches filled with money.

He peeled off about a couple dozen of the hundreds from each and returned to the bedroom. A little cold cash is always nice, but diamonds are forever. It had taken several minutes to select the diamond necklace he chose.

Out of superstitious fear he resisted the gold jewelry. The childhood stories told by his grandfather of thieves being blinded by the gold, resulting in their capture or death, still haunted his subconscious.

The necklace was somewhere in the five to seven thousand dollar range, he had estimated, so his Hasidic employer should be willing to pay fifteen hundred for it, which made the job profitable enough, especially with his temporary employer having also promised to cover the expenses.

It would have been easy to fill a shopping bag in that supermarket of delights, but Michael wanted to attract as little attention as possible. One necklace would probably not be noticed. The painting, which was the actual object of the break-in, he could do very little about, but he had found it in a stack of paintings in her closet, so the chances of it being missed in the near future were minimal. This looked like another nice, clean hit for Michael. It had been a very good year. But, remembering his surprise at Shemuel's visit, he had no desire to push his luck.

Besides, the guards at the airport are armed, and too much gold and diamonds just might catch their attention. Shipping them, while certainly not out of the question, could be risky if there were too many or they stood out on the package X-ray. And gold tends to be very heavy.

The coke on the table bothered Michael. As a professional thief, he had never liked drugs or the people involved with them, and one of his real and unbreakable rules was to try to avoid people who do. His life was based on control, careful planning and execution. Drugs don't mix well with that. Michael was tempted to destroy it, but knew that if he did, the hit would definitely be noticed right away, so he resisted. Michael had planned to be far away when the burglary was finally noticed.

As he left, Michael made sure the door was properly shut, then used a plug spinner to re-lock it. The act of having left the cylinder in the slightly picked open position for just that purpose, as well as its smooth delivery, rewarded the effort. Soon he was back in his car, whistling an old Elvis tune called "Treasures and Tears" as he drove away.

He had driven North on old 301 all the way to Duvall County, which is basically the Jacksonville city limits. He then followed a roundabout course into downtown, registering at a smaller hotel across from the public park. The rainbow effect of lights on the park fountain always relaxed Michael whenever he visited the area.

At a discount store Michael bought wrapping and shipping materials, a book, and a cheap necklace. Behind a family owned grocery store he picked up an orange crate. The painting, wrapped in party gift wrap, went into the orange crate and the diamond necklace replaced its cheap cousin in the display box it had been purchased in, along with the receipt. He cut out some of the pages of the book, and the cash bonus of about forty-eight hundred bucks went between the remaining pages.

The necklace and the painting were shipped to an address in the Diamond District of New York, to one Shemuel Levine. The book went to Michael's business address in New York City, along with a note saying:

"Mike -

Thanks for the loan of the

 book and the money. Sorry I was

so long in returning same.

Many thanks,

Jerry"

Once they were shipped, Michael returned to the hotel for an early start on a long needed good night's sleep. But at one a.m., for no apparent reason, he had awakened and could not seem to get relaxed enough to sleep for the rest of the night.

Chapter 8

The next morning

Very early the next morning, Michael O'Shea left the Jacksonville motel he had spent the night in, and got to Interstate Ten by the quickest route. He had not slept well the night before, which was unusual for him. He followed it to the cut-off for I-75, which he followed back down as far as Tampa. He took I-75 rather than taking the shorter but slower route down 301 because he could relax more, not having to constantly evaluate changing speed limits.

The signs for Route 60, the causeway into Clearwater, were impossible to miss, and even having taken a slight detour and stopped for an early lunch at a steakhouse in the Ocala area (where he paid by credit card, on the off chance he needed to prove he was not in the Sunset Cove area), he returned the rental car before noon, saving another day's rates.

There was a slight drop-off charge for gas and clean-up, which he accepted without argument, despite the fact that he had filled the gas tank only a half block earlier and left the car spotless. He was in a good mood, having had a very successful and profitable adventure the day before. The burglary had gone even more smoothly than he had hoped

Michael caught a local cab to the Tampa/Saint Pete Airport. The driver wasn't the talkative kind, and his idea of a comfortable temperature was similar to Michel's own, so Michael tipped him a ten-spot as he departed.

He was starting to get a little low on cash, having already sent the bulk of what he had attained in a package shipped to himself. Normally, being cash poor would usually bother him, but he thought "What the heck" an appropriate response under the circumstances. It wasn't like the job was just beginning. Michael was returning home soon, his assigned task completed. He had no real need to carry excessive amounts of cash on his person.

That's when he saw the headlines and the picture on the news rack. The picture was either Rebeccah Levine, victim of his previous night's work, or her twin sister. The headline read: "BURGLAR SOUGHT IN BEACHFRONT MURDER."

Trembling fingers counted out coins even as his mind noted that many people look alike in newspaper photos, and that Florida is just chock full of beaches. He was absolutely certain he was being paranoid.

Reading the article, however, did anything but allay his fears. The victim's name was withheld, pending notification of next of kin, but it listed the name of the condos as the Playa del Sol, and gave the name of the person who had found the body, a Mr. Jose Ramos, of the same address, which Michael recognized as the one he had hit the evening before.

According to the article, Mr. Ramos had returned from a business trip late that afternoon. He had expected the victim to meet his plane. When she failed to do so, he tried to phone her, but the phone went unanswered. When he arrived home, he discovered that the condo had been burglarized and ransacked. The body was in the bedroom.

Police refused to comment on whether the victim had been sexually assaulted prior to the murder, as well as on other details of the case. An anonymous source, however, stated that the methods used in the break-in were similar to those in a string of break-ins by a cat burglar in recent months.

Suddenly, some of the words in the article seemed to jump out at him - "pending notification of next of kin". The victim was Michael's employer's daughter, who had paid him to return the painting she had taken from him, and had reluctantly agreed to handle any jewelry Michael had retrieved from the condo.

NOTIFICATION OF NEXT OF KIN. The words echoed in Michael's ears. Knowing that he had, in fact, burglarized her place on the very night of the murder, would her father then keep silent about his, and Michael's, involvement? Michael doubted it severely. He knew it was vital that he had to reach him first.

Ordinarily, the last thing Michael would have done was phone anyone from anywhere near the scene of a burglary. But, as someone once said, "Extraordinary times call for extraordinary measures." And this fit the bill. He bought a throwaway celphone, the kind the cops like to call a 'burner phone', and placed the call.

The phone was answered on the second ring, in a very businesslike manner by Shemuel Levine personally.

Michael responded, "This is Mike."

"You've succeeded, then?, Shemuel asked.

"It's on its way to you, even as we speak, but there's something else", Michael answered.

"And what is that, may I ask? Or is it safe for you to talk?"

Michael found himself wishing that Shemuel wasn't so careful and considerate, wishing that he hadn't placed the call to Shemuel, wishing. . . just wishing.

"I've got some bad news for you", Michael started. "There's no easy way to say it. I've got to tell it like it is and hope you can take it."

"So?" he asked, with the slightest discomfort creeping into his voice.

"After I broke into the place and left, someone else broke in."

"And?", he responded, impatience replacing the discomfort.

"Sir, whoever it was, they. . . killed your daughter. It wasn't me. I swear on my ancestors' graves."

The silence on the other end of the phone was deafening. Michael wanted to hang up, to run, to hide. But he waited. Michael could feel Shemuel's pain coming through the telephone despite the silence and the distance. Still he waited. His life depended on it, and he knew it.

Finally Shemuel began to speak. "How…Why…", he began, barely audible. Then his voice raised to a feverish pitch. "So why should I

60

believe you--a goniff?", Shemuel fairly shouted into the telephone. Then he disconnected so fast it actually seemed to hurt Michael's ear.

Fear and panic began to set in more deeply now, and Michael debated what to do. Finally, Michael dialed him again. Shemuel answered, but said not a word.

"Listen to me, please", Michael began. "Give me a little time, and I'll prove it. I will find her killer. I promise. Look, you can always go to the police later, and if worse comes to worse, there's an eye for an eye. You know enough about me to see that it happens. All I'm asking is that you don't go nuts right now and do something we're both likely to regret."

With a trembling voice Shemuel asked, "And why should I not? What have I to lose? One thief, more or less, when I have lost my precious daughter?"

"Because you want her real killer as much as I want to prove it wasn't me", Michael replied.

Michael waited again. There was no more to say. If Shemuel didn't buy it, Michael would be looking over his shoulder for the rest of his life, however short that might be. It seemed like hours before Shemuel answered, though it probably was less than a minute.

"So prove it", he said, and hung up. Michael breathed a small sigh of relief. He had a temporary reprieve. Now he had to make use of it.

Chapter 9

That same day

Officer Kevin Wolf's cruiser slowly made its way through the tourist traffic on his way to the local morgue. It was not his favorite destination, but if he wanted the inside story on the death of Rebeccah, there was no better place to get it. He had not needed to visit it very often, but had mixed feelings about that. The receptionist there was someone Kevin found really interesting, and would have liked to get to know better.

Unlike the Pennsylvania Highway Patrol, the West Florida town of Sunset Cove did not require its officers to attend autopsy of bodies simply because they were the OIC. Being Officer In Charge of a crime scene carried no privilege or additional responsibilities here. But Kevin still felt the obligation to attend.

Kevin missed the PHP, but could not stand even the idea of another Winter of pulling children's bodies out of snow and ice induced auto wreckages. He had hoped to become employed by the FDLE when he moved to Florida a few years earlier, but the Florida State Department of Law Enforcement had a hiring freeze on at the time, and only Sunset Cove was hiring.

The first couple of years had been fairly quiet, and, although the department was often criticized for the actions of some of his fellow workers, which embarrassed him, he had started to become somewhat complacent.

But this year had proved different. First, the department had been faced with several series of burglaries, and now, without a clue on any of those, they had the grisly murder of a young, wealthy and attractive woman in one of the city's more expensive condominiums.

The morgue and office of the Medical Examiner was in what looked to be an older factory that had been converted into offices. Kevin greeted the petite blonde at the reception desk, presenting his ID card, even though he knew that she knew who he was, and stated he needed to see the M.E. on business.

She told Kevin that the M.E. was in the middle of an autopsy on a busy day, and asked if he could possibly come back.

"Joanie, there is nothing I would like more than to come back another day, but this case won't wait for me. I have more pressure on me than a gator in a steam cooker."

Kevin gave her his best smile and she giggled.

"Well, it isn't a very pretty sight in there right now", she replied.

"I really enjoy your dialect, Joanie? Chicago, if I recall?", Kevin ventured, trying to prolong the communication. He had wanted an excuse to talk to her more on previous visits, but somehow the opportunity had just not presented itself.

"Yes, Chicago. But I've been here for about three years. I'm surprised you can still hear it."

"Hey, dialects are something I always notice, a hobby of mine. Yours is faint, but still just enough to give me a hint. Before I went into the Pennsylvania Highway Patrol, I spent some time in Chicago, living in a suite off Michigan Avenue. I liked the ability to get steak and eggs any time of the day, by walking a couple blocks in any direction."

She laughed. "That's true. Seafood, too, and true Chicago pizza. Not like what they sell as Chicago pizza around here. I miss it."

"Well, Joanie, maybe some time we can try to find someplace almost as good around here", Kevin flirted, "but today I need to see the M.E., even if it has to be when things aren't ideal. Trust me, this is not my first rodeo. I can take it."

"OK. Down the hall, third door on the right and then through the double doors inside. Suit up." she answered with a smile. She watched him carefully as he walked down the corridor, then sighed and went back to her work.

As Kevin approached the inner double doors, the smells of the examining room drifted out slightly, and he was reminded of what he was about to face. He did not look forward to it, but he knew from his experiences in the military that he could handle it.

Kevin entered the room and announced himself.

"Better stand over there" the assistant to the Medical Examiner stated. "And suit up."

Kevin grabbed paper booties and a showercap-like head covering and a face mask.

He pulled on the face mask, head cover and paper booties, and pushed a gown on over his crisp uniform. As he was doing so, he watched the Medical Examiner, Jeff Staley, at work. Jeff was busy on the finishing touches of measurements of the open cadaver on the table, which was an elderly fat man. Jeff Staley was a thin man with bony features that reminded Kevin of a vulture. Probably had something to do with his choice of careers, Kevin thought.

Watching him and smelling the odors of the place, Kevin wished he had thought to put an odorant under his nose before coming here, but he knew he could take it. He also knew research has shown that the use of oils or petroleum jellies in such surroundings increases the chances of infections spreading, because they trap the contaminants in the nose, which is a sensitive area.

But it was his background that provided the most support against the visuals and odors. As a young adult Kevin had, against the advice of his tribal elders, joined the military and ended up in the intelligence field. Survival training had been required, where he had learned not to let his stomach rule his brain or the rest of his body. He could still feel the bile trying to rise, but he ignored it and stayed as relaxed as he could.

When the autopsy was finished, Kevin talked with Jeff about the case of Rebeccah Levine.

"She was not just strangled and cut", Staley confirmed, reading from his notes. "Not only had she been tortured, but she also had signs of severe vaginal and anal tearing which appear to be from extremely rough, probably forced, sex. There were no traces of DNA, but there were traces of spermicide consistent with use of a condom recently. I would point out, of course, that these traces last long enough that they could have occurred hours prior to her death, and may not actually be related. Her fluids were indicative, however, of a single brand of condom, and the violent sex itself had occurred shortly before her death."

"So are you are saying it is likely to be related to the attack or not?", Kevin asked.

"I am saying the use of the condom may or may not be related, but the rough sex almost certainly is."

"Ok, I understand now", Kevin answered.

Staley continued, "She had been tortured. She had long shallow cuts on various parts of both sides of her body, as well as many deeper cuts, each of which had occurred prior to death. The torture was extensive, and not something done quickly. She also had a head wound that was made by a blunt instrument, but which was not a factor in her death, and was likely to pre-date the other injuries. The actual cause of death, however, had occurred after all that, and was a single straight-in knife wound that had entered her back next to the spine, avoided the ribs and pierced her heart."

"Nasty stuff", Kevin commented.

"Yes, I doubt seriously if this was just a case of sudden rage. It seems almost rehearsed. It is my opinion of that the head wound was the initial attack, most likely rendering her inactive, during which time her hands had been bound with something roughly the size of the "chicken band tie wraps", often used instead of handcuffs by many large city police departments. Then the cutting and sexual assaults had begun. And each was rough and forceful.

"The rough sex could actually have occurred at any or all of the stages. There is no way to tell, except that it was not post-mortem.

"Strangulation was the next attack, and had evidently been accomplished more than once, probably separated by more cutting, without being fatal. The final strike had been with a knife with at least a six inch long, moderately narrow blade, driven through the spine area and into her heart."

Kevin had been fairly confident that the damage had not been done by the boyfriend even before learning all this, assuming his timetable was honest, and it had checked out so that was likely. Now he was fully convinced. No, they were looking for someone else, but someone in a close to a constant state of rage. So it was not likely to be simply an interrupted burglary, at least in his opinion.

This killer had a real taste for cruelty. If he had only recently began, he was learning fast that he enjoyed it, and that made him very dangerous. And with him indicating this heightened level of a state of rage, it was extremely likely that he had been committing other murders as well, and somehow they had not been classified as burglaries. That might make it harder to find him, but it could work in favor of solving the case if he could find the prior events and link them..

"Toxicology shows traces of cocaine usage, and her nasal passages confirm she was a frequent user, but these do not seem to have been a factor in her death", Jeff continued, "and the results of toxicology show she was not actually high at the time of her death. I'm sorry, but that is about as much as I have at this point and there is nothing indicating a need for further testing that I can see."

"Thanks very much", Kevin responded, almost automatically. He nodded to the Medical Examiner, turned around and left. As he reached the doors and was removing the protective attire, Kevin frowned, not looking forward to telling the Chief the results.

Chapter 10

Later that evening

Somehow, Michael didn't notice the cab on the ride from the airport to Clearwater, and without intending to, when he got there he rented a compact. The first realization of it came when he started to get into the driver's seat and got stuck halfway. The previous driver had probably been a college girl from USF. Michael moved the seat back as far as it would go, but it was still a tight fit.

As he drove, Michael's knee was constantly bumping the steering wheel. At least he wouldn't fall asleep at the steering wheel. As uncomfortable as he was at this moment, Michael wondered if he might ever be able to sleep again.

Having sent the bulk of his money North, Michael was now cash poor, and with the situation the way it was, he did not want to visit an ATM. He stopped at the fisherman's cove he had rested at on his way into the area the day before, and rested there again until slightly after midnight, watching the waves and contemplating his plans. The waves did nothing to rest him.

Michael then began to implement the first step of his plan. It was the middle of the night when he found the convenience store he had visited earlier, and he carefully started working the hand-made lock picks. The lock cylinder in the aluminum framed glass door was made of diecast pot metal. The tolerances in it were so wide Michael could almost have parked the compact there. It picked even as he was just inserting the tools.

As usual, Michael left the cylinder plug in the picked open position, and he entered the store, walking quickly across to the back room. He didn't bother with the toothpick because the cylinder keyway had an open back, so it would not slow entry with a key. But the plug being rotated would at least help a little.

A rubber floor mat covered the in-the-floor safe. Michael lifted the mat, turned the dial right to 95, and lifted off the door. He had correctly surmised that the sleepy-eyed blond had to have left the safe unlocked on his previous visit, in what some store employees commonly refer to as the "Day Combination", and that it was probably her habit to do so.

A "Day Combination" occurs when the employee turns the dial left far enough to extend the bolt, but not far enough to scramble the combination wheels. Then, when they need in, they simply turn the dial to the right to pull the bolt back. It is a tremendous savings in time for them. It takes an average person thirty-three seconds to dial the combination open normally. This way it only takes three to five.

That was Michael's clue in the early morning. She had clanged the safe lid back into place in roughly ten seconds. No way could she have dialed it open that quickly, especially in her condition.

Inside the safe Michael got an unanticipated bonus. Instead of one cash bag, there were three. He emptied the money quickly, folded it, and put it in his pocket, leaving the change alone except for a single roll of quarters and a roll of dimes. Michael then did a little shopping. He needed toothpaste, a razor, shaving cream, deodorant, after shave, and some Alka-Seltzer. What a day - his stomach was churning.

Michael gulped down two of the tablets in a cup of tonic water, feeling once more the tickling sensation in his nose that brought back glimpses of childhood recollections. The now-empty cup and the tonic water bottle joined the other goodies in the paper shopping bag, and he dropped a couple of sandwiches on top for later, in case the tablets did their job.

Michael left the building, using the plug spinner to re-lock the door. On his way out, after locking the door, he tossed the bag onto the passenger seat, and quietly surveyed the highway. When he felt absolutely certain he could neither hear nor see any other vehicles in the area, Michael returned to the door of the store. Finding a large cement block that was probably used to prop open the door on good days, he threw it through the glass of the door.

To his absolute surprise it shattered the whole door on the first toss. Usually they use special glass to prevent that, and Michael had expected to have to throw the block several times in order to break it enough to be convincing. Now the young blonde wouldn't have to go to jail for a crime she didn't commit. Instead of being blamed on the poor girl, unspecified teenagers would get the credit, and never be caught.

Michael got back in the car quickly, and steered back onto the highway. He had enough money now to relax and calculate the best approach to the current situation.

Before very long, Michael passed the Playa del Sol condos again. But this time he needed a place to stay in the area, in spite of the risks. He located a boarding house of the type that doesn't permit guests, on a side street slightly over a block away. A short while later, but still before everyone else's day was likely to have begun, Michael talked to the landlady and rented a room. The room was on the top floor, giving him a view of Florida on two sides.

Out the front window Michael could see bikini-clad northern girls on the beach carefully toasting their skin so that when they got older they could moisturize it. Young men kicked up sand as they chased their flying discs closer and closer to their real targets, as the girls pretended not to notice.

Out the side window, however, he saw only green and white. A few small green alligators scurried across a green golf course, as white-suited golfers chased their tiny white balls between them. In the distance, Palm trees swayed in the breeze, the wind carrying away much of the humidity. He laughed momentarily at the unusual sight of the alligators. He knew that even in this area they were a rather uncommon sight.

This was a good place for Michael to begin to really think and lay out a proper plan.

He awoke at a little past four-thirty the next morning, and again surveyed the areas outside his two windows. It was a lot different from the view in his home in Pennsylvania. Who would have thought that being a thief offered such fine travel possibilities. Now if Michael could just get out from behind the eight ball on the murder, it could be a decent vacation of sorts. He wondered momentarily how much time he had before Shemuel's patience ran out, but at least for now he felt somewhat safe. Shemuel was his only link to the condos, and he had agreed to wait.

The Sun was rising beautifully, though slowly, across the edge of the horizon, breaking pink, blue and yellow banners low near the horizon. The beach was empty except for one early swimmer, probably trying to wash the cobwebs out from the night before. Michael envied him his view across the water as the sun filtered through the early clouds.

 A group of birds that Michael took to be egrets were feasting on the green side. Interestingly, several were tuxedo colored, as though someone had squeezed a penguin into the shape of an egret with its long neck and long thin legs. Michael spent a long moment wondering if they were actually egrets at all, because all the egret pictures he had seen were all of glossy white birds.

He then showered and began his typical morning routine. It was kind of nice to see Michael O'Shea looking back in the mirror instead of the Hasidic look he had worn as a cover for the burglary a few days earlier in New York. Other than a tiny childhood scar over one eyebrow, Michael was satisfied with his looks. He had to admit to himself that there is a certain amount of narcissism in him. After dressing, Michael sat down, pulled out the small notebook he had grabbed in the convenience store, and began planning and calculating.

He knew would need access to more than the details in the newspaper account, even though that was much more than it was likely to show in the online version. That much was a certainty in his mind, and he also would need at least one more visit to the scene.

Michael also had to consider possible alternatives to the newspaper account of what had happened, because he knew for a fact that the burglar, being himself, had not killed the Shemuel's daughter.

Michael was also curious as to why the theft had been spotted so soon. If he had taken all the golden items or cleaned out all the jewelry, he could easily see them being missed. But Michael had taken very little of what was there, none of the gold, and more importantly, only things that should not have been missed until much later.

One possibility, of course, was that the boyfriend had killed her. But Michael had made a fine living by knowing a bit about police logic, and that would have been the first thing they assumed. So if they were looking for the burglar, they had probably at least primarily ruled him out. So, assuming they were correct, someone other than her had to have been in that apartment between the time Michael left and the boyfriend returned. If so, what was their motivation? Why were they there and why would they kill her?

Of course, the boyfriend could have hired someone to kill her and used the burglary to hide it. He would need to talk with Jose Ramos and see if he could pick up on anything the police might have missed. That meant he needed a viable alternative identity to use, to permit him to nose around. He marked that on the list he was beginning to form.

If Michael were at home, that would be a cinch. In New York City, Michael knew a forger whose work was impeccable and who was known for keeping his mouth shut under the worst of conditions. But he was here in Florida, where he knew no one in the business.

Michael considered a trip down to Gibsonton, the Florida town known as "Carnie Town", in the hopes of locating an alibi agent who might know a forger, but the risks and exposure of such a search seemed unnecessarily risky. Besides, Gibtown, as it was commonly known, was really more known for freaks, geeks and ride owners than for gamesters. Chances are, it would be a complete waste of time.

Could there have actually been a second burglar? It seemed unlikely, but it was another possibility to be considered. If so, local newspapers could give Michael a picture of crime in the area, and the local library would likely have the recent few months archived, perhaps even the past year. With a little diligence he should be able to piece enough of the jigsaw of articles together to see the picture fairly clearly.

The library also would also offer the possibility of an online search, but Michael knew that would likely give too many unrelated finds and waste his time. Michael knew he was not a detective, but that he probably knew a lot more about crime and criminals than most detectives do.

The large block of drugs on the table during his visit, and the large rolls of cash in the freezer posed another possible motivation. The murder may have been drug related, and if another burglary had actually occurred, it might be simply a matter of convenience while the killer or killers was there, or to send a message to Ramos. That was the first he had considered it might actually be multiple assailants. He added the possibility to his list.

By seven-thirty that morning, Michael had completed an outline of goals and questions, and it was time to acquire his alternative persona to allow him to "poke around" without drawing too much suspicion. Fortunately for him the room still had a local phone book, probably a few years out of date, but usable. Michael picked two names out of it, being careful not to choose local companies from within Sunset Cove, because they might be recognizable, but which were close enough for his purposes. He found two in Saint Petersburg, about a half hour away to the Northeast.

At seven forty-five Michael walked into the office of the Citywide Detective Agency, and asked to see Mr. Brown. Michael reflected on how many real-life detectives have names like Smith, Jones, and Brown. It's enough to make you wonder who's hiding what.

The entry room featured a tall desk with two chairs behind it, one occupied by a lovely brunette in a red tank top and black slacks. The room was carefully appointed with small items showing a fair amount of taste. The walls featured paintings, one of which, Michael noticed, contained a pinhole camera lens hidden within it. The walls were a pale yellow with white trim on the three dark doors, one of which seemed to be a supply closet, and which probably housed the DVR to store the camera images.

Michael had hoped that Mr. Brown wouldn't be in yet. The office didn't officially open until eight o'clock in the morning and it had been his experience that bosses rarely start at the same time as the hired help. But Mr. Brown was evidently either a workaholic or an insomniac. The tank-topped brunette flashed her bright green eyes and smiled as she asked Michael to wait just a minute while she got him.

Michael watched her tight blue jeans wiggle their way across the floor to the inside office, her high heels clicking a slow Flamenco that her hips were only too willing to dance to. He was so engrossed in watching and admiring that he nearly forgot what he had come for. One of the sad things about being a professional burglar is that it rarely left much suitable time for Michael to develop a meaningful relationship. So instead he accepted small visual pleasures as he found them.

On the desk was a healthy stack of high quality business cards in a tray that said 'Take One.' Not being one to follow instructions too well, Michael quickly pocketed a pack of about thirty of them.

If Mr. Brown hadn't been in, Michael's job would now be done. But he was, so the act had just begun. The secretary showed him into Mr. Brown's office and introduced Brown as "Sam". This must be the week for meeting people named Sam. She hadn't asked Michael's name, and he didn't offer it.

Sam Brown was standing behind his desk, and he was tall, maybe six foot two, which made Michael look up slightly to see Sam's steely blue eyes staring at him, sizing him up the way a butcher might appraise a side of meat.

Michael was careful to look as awkward and uncomfortable as possible, which was actually quite easy. Sam Brown was used to taking a dominant role in his life, and it showed. Michael guessed that Sam had probably been a State Trooper before going into private practice. He had that kind of look about him. That is what made it real easy for Michael to appear uncomfortable. He was.

Sam Brown indicated a leather chair in front of his desk. Only after Michael was seated did Sam move to his own high-backed plush swivel chair, where he sat quietly for a moment before speaking.

"What can I do for you Mister. . . . ?"

He let the sentence hang, waiting for Michael to fill it with his name. Michael didn't.

"Maybe I shouldn't have come", Michael started. "Maybe I should wait until I'm sure - After all, I'm not, you know. It might be nothing."

Michael ran the sentences together in a near-hysteric pattern that he hoped would convey the "real" message.

It did. As the message centers in Sam's brain filed away the signals, there was a nearly audible click as his entire manner changed, and he became your old football buddy, Sam, that you could tell anything to. The guy was good at what he does. Michael almost immediately felt like pouring his heart and soul out to him.

He didn't, of course. Instead, Michael sat quietly in the soft leather chair, seeming not to have noticed the changes in Sam's demeanor. The ball thus being in Sam's court, he served it well.

"Look, pal", he began, "I know what's bothering you. I can see it in your eyes. And you ain't gonna' feel better 'til you talk about it. I think you know that."

He waited.

Michael waited.

The first to talk would lose the match, and neither was budging. The silence lasted about two full minutes, with Sam poised like the cat waiting for a canary that would soon come too close.

"It's . . . my wife", Michael finally began. "She . . . I . . ."

Michael covered his face in his hands and forced real tears to stream down his cheek. "I'm sorry I bothered you", he shouted, the self-pity obvious in his voice as he bolted for the door.

Sam still waited. He knew the visitor would be back. It might be tomorrow. It might be next week. Maybe even a month would pass, and then he'd be ready to face the problem, and pay Sam's fees, as well as the fees of the lawyer Sam would recommend once he got the goods on the visitor's wife.

He'd have a long wait this time. At the very least Sam would have to wait until Michael got married, which he had no immediate plans of doing. This time Sam had read the client wrong. But then, Michael is a pro.

Michael's next stop was the Benevolent Insurance Company. He had chosen it the same way he had picked the detective agency. They were the first ones in the yellow pages of the phone book that didn't begin with an 'A' and were outside of Sunset Cove.

Michael was grateful the rooming house still had older phone books in the night table, next to a Gideon's Bible. He preferred to use the yellow pages rather than an online search because online searches are nearly three times as likely to give you the address of a company that does not actually exist at that address. And the older the phone book, the more reliable the ads might be.

In today's internet-enabled society, National calling centers are set up to flood the internet with their ads, and give false addresses, often turning out to be the address of a restaurant instead. These companies send out rip-off artists to scam money from unsuspecting would-be customers, especially the elderly, often using slightly veiled threats.

Fortunately, they usually get noticed by the Press and make the evening news, allowing locals to recognize the fake company by its name. But as someone not local, Michael would have had no way of telling them apart, wasting a lot of his time, or worse yet, the name causing someone to alert the police to his presence.

Of course, the newer Yellow Pages are not totally immune, either, which is why Michael was grateful the book in the room showed signs of age. Maybe it was even printed before the scam entries began filling the pages. He also always made it a point not to use any of the businesses that begin with an 'A' or use a full or half page ad.

Citywide Detectives and the Benevolent Insurance Company were the first in their categories not to do so.

Michael timed his approach to the insurance company so as to arrive near the end of the lunch hour. He asked the young lady at the desk to buzz Mr. Scheiner's office. As she turned to do so, Michael lifted about twenty of the professionally printed business cards from the tray on her desk. They had the feel of quality you don't get in cheaply printed cards.

Predictably, Mr. Scheiner was out to lunch, and could someone else help him? To which Michael replied by promising to return for Mr. Scheiner after lunch. No one would notice or care when he did not.

All in all, a good day's work. Now he could relax until the early evening, at which time he would drive to the scene of the crime.

Chapter 11

Two days after Rebeccah's murder

While Michael was resting the afternoon away, across town Police Chief John Lawson was not. The faded and wrinkled folder on John Lawson's desk concerned a twenty five year old homicide in the city. The Chief opened it again and once more reviewed the facts.

Responding to neighbor complaints of an odor, Police had found Sally Johnson sitting in the living room of her single family home, doing a crossword puzzle while her long dead husband sat in the chair next to her. She had killed him with a hammer in April. It was a hot August day when the police arrived. The odor was horrific and the view even worse. Yet Sally was found sitting in a wooden rocking chair only a few feet from the body, doing a crossword and chatting merrily with the corpse.

When asked what happened to her husband, she matter-of-factly told the officers her husband had cheated on her once, but was not going to do it ever again, without even looking up from her crossword.

John Lawson had been one of the responding officers. He was new on the force at the time and it had been a rough initiation. The woman was convicted, but today she was scheduled to be released, a few years early for good behavior. She was 72 now. He decided she probably posed no immediate threat to the city, and closed the folder.

As he did, the phone on his desk rang.

"Chief Lawson."

"Chief, this is Bill Thomas over at the bank on Paradise Lane."

"Hi, Bill. How's the golf game?"

"Doesn't change much, unfortunately. But that's not why I called."

"What's up, Bill?"

"Got a really bad situation that I need to keep private. Can you stop by?"

"You still have that single cup coffee brewing system?"

"Sure do. And lots of varieties of flavors."

"I'll be there in fifteen."

"See you then."

Lawson hung the phone up, organized the paperwork on his desk so it all was neat and orderly, grabbed his official hat, and started for the door. Passing a mirror he was reminded of how much the hat seemed more appropriate on a cowboy than a cop, at least to him. But rules are rules. City Council had chosen the uniforms.

Arriving at the bank, he removed his hat and was ushered quickly into the conference room, where he was given free reign of the coffee maker. He chose a French Vanilla blend, inserted the cup and pressed the button. Twenty seconds later he had a cup of hot fresh coffee with a smooth flavor. He pressed the arm on the face of the conference room refrigerator door and received a small handful of ice chips, which he used to cool it slightly.

Bill joined him less than thirty seconds later. Bill was a shorter man, but made up for his height with his professional demeanor. His suit was immaculately cut, obviously tailored specifically for him and of top quality materials. He wore a corporate tie with the small logo of the bank imprinted on a dark red background.

Even though his eyes betrayed the stress he was feeling, his smile was wide, open and friendly. He offered his hand, and Chief Lawson accepted it and shook hands. Bill had a firm but not overly strong grip, Lawson noted to himself.

Bill fixed himself a cup of the fresh brewed coffee, choosing a caramel flavored blend, and sat across from Chief Lawson.

"I'm in real trouble.", Bill began.

"How so?"

"Are you familiar with the kiosk in the center of the bank?"

"Where the blank forms are for people who need a deposit slip, withdrawal form, or whatever?"

"Exactly."

"Nope. Never saw one", Lawson joked.

Bill ignored the joke. "About a month ago, an elderly lady, maybe in her eighties, stood at that kiosk, crying", Bill continued, "So I went over and tried to see what was the matter."

"What was it?"

"She said she had a large number of smaller checks coming in soon, and would have to write up deposit slips for each and she was worried she makes a mistake when writing the account number on the deposit slips. Said she was getting a little senile and her memory was not always the best."

"Seems like a reasonable concern."

"Yes. And with a simple solution. I had a tall stack of deposit slips with her account number magnetically encoded on them printed up and gave them to her."

"So what is the problem?"

"A week later she came in, stopped at the kiosk, then made a deposit of two checks", Bill explained, "And while she was there, evidently left her stack of deposit slips on top of the bank's stock blank deposit slips."

"Whew.", Chief Lawson whistled gently through his teeth.

"Yes. For the next few weeks, everyone who used the kiosk to make a deposit put it into her account, and no one noticed."

"For real?"

"No matter what you write on the slips, the magnetic encoding tells it where to go."

"So how long before you get it all straightened out?"

"That's why I called you. Last week, she came in crying again, She said she needed to withdraw some cash but could not remember how much she had, or even whether she had enough to meet her needs. So I checked her account and she had over three hundred thousand."

Lawson whistled again.

"Oh, I don't need THAT much, she had said," Bill reported. "I only need $150,000. But I need cash."

"You're kidding."

"Wish I was. I arranged for her to pick it up the following Friday, and she did. Hasn't been seen since, and today we discovered the situation."

"And you want me to put out a BOLO for her."

"Wish it were that simple. Think about it. I can't prove intent. By her own words, she was 'a little senile'. All the bad decisions appear to have been mine. Even if you found her, chances are that all we can do is ask her to return any unused funds."

"Ouch."

"Ouch indeed. Any ideas?"

"None, but I will work on it."

"That's all I can ask", Bill answered, and stood, offering his hand again. "Thanks."

On his way out of the bank, Lawson thought to himself, "This is another unsolvable case. Just what we need right now."

Chapter 12

Later that same evening

Michael parked the oddly shaped little compact in front of the Playa del Sol condominiums just as the sun began its slow descent into the western skies, bathing the horizon in bold red and orange flame. It was now almost exactly forty-eight hours from the time of Rebeccah Levine's death. Michael waited quietly, reading a local paper and hating the day he had decided to give up smoking. Of course, in our new age of modern prohibitionism, he mused, it's probably just as well. If he lit up, someone would tell him to put it out anyway.

Finally a light came on in the Ramos household, and Michael went into the routine he had mentally rehearsed while waiting. It had a curious duality about it. It felt both totally natural and absolutely ridiculous at the same time.

When Jose Ramos answered the door, Michael handed him a business card.

"Mr. Ramos", Michael said, "I'm Sam Brown of Citywide Detectives. Got a minute?"

"What for?", Ramos asked, the clear defiance unmistakable in his voice. It reminded Michael distinctly of a backyard dog defending his territory.

"I might be able to get you back some of what you lost in the burglary the other night", Michael lied.

Ramos hesitated a moment, then invited Michael in. The poly bag was gone from the kitchen table, of course. Too many cops snooping around, Michael suspected. They sat on the plush white sectionals in the living room as they talked. Looking around, Michael saw that yellow police tape ribbons still covered the bedroom door opening.

"I've been hired by the Benevolent Insurance Company", Michael started, handing Ramos the other card, which he had collected from Scheiner, as though it proved the statement to be true.

"What kind of crap is that? I didn't have no insurance", Ramos interrupted. It was interesting to Michael that Ramos ignored the possibility of Rebeccah Levine having some, but perhaps that subject had already come up for them.

"You may not have, Mr. Ramos, but a lot of the victims in the string of burglaries in the area do, and too many of them are insured by the Benevolent Insurance Company, so the company hired me."

"So what's this got to do with me?", Ramos asked.

"Maybe nothing. But maybe it's the same guy, and maybe I catch the creep hot, with some of the stuff he stole from you and your old lady. And if I find it, instead of the cops, it won't necessarily have to be stored for years in evidence bags. I figure you'd want it back, right?"

"Yeah, I would", he answered sullenly.

"What did he take?", Michael asked.

"My old lady had some diamond jewelry. Her old man's in the diamond business in New York. I had some coins and stuff, and a small gold medallion. I gave descriptions and photos to the cops."

Remembering the abundance of golden items Michael had seen that night, the hairs on the back of his neck bristled. It is always the animal instinct in us that first senses when things are not right. There had also been a lot of diamond jewelry, but the gold had seemed to be of higher importance to Jose Ramos, so Michael decided to concentrate his interrogation on it.

"You mind if I get myself a drink of water?", Michael asked, and started for the kitchen.

"No, go ahead."

Michael selected a tall plastic cup from the top tray of the open door of the dishwasher, ran the water a few seconds, then filled the cup about two thirds of the way full of water. Quickly opening the freezer, he said, "You got ice?"

Before Ramos could object, Michael had helped himself to a pair of cubes and visually inspected the freezer contents. The aluminum foil covered packets of cold cash were still where he had left them on his first visit.

As Michael swung the freezer door shut, he considered the possibilities. Maybe the burglar didn't have time to properly toss the place. Or maybe he missed it. Or maybe, just maybe, he didn't need to take the cash and in spite of what the police might have been convinced of, was in the room with Michael at this very minute.

Returning to the sofa, Michael said, "Frankly, Mr. Ramos, I doubt that our thief will be the same guy after all. The guy I'm looking for is nuts about gold, and likes to hit places where there's plenty of it. Diamonds and coins sounds like someone else. If there was only one gold medallion included in your loss, I probably cannot help you."

The lie took Ramos aback and left him off-balance. Michael could almost see his mind sway, trying to regain the balance, weighing each side carefully. Ramos hesitated for a long second, then licked his lips and began.

"Look, man, this I didn't tell the cops because I didn't want no questions about where I got the money for it."

He paused. Michael waited.

"Man", he said, "I had a shitload of gold jewelry in the bedroom, and he took all of it - every last piece, including my favorite medallion, which was huge." His eyes flared. "If you catch him, I want him. I want to make him pay for what he did."

The last was said with enough hatred to convince Michael it was true. Killing Ramos' girlfriend was evidently one thing, but stealing his pretty gold toys quite another. It was too childishly selfish not to be true. In that moment, Michael felt confident the police had been right to clear Ramos. It would be hard to fake being that petty.

"Did the police tell you any details about her murder?", Michael casually asked.

"When they told me I could move back in here, except for the bedroom, they told me she had been raped and tortured before being killed, but would not give me any more details", he replied.

That was not good news for Michael. When Shemuel learned of it, it was likely to put an even finer edge on the sword upon which Michael was perched, but he kept his face calm. Michael's grandfather had taught him a technique that was almost always useful – a Japanese technique called 'Shiran Kao' - the face of he who knows nothing. It had won many a poker hand over the years, and came in handy during times of stress such as this.

They talked a short while longer, and then Michael excused himself for the night, promising to be in touch if anything developed. During their talk, Michael learned that the entry was apparently through the sliding patio door. The catch had been slipped with a butter knife or something very similar to one, according to the detectives who checked out the scene. Their finding was based on marks on the catch itself.

Because that is a method that would work on that particular lock, and the marks, which Michael examined, looked reasonably fresh and appropriately placed, Michael tended to believe the detectives were right, increasing the likelihood of a second burglar.

 However, the lock on that door used a disc tumbler cylinder that a kid could pick with a diaper pin, so Michael figured the burglar's skill level can't be too high. He could have saved himself about a full minute that way, and a minute of being exposed on the outside patio is a serious risk. Of course, one job isn't much to judge a person's skill level on and Michael realized he could be wrong about him. But regardless, it made it much more likely that there had, in fact, been another burglary, or at least that the killer had broken in rather than being invited.

On the way back to the boarding house and the solitude of his room, Michael stopped at a neighborhood bar called 'Smiley's Place.' Smiley was tending bar. Whoever nicknamed him must have had a keen sense of irony, because it didn't look like Smiley had ever smiled in his life. Nor did much about the place invite smiles. The stools were cracked red vinyl. The floors were sticky and rough with a dirty look and the smell of stale beer. But at least the draught beer was cold, and the glasses tall and clean. That was enough for Michael right now.

At the other end of the bar, a pair of rough looking guys were giving some grief to a bespectacled elderly gentleman. Then they were joined by a short bearded man, and the whole thing ended as quickly as it had begun.

"Damn Cooper brothers", Smiley muttered. "Good thing Emory was there."

"Regulars?", Michael asked, though he really wasn't interested.

"The kind of guys where once is too regular", the bartender replied. "Mean and always looking for trouble. And willing to create it if they don't find it. But no, I think they usually go someplace else, which is fine by me."

Smiley continued drying glasses with a small bar towel to remove any soap marks, and Michael went back to his beer. After two beers Michael headed back to his room.

Michael greeted the landlady as she peered out through her door to see if anyone was coming in with him, and climbed the long stairs. A quick hot shower rested any of the muscles that the beer hadn't, and he was sleeping soundly within a minute of when his head hit the pillow.

Chapter 13

Michael's next day was perfectly planned out. He was at the library when it opened, and proceeded to skim read every page of every newspaper in their files, going back for two years. He took detailed notes on anything even vaguely concerned with burglary, criminal trespass, fencing operations, or related to sex offenses. He also researched murders, but without a lot of hope. Most murders are clear cut and involve family members or close friends or neighbors, and have no mystery as to the perpetrator, only the motive.

Before noon Michael's hand was cramping regularly. There is a lot of crime in any tourist area and Sunset Cove was no exception. By the time Michael finished, he had gone through two pens and most of a very thick spiral notebook. It would take at least the rest of the night to sort out all the information he had extracted, but from it he hoped to build a picture of burglary in the area, including a who's who of the locals involved.

Even though he realized he would need to return for more searches as his answers began to take a more solid form, these would give him a starting place in planning the rest of the search, and hopefully even locating the killer.

Michael found it interesting that there were even more burglaries in the area than he would have expected. This made the possibility of a second burglar far more likely than he had at first believed it to be, and definitely a first avenue to pursue.

Interesting as well was the somewhat humorous fact that the lie Michael had told Jose Ramos turned out to very likely be true. Many of these had involved the theft of gold in some form or other.

Interesting, also, was that Michael got the distinct feeling in reading the articles that there might actually be several different cat burglars in the area. That seemed odd because cat burglars tend to be a fairly rare occurrence. Of course, there also seemed to be the usual number of amateurs as well, muddying the waters even further.

As expected, there were no other murders in the immediate area that seemed related. There were the usual high number of disappearances, but once again, none seemed related to this incident.

The vast majority of burglaries, of course, fell into familiar patterns. Paying attention to the competition, Michael had seen similar patterns before.

 Most were what appeared to be singular and unrelated events. Different people react differently to committing a burglary. A large percentage are so terrified and excited by the act of being in someone else's home or business illegally that they sweat profusely, and many times even lose control of their bodily functions. If they are able to get their pants down in time, the police reports may describe it as an act of vandalism, rather than the act of sheer desperation it truly is.

Either way, having had the shit scared out of them, most of these people never commit a similar crime. They correctly deduce that they are not cut out for a life of crime. This accounts for the large percentage of burglaries falling into the amateur range. When you do something only once, it is hard to learn from your mistakes and improve your ability to do it. Many of these are also juveniles, accounting for about 54% of all burglaries in any area, according to the FBI statistics.

Then there are people like Michael, for whom crime is a profit-making business. Their reactions tend to be somewhat cold and calculated, and if there were no profit anticipated, they would be likely to commit no crime. Caution is their watchword.

But for the third group, burglary is a stimulus much like a good sexual encounter. Like the first group, their body reacts to the idea of being in someone else's home or business illegally. But for these people, the fear and excitement cause an adrenalin flow and a blood rush. Describing it in early encounters, they use phrases like "For the first time, I felt truly alive."

They are the thrill thieves. Typically, in the beginning the mere act of breaking and entering is enough. Then they discover that by taking something from the premises the adrenalin high is extended. By this time, they could be accurately described as adrenalin addicts. Soon, mere burglary is not enough, and they escalate to being cat burglars.

A cat burglar is a thief who invades occupied premises to commit his burglary. It is a far more serious crime in nearly every state, and with good reason. It is far too often the last stage before the cross-over to crimes against person rather than against property.

Not every cat burglar crosses that line, of course. Most just keep taking more and more risks, becoming bolder and bolder until they are finally caught, which is, for them, the ultimate adrenalin flow.

One of the burglars Michael was tracking had, in a fairly recent burglary, deliberately awakened the elderly couple whose home he had just burglarized to say "Bye, Bye". Of course, among the items he had stolen were their eyeglasses and hearing aids, so they weren't able to describe him to the police, and they described his voice as being muffled beyond any recognition.

In another case, a middle aged man had awakened to surprise a burglar in his home. Picking up a baseball bat, he had told his wife to hide while he took care of it. No one knows exactly what happened next, but the homeowner has been in a coma ever since, a victim of his own baseball bat. The burglar probably thought he was dead.

If Michael's profile was correct, and of course, there was a good chance it was not, the guy he was looking for was most likely crossing over. So the question as Michael saw it was, how far back can the thief be traced by following his pattern? And could Michael correctly separate the various burglary patterns?

But who knows? If Michael could trace the burglary pattern back far enough, maybe he could find an early arrest. It was not overly likely, since that might tend to have altered the pattern, but stranger things have happened. In fact, his research already had exposed two incidents on which to focus his early efforts.

Of course, as he had already noted, other possibilities also existed. What if the attack on the Ramos residence was not a burglary at all, but something of a drug related attack. Perhaps it was a message sent to Ramos from a local gang or cartel.

Michael made a note to himself to investigate those possibilities as well, although it was somewhat outside his field of expertise, so it would take a back burner in his efforts for now. In his defense for this, there had been nothing in the articles in the newspapers that strongly supported any of the other possibilities..

On the way home, Michael picked up a copy of the day's paper which confirmed that Rebeccah Levine had been raped, apparently in more than one orifice, and tortured as well as murdered. There was no DNA discovered. How much longer could her father hold the pieces of his sanity together, Michael wondered, feeling the pressures of time closing in on him.

Shemuel was already angry at her death, and would be further furious that an autopsy had been performed (although a rabbi had likely been present and everything returned upon completion), but this newest piece of the puzzle would likely send him over the edge. And when he went over the edge, it was Michael that Shemuel was likely to land on if Michael did not find the real killer before that.

Michael made a beeline back to the room he was renting and began poring through all the notes he had taken at the library. He needed every bit of information to be burned into his memory and fully understood, and to cull out any unnecessary information.

He worked through the morning and into the afternoon. By then his eyes felt as though they were permanently crossed, his hands were cramped, his pens were all out of ink, and he still had about thirty pages to read, absorb, and fit into the picture. He halfway considered running an ad in the local classified for a research assistant, but decided that a late lunch would probably serve the same purpose, and maybe better and faster.

As Michael reached the ground floor, he heard the door creak, and watched out of the corner of his eye as it opened just a crack to allow the landlady to peer out, and once again monitor her territory. As tired as he was, it irritated him rather than amuse him as it usually would have.

As he started the little compact, he let the engine roar. He guessed that a part of him wanted to express the primal anger within. After he had done it, he felt foolish for having done so, which made him even angrier.

No one on the road knew how to drive that day. Some were too fast, some too slow, and some didn't know just where to go, although he was trying very hard to tell them. Michael usually did not take on the responsibility of teaching other people to drive, but that day was certainly an exception.

The diner he chose looked clean and yet well-traveled from the outside. The parking lot was oversize, which might mean that truckers sometimes make it their spot on their way through the area. While Michael had never held to the theory that the places truckers frequent have better food, he believed that at the least it is usually edible, which is more than can be said for some of the other eating establishments in places like Florida, New York and New Jersey.

Michael sat at a booth in the back of the diner. The light was higher than he would prefer it when he dined out, but it was not unbearably so. He kept watching the numbers speed by on his digital wristwatch. Fully three minutes later, he still had not seen his waitress come anywhere near the table, so he shouted out, "Hey, how about some service back here?"

The waitress that came out of the kitchen answered.

"l saw you looking at your watch so I figured that you were waiting on someone else to arrive."

She slowly walked across the room, and he became aware of a kind of quiet defiance in her gaze, as though she had just won a round in a challenging and exciting game, and was daring the other player to try her again. Although she was not tall, maybe only five foot two or three, she carried herself in a way that made her seem tall.

She wore a black mini-dress that had a small amount of white lace around the rather low cut front. Her legs were smoothly tanned as high as the eye could see, and she wore no stockings. The white soft-soled shoes contrasted with her tan, and had just enough lift to them to give appearance of being almost high-heeled.

Her hair was auburn, worn long and free, with a life in it that said she spent hours each day caring for it and pampering it. Michael could imagine her sitting in front of a mirror brushing it ever so carefully. He found the image strangely fascinating.

And then he saw her eyes. They wore only a slight amount of make-up, as did the rest of her face, but carefully applied to bring out the full sparkle of green and gold in them. But that was not what he noticed just then. Instead, he noticed that her eyes had changed from the defiant look he had noticed a moment earlier. Now they sparkled with a laughter and delight in observing his attention to her. She knew he had been captivated by her, and she took great joy in winning yet another hand in the game.

As Michael placed his order for steak, medium well, and mashed potatoes, and assured her that he definitely wanted coffee, he was repeatedly made aware of the tinkling of small, delicate bells when she spoke. Her voice was uniquely musical, gentle, and delightfully entertaining.

And then he saw her eyes again, and knew she had won another hand in the game. It angered him. After all, he was there to eat, not play games. Nevertheless, as she walked away, he felt an excitement as he watched the gentle sway of her hips.

Michael tried to be patient as he waited for the food. He knew that much of his anger was merely frustration and exhaustion. Nevertheless, by the time the food came, he was boiling inside.

Michael was not usually the type to complain, especially about food in a restaurant. Maybe in this case he just wanted to win one round in the game himself, and maybe he just wanted to let some of the steam out. At any rate, this time he chose to complain.

As she came out of the kitchen, he signaled her to the table, and then began a long tirade about the over-cooking of the steak, and the under-cooking of the mashed potatoes, and the icy temperature of the coffee.

Looking very distressed, she apologized and promised to have it fixed up promptly. Yet as upset as she had seemed, the sway of her hips did not change as she carried the tray back to the kitchen.

About two minutes later, she returned to the table, a tray carried high in her hand.

"I'm sure this will be much better, sir", she said with a full and warm smile. "I'm very sorry about the other, and I promise it won't ever happen again."

Michael felt much better, then. He had vented his anger, won a hand in the lady's own game, and was about to enjoy a splendid meal. Truth be known, the first platter had been very attractive looking, and well within the range that he would usually have found acceptable, even though it wasn't perfect. She was being so kind and apologetic that he almost felt sorry for having complained. Almost. But it still felt better to have done it.

Then she set down the tray and he was speechless. His eyes opened like silver dollars and all he could do was stare and gasp. It was the same platter he had before, but ketchup had been spread all over the steak and potatoes, and there was a pickle in the coffee.

"Enjoy your meal, sir", she said, as she turned and walked back to the kitchen door without missing a stride.

Michael must have sat for a full minute allowing it to sink into his brain, and then he began to laugh. Not a chuckle, mind you, but a full bodied, all-embracing guffaw that shook his sides and didn't stop until he thought his stomach muscles might never allow him to breathe normally again. Tears rolled out of his eyes and down his cheeks. His face was so red that it was a miracle that cars on the highway didn't stop to wait for the green.

92

Michael didn't know why it caught him the way it did. Maybe because it was so unexpected and delivered with such sincerity. Or maybe because what his body really needed to do right then was laugh away the pain, frustration and tiredness. For whatever reason, it did the job. He felt better than he had in days.

He ate every bite of the food, including the pickle, and drank the coffee to the last drop. As he finished it, she returned, and with a straight face, asked him if he enjoyed his meal, and would he care for dessert.

Michael told her he had enjoyed the meal tremendously, and that it was a big improvement over the first platter she had brought him. He declined the dessert, but asked if there was any chance of the cook sharing his recipe with him for that delicious meal.

At that, her face opened into a brief wide and beautiful laughter, ending in the kind of smile that once launched a thousand ships. Michael knew without a doubt where he would be having his meals whenever he was around here. He even for a brief moment considered relocation far away from the Pennsylvania winters.

Her name, he learned, was Nichole, although she preferred to be called "Nicki". She was originally from Louisiana, and wasn't quite sure why she had moved to Florida, except that it wasn't Louisiana. Michael thought about her all the way back to his room, chuckling occasionally as he remembered the way the platter had looked, and imagined how he must have.

Chapter 14

Once he was back in the room, Michael found it amazing how much easier the pieces were to fit together, and how much simpler it was to trace the patterns involved. Much of what he learned matched his initial impressions fairly closely, but there were a few things he had missed that now seemed obvious.

One possible suspect could be ruled out because Michael had run into him a few months ago on a job in Chicago. The guy had graduated to the big leagues, and was doing salaried burglaries for a group of businessmen that hate to be called the Mob or the Outfit. When Michael realized why the guy was hitting the same place he was, he decided to let him take it. Michael could choose any job he wanted. The guy was stuck with the assignments he received. That's a tough row to hoe.

As he had suspected earlier, most of the burglaries were committed by teenagers, reflected their skill level, and their penchant for things electronic. It was a simple matter to rule them out on a set of hits such as he was learning about.

One particularly interesting set of burglaries was from an unusual source - a group of elementary school kids were seen prior to each burglary, and were believed to be related to it. Most likely this was a case like that from Charles Dickens' Oliver Twist, where Fagin was an adult who ran a gang of child pickpockets and thieves. Still, it had been going on for several months, and it sounded like the police were still clueless, which he found curiously intriguing. Probably a bent cop running them, he thought briefly. But it also had nothing to do with what he was there to learn, so he crossed those off on his notes.

Most burglars prefer to strike between the hours of seven and ten at night, when the owners are out for an evening's entertainment, or during the mid-afternoon. The pattern of escalation was there, but because Rebeccah had died around Sunset, it was unlikely that any matching this string was related. Nonetheless, he needed to isolate them so they could be eliminated.

Michael had noticed one strong lead on his initial reading in the library. The police had been basically clueless on the crime, although they had interviewed one person of interest, a fellow with the unusual name of Laurence P Stickney the Fourth, and later released him. That would be the first one he would later check, he decided.

After all the sifting, after nearly three hundred pages of handwritten information, Michael had two obviously possible suspects, both of which had been questioned very early in the period he was checking, and neither of whom fit the typical profile for burglars, which he found encouraging.

Nonetheless, he realized both might turn out to be quite innocent of this particular crime.

These two were both older than the average burglar, but without showing any particular finesse that might indicate experience and skill. Both were accused of having taken jewelry and gold, questioned and released, but not before attracting the attention of the press.

Interestingly enough, both had also been picked up by the same cop, who then transferred to the State Police based on his successful record of arrests. That would mean it was possible none of the other police were particularly watching them, so they could still both be active.

Michael had also located what appeared to likely be three full-time fences, any of whom could be handling the stolen merchandise. It was almost a certainty that one of them was. They looked to him like one of his best starting places. But first, he would have to gain their confidence, which would mean that he would have to pull another hit in the area.

That was something that he truthfully did not want to do, even though it seemed like his best, and possibly only, chance of cracking this case before Sam Levine cracked instead.

Michael didn't like fences. They are only loyal to themselves, most talk too much, and all would sell you down the river before they even thought of doing time themselves. But those same traits might make them usable tools this time.

Michael knew that even if he found the killer, a fence was still his best hope of proving who was guilty. Knowing was not enough. He needed to be able to prove it, at least to Shemuel, and possibly indirectly to the police.

First Michael needed some bargaining power, though. That meant a hit that night was justified. Because birds of a feather really do tend to flock together, Michael headed for the Playa del Sol condos in the late afternoon. There he waited and watched until his target appeared and was chosen. Michael hadn't known specifically who he would be, but he knew what the target's traits would be.

The guy's gold chains glittered in reflection of the parking area lights as he left his apartment and his radio blasted from the sports car as he drove off. Like Ramos, he was more of the fast money crowd. And Michael knew that almost guaranteed what he would find when he got to the apartment. And of course, this condo was on the second floor also. That had been a deciding factor in his selection.

This time the lock fought Michael all the way, and he was almost ready to give up when he heard footsteps approaching. Just then it turned, however, and Michael was in.

Suitcases that from the luggage tags Michael suspected once might have contained coke were leaning against one wall, but Michael ignored them. He also ignored expensive watches and similar items he could see randomly placed around the rooms. This time he was strictly going for the gold. His research had indicated that there was a strong likelihood of a link between gold and the victims of the cat burglar he suspected might be behind the killing. So he wanted a fence who would handle exactly that.

The drawer of the nightstand offered his bounty, and Michael was halfway to the front door with his bag filled with delights when he heard a key fumbling to enter the lock. Out of habit, Michael had fortunately left the keyway in the picked open position, halfway upside down, with a piece of broken toothpick in it. The key wouldn't go in until it was turned around, and would stick a little even then. That gave him a little time, but possibly not enough.

Michael ran to the patio door, removed a broomstick placed there by its occupant to prevent break-ins, and slid it open. He leapt out, vaulted the small balcony fence, dropping the bag, which he followed to the ground. Michael's ankles and arches felt as though they had been clubbed, but he ignored the pain as he retrieved the bag and ran to the car.

Michael roared away, but he didn't drive back to his room yet. He drove around until he was absolutely certain that he hadn't been followed. The evening hadn't been a total washout, he reflected. At least Michael had the gold to bargain with a fence over, and he hadn't been caught yet.

He decided to stash his bounty at the fisherman's cove he had stopped at earlier on his way into the area. He picked up a small shovel at a hardware store on the way.

The cove was deserted, as Michael had expected it to be that late in the day. Fishermen like to get an early start and return to shore when the sun gets warm.

He selected a secluded but recognizable palm tree, used the shovel to dig a hole about three inches deeper than the bag required, and buried he bag of gold in the sand loosely .

He then covered it with more sand, and that sand with palm leaves. The palm leaves would probably keep the bag dry from small afternoon rains.

It would be secure until the next big storm, and if Michael was not out of the area long before that, he probably would not care if it was found. It was about a month before the season of afternoon storms, and Michael suspected Shemuel's patience was a far shorter period.

Michael decided to make another stop at the bar near his rooming house to relax briefly before beginning the next phase of his operation - contacting the fences.

He had barely reached the counter and not even chosen a seat yet, when his attention was drawn to a grainy video playing on the local news channel. The 'breaking news' banner at the bottom described it as 'video of burglar spotted at scene of burglary and murder'.

Although very poor in quality, probably from a cheap phone, the video showed Michael dropping from the balcony and retrieving the bag, then running around the corner of the building.

Michael ordered a double shot of Glen Fiddich 12 and sat contemplating this latest turn of events. He was astounded at how quickly the video had made it to a news desk, even more than he was frustrated that he had missed the fact he was being photographed.

Michael was not really identifiable in the photo, but it did not make him happy to see it. He knew that somewhere police IT people would be trying to improve the image to make a drawing of the suspect. He also knew it increased his risk in contacting the fences. He would have to put that on hold.

There was still some afternoon left, so he decided to instead begin running down the short suspect list he had put together.

Chapter 15

Michael knew the two potential leads he had were fairly slim, but slim beats none, and it allowed him to delay visiting a fence, with all its related risks, a little longer.

The first address was on the outskirts of town, in a cul-de-sac at the end of a widely spaced set of wooden single story houses. Apparently the original developers built on every third lot when they built the development, and sales never caught up enough to continue beyond that.

But much to Michael's dismay, the address was now an empty lot with the remnants of what had once been a burned down home. The concrete base was charred and small portions of the burned charcoal remained, but little else.

He was just about to leave when an elderly lady walking her Chihuahua addressed him.

"Are you thinking of buying the lot?", she asked.

"No, actually I was looking for the owner. I guess I am a little late. This was the best address I had."

" It burned down about a year and a half ago. Did you know them well?"

"No, I was a business associate of his."

"It was quite a shame. His wife was always smoking in bed, and one night when he was out of town, she paid for it with her life."

"Smoking in bed.", he muttered thoughtfully.

"Yes, she had done so twice before and the fire department was called in time, but I guess that time she had not replaced the batteries in the smoke detectors after the previous fire. She was not all that bright, you know. Heavy drinker. It's no wonder they were always arguing."

"Do you know where the husband is living now?"

"No. Mr. Stickney left once the insurances on her life and the house had paid off, and no one on the block has heard from him since. I keep expecting to see a 'For Sale' sign. I thought you might be here for that."

Michael thanked her for her time, and left, making a mental note to follow up on the former resident, although it seemed highly unlikely this lead would go anywhere. Laurence Stickney the Fourth seemed more like just another low- life loser.

He reminded himself that it had been a slim lead anyway, so he should not be too disappointed.

The second address Michel had obtained from the 'Police Blotter' in the newspaper turned out to be an aging block and stucco house, almost square in shape, on a small tract of land at the edge of town. From the outside, the house looked relatively cared for, although the Pensacola rye grass lawn soon would need cutting.

There was a one car garage, with its door closed, and a red and white Mini-Cooper sat uncovered in the driveway under a canopy. The house had a large screened room that stood empty except a small table surrounded by six swivel chairs. Other than a pair of tall cactus plants and a century palm bush, there were no signs of personality showing on the outside of the house, so Michael felt reasonably certain that Fentworth wasn't a family man, but the small car indicated he might not live alone.

Approaching the house, Michael knocked on the jalousie door. The first time he knocked, the only response was the rattling of the slats of glass that made up most of the door. His second knock was rewarded by a feminine voice inviting him to "Come in".

Opening the door, Michael walked into the living room of the house. It was a world apart from the outside. The furniture, though modern, was impeccably chosen, and hadn't been cheap. A handful of small crystal sculptures were tastefully arranged around the room. Michael recognized a painting on one wall from a gallery in New York, where its price tag had been over two thousand bucks. He tried to remember if he knew who had purchased it, but couldn't.

Although the decor could all have been the rewards of successful burglaries, the arrangement told Michael it wasn't as likely as he wanted to believe. The kind of taste that went with this was usually bred, not acquired. Also, the flavor was New York, not Florida. Michael began to wonder if he even had the right place. His hostess still hadn't appeared, so he called out a questioning hello.

"I'm doing my eyes. Who are you, and what do you want?"

The voice came from the bathroom in the far corner of the small house. Michael could see the kitchen ahead to the right, and the bedroom down the hall to the left. A very functional and unimaginative arrangement, which he knew was typical of this type of house in Florida.

"I'm looking for Jim Fentworth", Michael answered.

"Wrong house", the voice responded, "He moved out about a year ago. I bought the house from him. What do you want him for?"

The question, though casually asked, brought up the hairs on the back of Michael's neck, and told him there was more to the story than simply buying the house a year ago. Why else would she care what he wanted?

"Do you know where I can find him?", Michael asked, ignoring her question.

"Yes, but who wants to know?"

Michael thought about it a few seconds, then decided. "Sam Brown, Citywide Detectives", he answered.

"Is he in trouble?"

"Maybe. I won't know until I talk to him. But I won't cause him any trouble. What's your interest in it?"

"I know him. I don't particularly like him, but we have a lot of friends in common. As a matter of fact, I'm going to a party at his house early this evening. It might be fun to bring you along. Interested?"

Before Michael could answer, he heard the door open and the quiet slap of bare feet on the terrazzo floor of the hallway. Not exactly a rare sound in the Sunshine State, but as he turned to answer, Michael found that all he could do was stare. She had been doing her eyes, all right, and they were beautiful. But the rest of her was stunning.

Her hair was cut in a Mohawk, of the style that was popular among some of the people for about a minute in the mid-1980's, and it was dyed a rich sky blue. Michael had always thought this sort of thing was ugly, whether on a male or a female, but this one was all female and anything but ugly.

He was accustomed to seeing brightly colored hair on teen aged girls from time to time, but this lady was obviously matured.

She stood, as nearly as Michael could guess, about six feet tall, but there was nothing big or awkward about her. Everything about her was perfectly proportioned. On her, the bizarre hairdo looked just fine. On her, anything would look just fine. But nothing looked even better, and that's what she had on right now.

She stood gracefully, and when his eyes finally got back to hers, Michael saw that she was appraising him, also. When she smiled, it seemed to light up the already bright room, and Michael couldn't help returning the smile. He stopped thinking much about why he was there. It was as if she had taken over his entire being.

"I'm sorry", Michael stated awkwardly.

"For what?", she asked.

"You.., I... , you're not dressed...and I'm ..."

"You're not the one who undressed me, Sugar, so why are you feeling guilty? I'm the one who is naked and if I'm not embarrassed, so why should you be?"

"It's just, I ...", Michael paused, not really knowing what to say.

"Look, if you are going to the party with me, you had better get over this pretty quickly, okay?"

"Okay", Michael answered, using up the full measure of his available wittiness. "So what should I call you, sweetheart?"

"Sweetheart will do just fine", she said, and laughed again, "but my name is Linda. What's yours?"

"Mike", he answered, without thinking about it.

"Linda Beecher," she continued, "And to think you were only a Sam when you first came in."

Seeing Michael's embarrassment, she laughed again.

"Best little old lie detector in the whole world, right here between my legs", she said. There was a certain bawdy flavor to her laughter this time, as though of shared secret awarenesses.

But the name correction did not seem to bother her as she quietly slipped into a pullover low cut very short dress of soft silk-like material in summer flower colors. She wore nothing underneath, but put on a pair of medium heeled shoes that made her seem even taller.

After she was as dressed as she intended to be, they started the drive in Michael's rental car to the other side of town, where she told him Fentworth had moved. Getting into the little car, for the first time Michael was truly aware of her size.

"Need a shoehorn?", he asked. "Sorry that unlike your car, this isn't a convertible."

"I'm skilled. I'll make it."

"Sweetheart", Michael said, grinning at her, "I suspect you are surely skilled."

They laughed a familiar laugh, one that belied how briefly they had known each other. Michael followed her carefully offered driving instructions and they continued to laugh often as they talked of many things along the way. Somehow they kept from laughing after their drive, as they pulled into the Fentworth property. The sun was just beginning to cast long shadows, and the sky was beginning to look like a vivid watercolor. Somehow it made the Fentworth estate seem surrealistic.

And estate it truly was. As they entered the extremely large parking lot at Jim Fentworth's home, Michael was intrigued and pleased by both its proximity to the Playa del Sol condos, and its' obviously tasteless wealth. Most homes in Florida are either ranch style or split level, but this one was actually several three story buildings merged together in nearly a C shape. Around the perimeter of the property was a tall block wall with turret stations in each corner. There were large metal gates that could be swung shut, although they were open currently. They appeared to be electrically activated. On the West end of the property, the driveway passed a series of about twenty garages, and beyond that was a small inlet with a large boat dock, currently empty, complete with a large boathouse. Although the home it was not very distant from its neighboring houses, it felt as if it were.

The driveway split off into a large circular drive with a fountain in its middle and another straight portion that led to a Spanish influenced style of port cochere. Michael followed the circular drive and parked in one of the spaces on the far side of it.

Chances were very good that the telescope Michael spotted on Fentworth's roof could see a great deal of who and what went on in the Playa del Sol condos if it were pointed in that direction. Hope for an early end to this search made his heart pound almost as much as looking at his current companion did, and that was no small task.

As they entered the house without knocking, Michael observed that the wall in front of the entryway had doors on each side leading to a sunken and sloped movie theatre with cathedral ceilings. He estimated the seating at about 150 seats. This was not a modest person's home by any means. It was quite the change from Fentworth's previous residence, possibly funded by gold and jewel thefts. Michael's hope was rising steadily.

The swimming pool in the center of the kidney shaped home was overly decorated around its circumference by bold statues of male and female forms in difficult poses. That they were expensive went without saying. That they were in doubtful taste also did. Furniture visible through the large windows of his home were also undoubtedly from the finest stores, but arranged in such a haphazard way that all of them looked cheap.

All of this made it more likely that Fentworth was definitely worth consideration as a suspect in the recent burglaries in the area, and maybe the murder of Rebeccah Levine. His wealth was fast money, not old money, and not very likely to be earned money. Passing by Fentworth's master bedroom Michael saw the glint of gold on a nightstand next to the bed and became even more hopeful.

The party they were attending was obviously an excuse for wanton abandon more than a social gathering. Michael and Linda were not even among the early guests to arrive. Many had obviously been relaxing for quite a while before Michael and Linda got there. Bodies caressed each other openly in various areas of the house and grounds. Linda and Michael circulated through the wide variety of guests that had come for the party for nearly four hours, and saw most of the house, including a more than brief and very private stop in his boat house.

In the boathouse, Linda turned toward Mike, and gazed thoughtfully for a moment before speaking.

"Interesting party, eh?"

"A bit bold for my tastes, but I would have to agree it is interesting.", Michael replied.

"I find you very interesting, too" Linda stated. Then she was coming toward him, and his eyes watched her lips, longing to taste them, aware of the nearness of her. Michael's mind went blank as he almost automatically put his arms around her body, and sought her lips with his.

But before they could touch, Michael felt a tugging at his zipper, a pulling freedom, and then suddenly the lady was only three feet tall, and he was fully experiencing the warm moistness of her soft lips, lips that he had yet to taste. But suddenly Michael didn't mind that at all. He nearly went into shock at this somewhat unexpected and unprecedented turn of events.

Her hands gripped Michael for support, while his sought the fullness of her magnificent breasts, and traced the sleek lines of her shoulder and neck, to the shaved baldness of the sides of her head and the delicate lines of her high cheekbones. Michael was admittedly still a bit confused by the suddenness of these events, but he did not care.

 She brought him along skillfully and wonderfully until he felt the muscles of his body draw tight, the motion of his hips uncontrollable, and knew that he was about to explode in completion and satisfaction. Then just as suddenly as it had begun, it stopped, leaving Michael hanging on that cliff, wanting to fall off, but unable to.

She was six feet tall again, and gently leading him onto one of the larger flatboats. She helped Michael out of his clothes, and they both helped him out of his clothes, and he helped her out of her clothes, which went very quickly. One button on Michael's shirt popped off and flew to a skittering halt along the wall, but he didn't mind it at all.

Michael had to admit to himself that he was more than a little baffled. Maybe somewhere there are guys who on a regular basis get a response like this to meeting someone, but Michael certainly did not consider himself to be one of them. Even as Brian Stonewell, whose money was often an aphrodisiac, he had never experienced anything sudden like this. But it was impossible for him to concentrate on that confusion for very long.

 Their lips met for the first time and explored each other, and their hands searched the lines of each other's body, and they tumbled toward the flatboat.

Her knees reached for the ceiling, and her thighs massaged Michael's cheeks as he experienced the other tastes and textures of her, slowly working his way back to her face and those wonderful lips. Only then did their bodies join to become the four-footed writhing see-saw beast, her hips rising as his fell, and dropping as his withdrew.

When Michael felt her hips quiver and drive toward his in small staccato rhythm, and her breath become reduced to gasps and incoherent moans, he knew, and in that knowledge came the satisfying completion that he had thought he needed before they moved to the flatboat, and Michael was carried off that cliff into the depths of her, exploding his whole being until nothing seemed to exist except that completion.

The second time, a few minutes later, lacked the hunger and need of the first, but replaced it with textures and tenderness, warm explorations and a delicate familiarity.

Nearly an hour of touching and small familiar kisses passed before the time came for their third joining, and it was a warm comfort that brought with its end the knowledge that the experience was, at least for now, fully a complete knowing.

They showered together using the boathouse shower and a bottle of liquid soap from its shelf, the soft lathering of each other's body bringing with it the warm awareness and the little hungers. Then, when they had rinsed, their lips sought each other again, and other bodies started to forget the completeness they shared, and to hunger again for the fullness of touch.

Michael felt a sharp slap on his butt that brought him out of it.

"What's that for?", he asked.

"To break the spell cast by carnal lust, darling", she said, and scampered out of the shower so quickly that at first Michael thought she had slipped. Then she threw him a towel from the rack next to the shower, and began drying herself with its mate.

"If we kept going the way we were, we'd never make it out of here and meet Jim ", she said, "And we'd miss all the fun of whatever you are really up to." Her eyes sparkled with humor as she said it, and Michael knew that it wouldn't take much to get them both back into the boat.

"Do you think that we could do it again next week", she asked, "when I turn fifteen on my birthday? That would really make the day special."

Michael's jaw dropped momentarily, and his eyes opened like silver dollars had filled them, and the part of him that had heretofore stood at attention from the shower, even after the slap, withered and tried to hide in the dark hairs that surrounded it.

Then she laughed, a tinkling of bells mixed with a hearty robustness, and she said, "No, dear heart, just an old joke from a movie I once watched."

Michael knew, of course, that she had been joking. Obviously, if she had bought Fentworth's previous house she was no child. And the body he had just shared had been fully matured and knowing in a way that could only come from time and experience. But at the moment she said it, shock had made him forget all logic momentarily.

Even now, knowing the reality of it, Michael realized that its effect was a reminder that he actually knew nothing at all about her. Well, not quite nothing, but certainly not enough.

They left the boathouse sweating again, but not from the Florida heat. There was actually a cool breeze that had cooled their naked bodies in the boathouse earlier, but they had managed to work up quite a sweat anyway.

They had just gotten back to a reasonable vestige of their normal selves, when they were approached by a short man in his mid to late thirties with a white short-sleeve shirt that was obviously custom tailored and made of an excellent material. Smiling, Linda introduced Michael to James Fentworth.

"Jim", she said, "I'd like you to meet Sam Brown, an old friend of mine."

The joy Michael had been feeling dissipated quickly when he met James Fentworth. Michael was a little disappointed, although at the same time a little bit intrigued. Contrary to what he had expected he was neither a native Floridian nor James Fentworth.

Michael recognized him from newspaper and magazine photos in the New York area. He was Jimmy, true enough, but Jimmy DiCenzo, the wild son of the Johnny the Dentist, an enforcer for the Outfit in the City.

Jimmy had gotten into a few scrapes with the law involving partying, women and drugs, and had disappeared a few years ago. Now Michael knew where Jimmy had gone.

Had Jimmy decided to follow in his father's footsteps and make murder a family tradition, starting off by combining it with burglary? It was certainly believable. On the other hand, being the son of a professional killer would he be likely to show such rage as the killing of Rebeccah had demonstrated? That part seemed unlikely, although not impossible.

Michael and Linda circulated a little more, got the two-penny tour of the antique and luxury cars in the 24 garages they had passed earlier, and before long decided that no more was to be gained there for either of them and left.

"You're probably wondering if I do that with every guy who knocks on my door. The answer is No", she stated as Michael drove her home.

"Then why me?", Michael asked, genuinely a little confused.

"I could see into your soul", she replied " and I could see you were a very honorable man, mostly very honest, with a real set of rules and values, but that you were in pain and you were not being honest with me, probably out of some kind of fear. The only way to break through all that in a hurry is to break down all the walls. So I did."

"Believe me, I am not all that honest", Michael answered.

"See? Even that proves what I am saying. Your pain and fear are none of my business. But I can at least make you able to be more open with me. I can sense you are a very special person. And I can help bring that out, making us both happier."

Michael mused a short while on this strange woman and her ideas. He had certainly never met anyone like her. Most of the women he dated seemed shallow to him. None made him wonder what it would be like to spend a lifetime with them, much as he wanted to find someone to share his life with. In a really short while, almost inexplicably she had.

Somehow, and Michael could not say exactly how, this felt like something much deeper than just great sex. He had great sex before. This was something else, something special about her that Michael could sense in every part of his being, but could not explain, even to himself. She said she could see into his soul, and as unlikely as Michael found that, a part of him felt like he could see into hers as well, and it was beautiful. Her world was not grey and analytical as was his, but was full of color and light and hope. Could she be what Michael had been searching for without knowing it? He doubted it, but still...

When they got back to Linda's house, though, they found plenty to be gained for both of them, and it was well into the next morning when Michael finally awoke and showered to face the day.

"Do you want a copy of the video from the boathouse?", she asked, as Michael was drying off.

"What video?"

"Darling, you mean to say you never noticed the cameras there, not even the ones in the boathouse? Jim has an absolute penchant for voyeurism, but he'll only share the videos with the couples involved. I'll bet ours are absolutely thrilling. After all, you are."

This was a twist Michael hadn't planned on, and wasn't particularly pleased with, although he had to admit to himself and to her that it might indeed be very thrilling. It was not as disconcerting as it might have been, however, because Michael was already planning an unannounced visit to the house to check out the gold, and see what he could find connecting their host with the murder. The original of the video was merely something else to pick up there while he shopped for clues.

Michael told her a copy might be very nice, and they parted with a familiar kiss.

"By the way, you did not ask, but in case you are wondering, I see my doctor regularly and I am in perfect health in every way. No diseases." she stated.

Michael was shocked to realize that the thought had barely crossed his mind, but felt very relieved that she had told him. Sooner or later the spell would have worn off and he might have been very worried. They kissed again, even more tenderly and he left, looking back in his rear view mirror frequently until he could no longer see her or even her house.

Chapter 16

Officer Ed Camponi drove past the burned down Spaghetti Palace on his way home from the station house. He grimaced, remembering the years of torment he had received over that.

When he arrived at his home, he observed his neighbor berating her husband as he so often did. It made him very glad his wife was now long gone. Still, the bickering brought back vicious memories, and he could feel the bile rise in his throat as his anger built. He honestly did not miss her a bit.

He went into the study and closed the thick curtains, muffling the sounds somewhat. Then he put an old 33 and a third vinyl record on the antique stereo and listened to Frank Sinatra singing of his love of New York.

It calmed him slightly, and he opened his liquor storage cabinet and retrieved an expensive bottle of Glen Fiddich 18, pouring himself a healthy sampling in a tall glass. He had been hitting the good stuff a little more frequently lately as memories of the night of the fire kept coming back to him.

He replaced the bottle on the shelf and sat down in his recliner to let the smooth flavor and scent to follow the music into the depths of his mind, beginning to calm him. The recliner was soft, and very spacious around his thin body.

His mind was full of torment. Part of it was anger at the behavior his neighbor had exhibited, but the biggest portion was insecurity about his job. He wondered how long he would still have a position with the Sunset Cove Police Force. He knew that he had almost been let go once before, and if the City Council was indeed looking at cutting back, he imagined he would likely be the first to go.

Although his finances meant he did not really need the job, his ego did. It was the first mask people saw when they looked at him, and it excused the fact he was getting older. He often told himself that people had more faith in an older policeman than a young one. And at times he was sure of it. Or almost sure, at least. But sometimes doubt replaced the opinion.

Then the music did its job and he drifted off to sleep, barely remembering to set the glass on the coffee table before dropping off completely. Fortunately he had already set the alarm to wake him up before his next shift.

This was the night before what he called the short shift change - only a few hours between shifts - as opposed to the long shift change where he actually had thirty-six hours to do with as he pleased. He always looked forward to those shift changes, and made the most of them.

.

Chapter 17

Jose Ramos was on the phone with his supplier in Fort Lauderdale, and neither side of the conversation was very happy.

"I know it is a lot sooner than you would have expected. That should normally be a good thing and I could understand you wanting to charge a premium. But you gotta look at it from my side, Manny", Jose said.

Manny snorted into the phone. "Some cock and bull story about someone stealing thirty blocks of coke from you and you want a better price?"

"It's NOT a cock and bull story, Manny. They killed my old lady. You saw the news, right?"

"So kill them and get it back", Manny responded.

"That's just it", Ramos stated, "It has been almost a week, and the shit hasn't hit the streets. If it had, I could do just that. But it didn't. There was even a private investigator hired by the insurance companies and nothing has turned up, not even the jewelry."

"Bullshit.", Manny shouted into the phone. "Why would somebody steal it and not sell it or share it?"

"I been thinking about that, Manny, and the only thing that makes any sense to me is that it's the fucking cops. They must have come in to bust me, and when I wasn't there, they got pissed and killed my old lady trying to find out where I was. Then they confiscated my shit."

"That don't make any sense", Manny said. "Why wouldn't they just come get you now?"

"Because they killed my old lady", Ramos shouted. "They gotta hide it now, and lay low because even a cop can't get away with torturing a rich chick. So they make it look like a burglary gone wrong."

"So let's say I believe you", Manny said, "that still don't tell me why I shouldn't charge you a premium to replace what you lost."

"Come on, Manny. We been doing business for a long time. It's bad enough I gotta dig into my reserves at all to pay for it, but paying EXTRA? Don't do me like that, guy. Not after everything we been through?"

"Ah, hell.", Manny stated, pausing for a moment. " What the hell. I'll give it to you at regular price but I'm not cutting back from that. Business is business."

"Okay, if that's the best you can do.", Ramos answered, "Use the regular delivery guy. I'll be down with the money in the morning. "

They both clicked off their burner phones and stripped them of their SIMM cards before disposing of them.

Chapter 18

Officer Mickey Clements was smiling as he entered the back door at Johnson's Fish-o-Rama Tavern. He had a box full of bags of boiled and salted peanuts for the tavern to sell. They were always one of his best customers, because their customers fell into that grey area between the wealthy tourists and the often dirty independent fishermen. They had plenty of money to buy the treats and were not too proud to do so.

"Mickey", Gary, the owner, said, "Your timing is perfect."

"Running out?", Mickey said cheerfully.

"Well, yes, I guess so, but that isn't what I meant."

"I don't get it."

"I'm sorry. Let's start over. Mickey, a guy just tried to pass a credit card for his drinks, and it is stolen."

"On the list?", Mickey inquired.

"No.", Gary replied, "It isn't his. It belongs to the dead girl from the news."

"You're kidding me, right?", Mickey said, laughing.

"No, I'm serious as Hell. The guy is just sitting there drinking like nothing is going on and hands the waitress that card. And you walked in just as I was about to call it in."

Mickey set the box down on the small counter in the tavern's kitchen where Gary normally made sandwiches and snacks as needed. He keyed the mike.

"833."

"Go ahead 833", Sue answered.

"Need backup at Fish-o-Rama. Possible 187 suspect."

"10-4, 833. I will send 813."

"10-4 - I'll watch for him. Tell him to come in slow. I don't want to spook the guy."

"Will do", Sue answered, and switched her microphone to Camponi's direct channel. He stated he could be there in three minutes, and she then informed Mickey of the anticipated arrival .

Mickey released the safety strap on his holster and took out his 9 mm Ruger. He chambered a load and tested the safety. Then he quietly walked to the connecting door between the kitchen and the main barroom and edged the door open slightly to give him a view of the room.

"Which guy?", Mickey asked.

"Thin Hispanic looking guy at the corner table, wearing all black", Gary answered.

"Ouch", Mickey commented, "from there he will be able to see both myself and Camponi approaching."

"Maybe I can get Katie the waitress to distract him", Gary suggested.

"No, if we did that and she got hurt, the Chief would have my ass fried", Mickey answered.

Looking again at the large box of peanuts, Mickey had an idea. " Are you willing to donate some bags of peanuts to the cause to keep your place from getting shot up?", Mickey asked.

"Whatever it takes to make this as painless as possible", Gary responded.

Through the large front window of the tavern, Mickey could see Camponi's cruiser pulling into the lot.

"Showtime", he said.

He put his gun into the large box of peanuts, and raised the box to cover his badge, uniform shirt and tie, then pushed the door open.

"Free peanuts, folks, courtesy of Gary", Mickey called out and entered the barroom, handing out bags to individuals as he passed them, working his way to the back corner of the room. When he got there, instead of a bag, he pulled out his gun, dropped the box and shouted, "Don't move a muscle."

The large Hispanic in the black tee shirt looked like he was going to go for it anyway, but just then Camponi came in with his gun drawn as well. The guy stared at him a moment, shrugged, and relaxed his muscles. He then maintained steady eye contact with Officer Clements.

Camponi approached him, then ordered him to stand and put his hands behind his back. The suspect did exactly as he was told, and the arrest went without any difficulties. Camponi patted him down and cuffed him using a plastic tie band before transporting him to the station.

As Mickey followed, he was pleased. Not only had they very likely caught the girl's killer, but Camponi would have to do the paperwork. And he would charge Fish-o-Rama for that box of peanuts as well as one to replace it for them to sell. What could be better?

At booking, the contents of the suspect's pockets revealed several small bags of cocaine and a rubber band surrounding a relatively small roll of twenty dollar bills. There was a burner phone, but no wallet. Because the collar technically belonged to Camponi, based upon his transport and paperwork, he led the interrogation, but Mickey sat in.

"You've been read your rights during booking. Do you acknowledge this for the recording?"

The suspect nodded grudgingly.

"I need you to say it aloud", Camponi stated.

"Yah, I know my fucking rights", the suspect responded.

"State your name", Camponi continued.

"No." the suspect replied.

"What do you mean, no?", Camponi asked.

"I mean, No, I don't gotta tell you that."

"You think we can't find out who you are?", Camponi sneered.

"Don't mean I gotta make it easy though, do it?"

"Okay, you were using a credit card with the name Rebeccah on it, so I guess we will just call you Becky and book you under that name. Ought to make you popular in prison", Camponi threatened.

The suspect snarled a little, scowled and then shrugged and said "Antonio Rivera".

"Then I'm going to call you Tony instead. Is that ok?", Camponi asked.

"Whatever."

"Tony, right now we have you on a stolen credit card and felony possession with intent to sell. And it looks like you are also going down for murder one, unless you tell us what happened with the girl. If she got smart with you and gave you some shit, maybe we can convince the judge you didn't intend to kill her. Take the death penalty off the table."

"Death penalty? What the hell you talking about. I didn't kill nobody."

"You had the dead girl's credit card", Camponi stated, "I can't believe you were stupid enough to use it right here in town. If you don't start talking fast about what happened and how she got killed, I'm not going to be able to do anything to help you."

"No, man. I BOUGHT that fucking card. I didn't know she was killed. I didn't know who she was at all. I bought a dozen cards and that was one of them."

"You're trying to tell me you didn't know she was dead, even though it's been practically the only thing on the news the last couple days?"

"I don't watch no news, man. Got no interest in it. All about people I don't know and don't care about."

"So where did you buy the card?", Camponi asked, "assuming for a minute that I believe you?"

"Come on, I ain't no snitch."

"Fine, so we go back to the death penalty."

"No, wait, man. ok. ok. I bought it from Crazy Larry up in Saint Pete."

Camponi recognized that Crazy Larry was a well-documented fence. He kept being busted, fined, and doing a short term in jail or doing no time in exchange for providing the police with information. Camponi reflected that it could be true, or it could be that Rivera also knew the same stories, and was just using them as a smoke screen.

He thought about it a moment, then looked at Mickey. "What do you think? Do we check out his bullshit story or not?", he asked loudly.

"It's not bullshit. I swear it's the truth", Rivera shouted.

Mickey pretended not to have heard Rivera, and nodded, "I agree, it's probably bullshit, but if he gives us his address and permission to search the place, maybe we will find out one way or the other."

"I will", Rivera shouted, and began listing his two addresses. Mickey wrote them in his notebook. Then they took Rivera back to his cell and locked him in.

After they were back in the main section of the station, Mickey asked Camponi, "What do you think?"

"He seemed sincere enough. Pretty damned stupid, but I don't think he's lying about the card."

"Well, let's toss his places, and see what we find. If there are eleven more stolen cards, we can add them to his list of felonies, but we will know there is a chance he might not be our killer after all. It'd be a shame, though. I really thought maybe we had him. Could have gone a long way with City Council."

Chapter 19

As Kevin Wolf entered the back door of the precinct house he could hear the muttered arguments at the front desk. Sue Bennet was on duty and her ex-husband, Harvey, was at the service counter engaged in heated, but quiet, debate.

At six foot four and 235 pounds of mostly muscle, Harvey had seemed like he had the world at his feet in high school, and Sue had fallen there as well. But once the days of leading the football team were over, Harvey really did not amount to much. He scraped his way through college at USF, and received a Bachelor's degree that he could always hang on the wall wherever he worked.

But somehow the real meaning of that degree, the promise it seemed to hold, never really came through. Much like Harvey himself, it was a hollow reminder of what might have been.

Unable to keep a professional job for more than a year without his ego interfering, Harvey burned through opportunities like Sherman through Atlanta. And with his wife working to support them, his ego had made him unbearable and cruel, resulting in their rather torrid divorce a few months earlier.

Since then, Harvey had needed to be physically removed from the building on several occasions. It appeared to Kevin it was probably about to need done again, and he was the one who would need to do it.

But Harvey looked up when Kevin entered the room behind Sue. His eyes looked around quickly, as if wanting to melt into the background, and he stopped his argument mid-sentence. Despite his size, Harvey was more a bully than a fighter, and he secretly was quite afraid of Kevin.

"Screw this.", he muttered, and with an angry look cast in Sue's direction, he left, doing his level best to slam the outside door, but finding that the resistance of its door closer made it impossible to do so.

After Harvey was gone, Sue turned to Kevin and said, "Thanks for showing up when you did. That man is going to hurt someone someday. He is just so frustrated with himself that he hates the whole world, and me even more."

Kevin nodded agreement. "Too much anger", he stated flatly, "and he needs someplace to direct it. That man needs to find a hobby if he cannot find a job. Something to take his mind off himself."

Sue nodded back.

"You're right. And I think he really hates ALL women, not just me", she commented. "Maybe he always did."

The moment over, Kevin showed Sue a sheet from his notebook describing the murder scene. "Would you make a copy of this and check with NCIC for any matching activities?", he asked.

"Certainly", Sue replied, and quickly made a photocopy of the sheet. Reading it, she shuddered little. "Kind of gruesome", she commented.

"Yes, that is why I doubt this is the first time something like this has occurred. But I know we have had nothing like it around here. It is a long shot, but I think it needs pursuing."

"It shouldn't take long for a response", Sue said, and began typing details from the photocopy into her computer. She sat quietly for about a count of ten, and then the screen showed several possible matches. She printed a copy out for Officer Wolf as she read from the screen.

Reading the printouts, Kevin commented, "Whew. I was expecting some responses, but this is nasty. It looks like our killing is not unique, and especially not here in Florida. There have been six murders in as many months, spread around the state, though mostly here in the center, that all sound very much like our victim, Rebeccah

Levine. However, in almost all of them, it was a couple who were murdered."

"Yes", Sue answered, "in all of them there is a primary head injury, followed by serious cutting and beating, with the final death-dealing cut to the heart. All involve primary attention to the female victim, who has also evidently been raped. All of these are pretty much exact matches for the details you asked for, not even a little variance except for Rebeccah Levine's boyfriend ...Scary."

"The fact that the murders are so widely spread seems to me to indicate that either our killer is moving around a lot or it is more than one killer following some sort of ritual. I wonder if this could be some sort of gang orientation thing?", Kevin asked.

Sue typed again on the computer and waited. "No matches found", she replied.

"That does not necessarily mean the answer is no, though", Kevin noted. "Could be simply that no one made the link and entered it into the system. But it does move it down on the likelihood scale. Thanks. These details will give me a starting place beyond just the initial assumption of a random act by a surprised burglar. It could very likely be that it was an intentional planned act, as well as that the killer might not be local."

"Certainly does", Sue agreed. "Do you think whoever did it will come back for the boyfriend in Rebeccah's case?"

Kevin pondered that a little while before answering. "I am going out on a limb here, but I will say I do not think it is a high risk. Seems likely the male victims were simply there for the event, not the target. And to be honest, we do not have the manpower to watch over Jose Ramos without a much higher indication of risk."

"True that", Sue replied. "We are already swamped. This has been a heck of a year."

"Do me a favor, though, and run as much information as you can find on the victims of these other cases and compare them for similarities.

Perhaps we can find what made them targets, and that might lead us to whoever murdered Rebeccah."

"I'll start right away. That could take a day or two, though. It's not something easily catalogued.", Sue replied thoughtfully.

"Also send emails to the OIC in each case, and see if they had any solid looking leads.", Kevin continued.

"Will do", Sue replied.

Kevin stood in place, for a moment, then nodded to Sue, turned and returned to his cruiser.

Chapter 20

Michael left for breakfast at what had been his favorite diner until that morning. In fact, it was, right up until he walked in and saw Nicki still on duty, and began to feel embarrassed and guilty about his experience with Linda at Fentworth's for no reason that he could determine.

Her sparkling eyes seemed to see right through him, and his mouth didn't know quite what to say.

It was as if she knew that, because she suddenly laughed and said, "Try Good Morning, dummy." When Michael sputtered unintelligibly, she said, "Definitely a coffee, steak and eggs, and coffee order, if I ever saw one. Lots and lots of coffee."

She brought the order with a speed that made him wonder if she had instead decided to give him an order prepared for someone else, but he didn't ask. In fact, Michael didn't say much at all.

After the meal, she brought him the menu again, and offered him dessert. Because Michael had not taken dessert on his previous visit, this surprised him a little, but when he looked into her eyes again, he understood why.

"Was the main course so good that you couldn't enjoy a little dessert?", she teased.

Her cheek muscles turned down in what should have been a frown but became one of the most beautifully twisted smiles Michael had ever seen, and her eyes were emeralds of untold depth but somehow with a golden hue.

"Pick me up tonight at eight at this address", she said, and began writing on the napkin.

This was certainly turning into one of the most interestingly different weeks of Michael's life. He just couldn't help hoping that his life as he knew it lasted long enough to enjoy it. But Michael had no doubt that he would if it did.

Michael quickly agreed to the time and place, his mind justifying it easily because he was going to work so hard this afternoon on solving his problem that he would both deserve and need the break tonight.

Michael took care of the bill and the tip, and left for his room and his tools. He needed to find out how much gold was hidden in Fentworth's place, and whether any of it was familiar enough looking to remind him of the night that had started the nightmare side of this experience. Michael returned to his room, via the landlady's suspicious and critical eye, and rested deeply throughout most of the afternoon. His body was exhausted from all of its recent tensions, both good and bad, and he needed to be alert for the evening's efforts.

It was late afternoon when Michael parked a block from Fentworth's huge house and approached the house, walking in the long shadows of the palm trees wherever possible. The bold statues made a perfect cover for his approach, while allowing him a reasonably good view of the premises. Michael had chosen this time of day rather than a night approach figuring it to be likely to be the safest time, given the events he had seen occurring earlier. Fentworth seemed like a night owl.

Michael had expected the gate, entrance doors and patio doors to all be secured, but they were instead all standing wide open. The guests all seemed to have left the area, though, as he had hoped. Being cautious this time about cameras as he moved, Michael carefully entered the home and started up the stairs toward the bedroom and his goal.

But as he neared it, a soft set of sounds inside tugged at his consciousness and he crept ever slower to the thick door, which was now closed.

The sounds were now identifiable. It sounded as though two couples were engaged in an extremely mutual sharing of experiences. Then Michael recognized one of the voices as his own and another as Linda's.

Michael carefully turned the knob and cracked open the door just far enough to see inside. He could see the obvious glint of a large amount of gold on the nightstand, but that took very little of his attention. The far wall was filled with his recent boathouse experiences, which Linda and Jim Fentworth were watching while groping and caressing each other. She had evidently decided to get her copy of the video early, and to preview it fully.

For someone she had said she didn't particularly like, she seemed to be getting along pretty well with Jim. In fact, he seemed to be bringing her along quite nicely. Obviously, Jim Fentworth wasn't only a voyeur.

In all honesty, Michael felt like he was the voyeur, feeling the mixture of arousal and a slight twinge of jealousy rising, with the arousal clearly in the lead. It was a side of himself he had never seen before, and wasn't quite comfortable with.

Michael quietly closed the door and crept back down the stairs. This wasn't the best possible time to steal the gold or the video from the bedroom. That would have to wait.

Upon reaching the car, Michael felt the tiny engine roar into life, and he pushed the gas pedal farther than he needed to as he pulled away and on down the road. Michael wondered at this unusual reaction, and slowed the car down to the legal limit after about two blocks had passed.

Chapter 21

Officer Kevin Wolf truly disliked swing shifts. He had been accustomed to a reliable shift while with the Pennsylvania Highway Patrol, but the Sunset Cove police department was too small an organization to permit such a luxury. So instead all the officers had to rotate shifts almost constantly. That resulted in less efficiency due to the constant changes in sleeping patterns, and Kevin truly disliked anything that interfered with efficiency.

He was at the South end of the city when the radio called out his badge number, 827. The dispatcher was Sue, which reminded Kevin that even the dispatchers had to rotate shifts. Before answering the call, he shook his head in disgust at such a wasteful procedure just to save the city money.

"827". he responded

"827, return to the station ", Sue answered.

'Ten-four, on my way."

It took him about six minutes to cover the distance back to the center of town. He entered the station half expecting to see Harvey there causing a problem again. But instead he found Sue all alone in the office.

"What's up, Sue?", he asked.

"Couple of things.", Sue answered. "You asked me to follow up on the similar incidents to the Levine killing with the various departments involved . I just got off the phone in regard to one that yielded something which might be worth noting. They had two similar killings in the Fort Lauderdale area about a month ago. When I mentioned why I was calling, I got lucky and the officer I spoke with was familiar with both the incidents as well as another possibly interesting fact. Seems that her boyfriend Jose Ramos was the focus of a drug related surveillance in the Fort Lauderdale area, where

Ramos had flown that day. The officer recognized the boyfriend's name in the news, so he mentioned it when I asked about the killings. There's nothing else to make a connection between the killings and Ramos, but it does seem like a big coincidence."

"So it is possible that the killing could instead be drug related after all", Kevin commented, "Interesting. That would explain a lot. You said a couple things?"

"Yes. Sort of. Just that I looked into all the incidents, and there was nothing else I could find that seemed to be of any interest. I contacted the Officers in charge of all the murders in the central part of the state, and none had any leads whatsoever.", Sue stated.

Just then the phone rang, and Sue answered it. Kevin, focused on the new information and its possible ramifications, did not pay much attention to what she was saying. But when she ended the connection and turned to him, he could not help but notice her face had gone very pale and her eyes showed a level of fear.

"It sounds like we have another one.", Sue stated. "Guy just called in and said he was visiting a friend to pick up something the friend was holding for him, but when he arrived, he found the doors open, and the friend and a young lady dead, with blood all over the place. That's pretty much a direct quote."

"Let's do this by the book just in case", Kevin responded. "Who is next up?"

"813 - Camponi. And he is in that area of the city already."

"OK. Give it to him.", Kevin suggested. "I will return to the cruiser, and you radio me to provide backup as if we had not been here discussing the case. I don't want to draw any attention to what we are looking into until I am sure it goes somewhere."

Sue nodded, and that is what they did.

Sue called out "813"

"813", Officer Camponi responded.

"1234 Palmetto Way. Large home inside a gate. See the gentleman, possible 1-8-7."

"10-4".

Sue then called out "827".

"827.", Kevin responded.

"Can you provide backup for 813?"

"10-4, on my way".

Kevin drove to the West end where the larger, more palatial homes were located. 1234 was a particularly large one, with a winding driveway leading to a port cochere. It had several large buildings on the rear of the property including a boathouse.

Although Camponi had supposedly been in the same area, Kevin arrived almost simultaneously with him. As they both got out of their vehicles and approached the main building, Kevin immediately spotted a young, rather thin fellow, his face red, apparently from crying and his breath foul from a recent bout of vomiting.

"They're in the master bedroom", the man said to the pair. "They are all cut up and there is blood all over the place."

"First things first", Camponi said, taking out his small notebook and a pen. "Your name and how you came to discover the bodies."

"My name is Jeffrey Burke", the man responded. " I am a regular visitor here, not exactly a friend of Jim's but something like that. I was supposed to pick up something here tonight, but when I arrived, I found all the doors open and him and that girl were dead."

"He and that girl", Kevin responded without thinking.

"Yes, the two of them", Jeff confirmed, thinking Kevin was requesting confirmation.

"What were you picking up, Mr. Burke?", Camponi prompted, "Drugs?"

"No sir", Burke answered, " a video he made for me."

Kevin noticed the man did not seem offended at the suggestion of drugs, so they might still be a factor, especially if this killing did turn out to be related to the string Sue had found. He made a notation to that effect in his notebook. He noticed Camponi had not picked up on it. Kevin would need to suggest it to him later.

"What kind of video?", Officer Camponi asked.

"Umm…does that matter? Just a video.", Burke said.

"I won't know if it matters until I hear the answer", Camponi stated firmly. "What kind of video has you picking it up at this hour of the day?"

"Umm, Jim threw parties of a kind of special sort, and this was a video of my participation at the party."

"Mr. Burke", if you continue to give me evasive answers, we can continue this discussion in the jail.", Camponi threatened.

"Okay, Okay. It was me and my girlfriend having sex at the party", Burke answered." It was that kind of party. And this was not an odd time for Jim Fentworth. He kept different hours from people who work for a living."

"Fentworth. Is that the victim's name?"

"Yes."

"And the female victim?"

"I don't know her", Burke said, "Honest, I don't. Probably just someone else picking up a video."

"What else can you tell us?", Officer Camponi asked.

"Nothing. Jim Fentworth bought this place about a year ago, from a Federal judge from New York City who decided to move to Alabama where it is less crowded. Jim has been throwing parties here almost every day since. I knew the judge and was introduced to Jim shortly after he bought it. I really like his parties. Don't get me wrong. My wife and I aren't swingers or anything. I don't think most people at Jim's parties are. It's just kind of thrilling to do it in public like that."

"Was he blackmailing anyone with these videos?", Kevin asked, "You, for example?"

"No, I think everyone who came here knew what they were doing and wouldn't have been very good blackmail material. He didn't even charge for the videos. I think he was independently wealthy."

"What about you?", Camponi asked, picking up on Kevin's line of questioning. "What do you do for a living?"

"I am a real estate agent", Burke answered, "High end properties like this one, although I didn't sell this particular property."

"Mr. Burke ", Camponi continued, "I am going to ask you to show me some ID now, and then I am going to ask you to wait here while I check out the crime scene. When I do, if you try to leave, I will arrest you. Are we clear?"

"Crystal", Burke said. "If I was going to run, I wouldn't have called it in."

"Possibly. Or possibly you thought that would clear you of any suspicions.", Camponi answered.

Burke frowned, then presented his driver license, and both Camponi and Kevin noted the number and address in their notebooks.

"Where exactly is the master bedroom?", Camponi asked.

"Up the stairs and second door to the right", Burke said.

Kevin followed a step or two behind Camponi as they slowly approached the bedroom, cognizant of their surroundings, watching for anything that might relate to the case, but they saw nothing worth documenting. Nonetheless, Camponi took the small camera off his belt and photographed the scene as he went.

Entering the master bedroom gave Kevin a sense of déjà vu. It was almost identical to the Levine killing except that Fentworth was also there, seemingly positioned on the floor as though watching the female victim. Both had a head wound that had bled severely.

The blood patterns told Kevin that the male had been moved to his current position while still bleeding, and therefore while still alive. The female had been bound with 'chicken band' plastic ties, with her hands behind her back.

Unlike Levine, the ties were still attached. She had been cut several times, in what appeared to be a random sequence of slashes of varying depths. There was one clean straight-in cut, just to the left of her spine that would have pierced her heart if deep enough. The Medical Examiner would determine whether it had.

Kevin noted the blood stains did not appear to have been disturbed, and wondered for a moment how a killer could do so much damage and not manage to leave a footprint in the blood.

But what really got Kevin's attention was the image frozen on the video screen on one wall of the room. It showed a couple engaged in sex in a darkened room. Kevin estimated it had been taken at about sunset based upon the light visible through windows in the building, The faces were not especially clear due to the lighting, but Kevin felt reasonably certain the female on the screen was the victim on the bed. But the male was not the victim sitting on the floor. That made whoever it was a definite person of interest, at least in his opinion.

Kevin tapped Camponi on the shoulder and moved in close to speak quietly, so the witness could not overhear them.

"This is almost identical to the Levine case I am working", Kevin commented. "Only important differences I see so far are the added victim and the video screen."

Camponi nodded, "What do you want to bet the guy on the video is her boyfriend and got jealous about what she and Fentworth were apparently up to here?"

"That was my thought too. It is a shame the video is not clearer."

"Yeah", Camponi stated "the lighting on it is really bad. "Let's keep this to ourselves for now, and see if we can find the guy and bring him in for questioning. In the meantime, maybe Saint Pete's IT guys can do something to bring the video in more clearly."

"I think that is an excellent way to proceed", Kevin answered.

As Kevin was leaving the room, he heard the approach of vehicles. Looking out the window, he observed it was channel ten news. Kevin, being younger and faster than Camponi, hurried down the stairs in an attempt to keep them back and to prevent access to the witness. He managed to keep them back, and at least limited the amount of access to the witness, but Burke had already answered several questions before Kevin got there. And from what Kevin was able to hear, Burke had also noted the image on the screen and had told the media representatives this.

Kevin frowned, knowing Chief Lawson would not be pleased by any of this. He glanced toward Camponi, who had evidently also overheard the interview. Camponi shook his head in disgust.

Once he had the news people back from the building, Camponi keyed his radio and called for the Medical Examiner and the Crime Scene technicians. It was close to forty-five minutes before either arrived, but they arrived close together.

In the meantime, Kevin left the scene. Camponi was primary on this one, allowing Kevin to pursue the Levine case independently. That allowed for a forked attack, which made Kevin happy because he knew it was one of the best aggressive moves. Camponi spent the time until the Medical Examiner arrived making a lot of statements of "No comment". When asked if the guy in the video was a suspect, he replied "It is too soon in the investigation to have any actual suspects."

Chapter 22

Mickey Clements pulled his cruiser up to the first of the two addresses Tony Rivera had provided. This one was an apartment he used as his residence, and used a simple push button combination lock on the entry. Rivera had said it was set to 1295 and Mickey was pleased to learn he had told the truth for at least this fact.

Mickey turned the lever handle, opening the door. Black cardboard had been taped over most of the windows, so it was necessary to put the lights on before entering. It was a single room except for a small bathroom, of the style of room which Mickey considered as a studio apartment.

There was a stench of dirty laundry, ignored garbage and odors reminiscent of both cigarette and marijuana smoke. The place was pretty much a mess, with clothes lying on the floor and on most of the furniture. Drug paraphernalia littered the table and coffee tables, as well as the nightstand next to the bed.

Mickey searched the place carefully, knowing he might not be lucky enough to get the fool to give him permission a second time, especially once a lawyer got involved which was bound to happen eventually. He used the small camera from his belt to photograph everything of possible importance.

But when he had finished, he only had a small amount of cocaine and less than an ounce of marijuana to show for his efforts.

'On the bright side", he thought, "there were not eleven cards here. If they aren't at the other place, we might have our killer after all."

He locked the apartment and returned to his cruiser, where he checked his notebook for the other address Rivera had given them. He then drove there, hoping at every turn there would not be credit cards there either.

The second address turned out to be a free standing garage in an alley on the edge of town. Rivera had said the key was in a double planter in front of the building, and sure enough, Mickey saw a planter there. Lifting the small cactus by an area of the plant where the needles had all been removed, the pot came up with the plant, revealing a second pot beneath, in which lay the key. He returned the potted plant to its mate, and opened the door.

Inside was a studio of a different sort. Rivera evidently considered himself an artist. The room was full of paintings, many of them with price tags on post-it notes. Mickey found the paintings strangely compelling. They were modern art, with broad strokes, and although done with oil paints, had a visual flavor similar to watercolors. In each, Mickey could see a shadowy figure that was not quite there.

But that was not Rivera's only business, it seemed. There were also two very organized boxes, one of small bags of cocaine and the other of small bags of marijuana. Mickey was a little surprised not seeing boxes of meth or oxycodone. He surmised Rivera must be pretty low on the scale when it came to dealers. He photographed each.

But in the center of the room was the current painting, barely started, in front of a small chair. And next to the chair, on a side table, was a small amount of cash and thirteen credit cards, all with different names on them. He had been expecting only eleven, but this was evidently not a onetime purchase for Rivera.

Mickey was disappointed. They would have Rivera on drug sales and identity theft, without a doubt, or actually Camponi would, but it meant they had no evidence against Rivera for the murder.

Reluctantly he phoned in his find, and asked dispatch to send crime scene technicians to the address to pick up the evidence. Maybe they would find something more to tie Rivera to the murder, though Mickey honestly doubted it at this stage. He waited until they arrived to leave.

When he returned to the station he saw Camponi entering as well, and approached him.

"Bad news, buddy", Mickey began, "The credit cards were at the second address, so we don't have any evidence against Rivera for the murder. We definitely have him on dealing and ID theft, though."

There was plenty of evidence to support those charges, so it's better than nothing."

"Don't worry about it", Camponi answered. "We just had another killing and it looks like the same guy did it. Rivera is in jail so it wasn't him. A drug bust is better than nothing, right?"

"I guess so, but it's still disappointing."

Chapter 23

Michael returned to the room and took another quick shower before dressing. By seven-thirty, he was on his way to the address on the napkin Nicki had given him. He didn't want to arrive too early, so Michael stopped at a little shop on the beach that sold magazines, cards and gifts. He thought that a small present might start the evening off on a nice note.

Michael carefully selected a tasteful little crystalline sculpture, and while it was being wrapped in tissue paper he took a few moments to admire himself and his cleverness in the mirror behind the counter.

Michael also, somewhat less appreciatively, admired himself on the grainy image showing on the television above it. The banner read 'BREAKING NEWS. COUPLE MURDERED', with a sub at the bottom of the screen of 'BOYFRIEND SOUGHT FOR QUESTIONING.' The picture between the two was not especially clear, but Michael recognized it easily. He had seen it just moments earlier, looking in the mirror.

Fortunately for Michael, the remote camera Fentworth had used in the boathouse had not created a high resolution image, and the lighting in the boathouse made the photograph much less clear than it might have been. Nonetheless, it was still recognizable enough for him to know it was a picture of himself.

Michael's face in the mirror didn't look so smug anymore, but he managed to maintain a reasonably calm exterior until he had collected his purchase and left the shop. Michael then made a beeline for the nearest bar where in a dark corner he sipped a non-alcoholic drink and watched a 24 hour local news station on the television for the next announcement regarding it.

Jim Fentworth was no longer a suspect on Michael's list. He was now a body in the morgue. And from the description, so was Linda Beecher, and the police had Michael figured as the prime suspect, or at least a 'person of interest', obviously because of the video. Michael was hurt and shocked, but it was too much. It reached something deep inside him and turned off his responses. All of his body and mind worked as before, but there was something grey there instead, controlling it all. Michael wasn't there, and he couldn't feel anything.

Then Michael thought about who Fentworth's father really was and felt something very small and primordial, deep inside - a fear on a level he had never experienced. But a part of him knew he had to fight it because if he gave in to fear that deep, Michael would likely be dead in a day or two. He would just make too many mistakes because all his mind would be capable of handling was the fear. So Michael pushed it back down and concentrated on the task at hand. He wasn't being brave. He was just moving his fear to a different part of himself so he could better control his reactions as he had learned to do in Military Intelligence in the war.

But in spite of that, another part of Michael suddenly awakened. It was a strange part, he thought, under the circumstances. It was a part that remembered a joke about a debutante that got drunk and fell off her balcony into a trash truck. Two elderly black men watched as the truck went under the overpass where they sat. One said to the other "Look at that perfectly good white girl them rich folks throwin' away. Seems like such a waste." And it did.

It was so funny that Michael started laughing and couldn't stop. The bartender eyed him as he made his way out of the bar leaving all of his change still on the table. Michael couldn't stop laughing, even when it turned to tears, and then finally to an uncontrollable retching. When it was over, Michael lay in the sand, vomit staining his clothing, tears and dirt streaking his face. He kicked sand over the vomit and looked around.

Michael had been lucky. No one was near. If they had been, they might have called the police and his ordeal would probably have been over, and Michael wasn't anywhere near ready to stop suffering. He was locked into this thing now to the bitter end.

One thing seemed certain. His date for tonight was out of the question. His time of running around freely was too limited to spend it that way. Michael walked toward the beach and continued into the water. Salt water is quite an effective detergent, though it is a little harsh on the fabric. Michael was grateful that the evening was hot but not humid. His clothes and body would dry off fairly quickly.

Once they had, Michael went back to his car and drove to the rooming house. He needed time to think and plan, and he knew that time was getting more precious every second. Fentworth's (it was easier to think of him as that) father would very likely have skilled help making arrangements to travel to the area much sooner than Michael would have preferred. And with his picture all over the news, police would likely be closing in on Michael with equal or greater speed. In his mind's eye, Michael could see the lab guys working furiously to enlarge the photo section by section using bicubic and 'nearest neighbor' algorithms to enhance the image until it showed the suspect clearly. Until it showed HIM clearly. Then one or the other was likely to find him very quickly. Or the police might simply find his bullet-ridden body.

Very early the next morning Michael snuck out of the boarding house as quietly as he could and bought a newspaper from the rack on the corner. Newspapers tended to carry more details than television news, and he needed as many details as possible to evaluate his next steps. Sure enough, the story began above the fold. Michael's body read the article and absorbed its information, processing it mechanically. Description in section C-7. Quotes in D-5. All of which Michael would need to file neatly away for future use.

From the newspaper accounts, the couple had been apparently been surprised in the act of making love by their assailant. They had been brutally murdered. Because of the circumstances involved, police could not speculate as to whether a sex crime had also occurred until the coroner results were back. The body had been discovered soon after the occurrence by a visitor to the home who was there to pick up an item belonging to him from the victim. He was not at this time considered a suspect. At this time, a previous lover was sought for questioning. He also was not yet a suspect, merely a 'person of interest'. It was unknown if robbery was a possible motive, but nothing of value was found in the immediate area of the couple. NOTHING OF VALUE.

There had been something quite precious there, but they couldn't see it because she was dead. Michael realized some would judge her for her freedom, and acknowledged that a part of him did resent that she had so quickly found another partner, but that was just a small part of who she was. Others might be blinded by it. They would never know what a special and wondrous thing a person with such an open and almost innocent approach to everything could be. Even he would never really know.

A part of Michael realized that he had not known her very long or very well, but that was drowned out by the fact that he knew that he had wanted to, and that now not only he, but no one else, would ever get to know her more completely. What a waste.

Michael reviewed his recent visit in his mind and was sincerely glad he had managed to take the time to avoid the cameras on that second visit. He wished he had done so on the initial trip as well, but it was too late to do anything about that. Michael had missed his chance and as a result had probably elevated himself to the status of a prime suspect, no matter what the police told the news his role was.

Feeling his stomach trying to turn on him again, Michael concentrated on remembering the facts. Nothing of value. Yet earlier, there had been a sizable amount of items of gold in plain sight in that bedroom. Had it been removed prior to the session? It didn't seem likely, since it had lain so openly the day before with many more people in the building. It seemed to be more of a showcase to Fentworth than a group of items of value. But Michael could not honestly remember if it had been there on his latest visit, although in his mind's eye he felt as if he recalled perhaps a glint of it. But he had been too focused on the images on the screen and the sight of the couple on the bed to pay attention to much else.

More likely, if the killer was a cat burglar, had he just escalated again? The hit had occurred sometime just after sunset, as presumably the Levine Killing had, but the deliberate murders of Jim Fentworth and Linda? How had the killer chosen them? And how was it that the killer had found them just when Michael was looking at Fentworth for the condo burglary and murder? Michael knew the path that had drawn him to the area. Could he then calculate what drew the killer there? And if so, perhaps to his next target? Or was the killer somehow following Michael, and if so, why and for how long? The questions made Michael's research more necessary than ever before, and he needed to find the answers within a very short time .

It was up to Michael to make that time matter, because it was all he had left. When it was gone he would have very neatly framed himself for three murders and all of the cat's burglaries, and Michael knew that neither Shemuel Levine nor Johnny DiCenzo would let him languish in prison filing appeals. Michael would be lucky to last a week there.

Before leaving the room, Michael wiped down everything that was likely to have distinguishable fingerprints. He suspected there were probably so many prints there already that a match would be next to impossible, and that fingerprints were not usually used very much by the police except to intimidate suspects, but he did not want to increase his level of risk even a little. When he left, Michael took what little he had brought with him, including his notebooks.

Chapter 24

Michael went to a nearby tourist bar and nursed a couple of tall drinks in one of the dark corners while he tried to think. It was not an easy task. His head felt as though every nerve had short-circuited and the brain had melted in place. Michael would begin to get a direction for his thoughts and then find himself awakening from a time of staring into the fog where his mind had once been.

Occasionally Michael would choke back the urge to cry over such a wonderful and wild creature being removed from the face of the earth, and occasionally he would force down anger at having been pressed deeper and deeper into the situation until no place was safe for him. But gradually the Long Island iced teas and the solitude did their job and logic began to return.

Michael began to break the problems into groups and to work on each group individually instead of being overwhelmed by their massive combined weight. The first problem was housing. He could not go without sleep for very long and still function effectively, yet he knew his rental room was out of the question. Too many people could have seen him entering and leaving, and Michael knew for certain that the landlady had. Fortunately Michael always traveled light and had been cautious not to have left anything of importance behind when he cleared out. He had no reason to return there again, and if the police found the room, it would only serve to slow them down. But renting a motel room or finding a different rooming house would only complicate the situation worse, and not provide any real security.

The second problem was that Michael could not go out in daylight without some form of disguise and Florida is not an easy place to disguise yourself. The hot sun melts makeup and prevents the comfortable wearing of baggy or misleading clothes. Michael's best bet would be to hide in plain sight by wearing slightly over-sized tourist clothes and sunglasses and carrying a camera. But even so most of the leg work would have to occur at night, or at least late afternoon.

The third problem was that Michael was now in possession, although hidden in the fisherman's cove, of a goodly and heavy amount of gold that he had intended to sell to a fence or fences. But he realized that under the circumstances a fence would be far more likely to sell him out to the police to curry favor than to deal with him in an honest fence and thief relationship, now that three murders were related to it.

He had not thought that through when he hastily decided to perform the hit. But then, he had not expected to be on video leaving the scene, or to later be on yet another video at the scene of a murder. That gold would be an anchor around his neck because if he was caught with it, it would be one more nail in his frame.

He regretted his impetuous decision to move ahead with the heist, but at the same time knew that he had to find a way to get it to a fence, and hopefully the right fence, to have any hope of finding Rebeccah's, and now Linda and Fentworth's, killer. And finding that killer quickly was about his only hope of survival.

Michael needed to find out who the killer is. Logic told him that he needed to connect the dots and find the similarities between the Playa del Sol and James Fentworth's home. The burglaries might have been a part of the answer, but it was becoming unlikely they were the key to solving it. He needed to examine the premises and look for other links. The difficult part of this would be the fact that both were now crime scenes, and would probably be under police watch. In point of fact, the police may even have already removed whatever evidence there was at either site, probably without recognizing its real value.

Of course, experience told Michael that police are rarely very intelligent and thorough when it comes to investigations. Nor are they typically vigilant about standing guard at crime scenes. Even a full around the clock stake-out would have gaps, and with resources typically thin, an around the clock watch was almost out of the question. The bigger question was whether Michael could fit between the gaps in coverage without getting crushed.

He needed a base of operations, someplace to rest moderately safely. Michael figured he had two choices, neither of them very ideal.

He could go up to the fisherman's cove he had used as a rest stop on the first visit and use that as a base of operations, or he could try to persuade the waitress at the diner to help him.

She was the only one who might, and something told Michael that she was not a stickler for the letter of the law. But Michael also knew this was a lot bigger than one little letter.

On the other hand, the cove was some distance away and staying there would make it difficult to carry on the business of finding out what was really going on and who the murderer was.

Also, he would be close enough to the gold that it might be linked to him if both were discovered.

So he decided to take a chance on the waitress.

Michael drove to the address she had written, and discovered it was a 24 by 72 foot double wide mobile home on a large wooded lot deep within the Florida Pines and palm trees. Someone had placed the pad there and run the utilities from a house a short distance away, though barely visible. The surrounding Florida pines would shade the mobile home from both the sun and the eyes of passing motorists. That was a break in his favor.

Also in his favor was the presence of a single car parked near the door to the mobile home. It was a cherry red Volkswagen Beetle, one of the near look-alikes to the original VW bug, with the engine in the rear and a fairly large trunk under the hood in front. Cherry red tends to be a single person's color choice for a car, and the Beetles are more popular amongst females, so there was an excellent chance that Nicki was home and probably alone.

Michael parked the rental car on the side of the approach road among some palm trees, using their branches for driving leverage so he would not become stuck. The car was fairly secluded, and Michael walked in so as to not give too much advance notice to the resident in case his evaluation was wrong.

It wasn't. Through the bay window, Michael could see Nicki clearly. She was singing quietly to herself while hand drying some dishes and returning them to the cabinets. Her voice was angelic, and Michael felt guilty interrupting it for the reasons he was about to.

Nicki quickly answered his knock on the light aluminum door, and seemed both pleased and confused to see him.

"A little late, aren't you, sugar?" she asked. "But then you have been a bit busy lately, haven't you?" In the gap between her slim waist and the door frame Michael could see the newspaper lying on her couch. "Anything to say for yourself, or did you come all this way just to murder me too?"

Despite her words Nicki did not seem afraid. In fact her eyes still seemed to shine with humor. Or was that just what Michael wanted to see?

"Look, I did not kill anyone. I swear it." Michael replied. "I just seem to be having a run of bad luck that is putting me in the wrong place at the wrong time. I made some stupid moves, but I am not a killer, even though the police probably have a lot of really good evidence to the contrary, and will have even more before long."

"So why are you here?" she asked. "Why aren't you running as far and as fast as you can?"

"It is a really long story" Michael replied. "May I step inside to talk? The mosquitoes are having a field day with my Northern blood out here."

Without a word or a second look Nicki stepped aside and turned back into the mobile home. "Have a seat", she invited. Michael climbed the three steps into it and followed her, sitting on the black leatherette sofa facing the door.

"Want a beer?" she asked, and before he could answer, Nicki removed one from the refrigerator, popped its cap off and handed it to him. It was an Old Dixie, which Michael was not familiar with. He took a sip of it. It wasn't bad. She then removed a raspberry wine cooler as well and sat across from him on a tan tweed recliner chair. "So?" she asked.

Michael was embarrassed to talk about Linda and would have given almost anything not to have to, but he had decided that his best chance with her was to come completely clean and tell her the whole story beginning with the heist in the jewelry district. When he finished, uninterrupted except for some slight gasps and chuckles at the appropriate spots, Nicki sat quietly, as though waiting for it all to sink in.

Michael looked around the room to keep from breaking the silence as long as he could. There were a few surprises, including some archery trophies on the shelf and deer antlers mounted on the wall. Not what Michael would have expected in a single woman's home.

When Nicki finally spoke, it wasn't about the murders or the burglaries, much to his amazement, but about Linda.

"Did you love her?" Nicki asked.

Michael thought a moment and then answered.

"No. I did not know her very long, but I do think I sort of loved who and what she was. She was wild and free and beautiful in a world that usually is full of fear and ugliness. She held nothing back in a world that holds everything back. I guess some people would see her differently and judge her for not being afraid to share herself so freely, but she did it with an innocence and openness that was refreshing. I think I was impressed by her freedom. I guess that is the best answer I can give."

"It sounds like you were lucky to have known her, even for such a short while. I envy you that feeling. To punish you for not keeping something that special closer to your heart, I think you will sleep on the couch tonight. In the morning we can talk some more."

For no apparent reason, Nicki laughed with the tinkling of small bells in her voice again as she had in the diner, and Michael watched the gentle sway of her hips once again as she walked into the bedroom.

Nicki left the bedroom door open and Michael could hear as each piece of her clothing dropped to the floor. Nicki apparently slept in the nude and in spite of current events was not afraid of him. That somehow seemed like two very good things in the midst of so many things that were anything but good.

Chapter 25

Michael rarely had nightmares. In fact, most of his dreams were just practice runs or re-runs of his latest planned caper. This night was an exception. Perhaps it was partly influenced by the sounds of high winds outside the mobile home, but whatever caused them to begin, the deep nightmares did not stop throughout the night.

One nightmare stuck in his mind as he began to awake. Michael had been in a world much akin to a Tim Burton film where he was trying desperately to survive against monsters when he came across a young lady very much in need of saving. Michael rescued her with the help of a very large sword that would have shocked even Errol Flynn, and together they braved the nightmares until they found the way out into the real world.

Together they laughed as they told friends over drinks at an outdoor café the strange story of how they had met in that strange land and fallen in love and would now be together forever.

But as Michael reached toward awakening he had realized who she was and that he would never be with her again in this world. Michael would never again see her strange blue hair or hear her voice.

He might have cried alligator tears with the realization if not for the pleasant reassurances of his surroundings as he awoke. Crying would not have been typical for him either, but it was a strange night.

Michael's awakening was accompanied by the smell of steak, eggs and coffee and the soft sounds of a crackling skillet, bare feet on vinyl tiles and a background murmur of gentle rain drops landing on the roof of the mobile home. It was not an unpleasant awakening, especially after the nightmares.

Nicki had pulled on a thin house robe and was making steak and eggs, along with mashed potatoes and coffee. No ketchup or pickle was visible, which pleased Michael immensely.

"Thought you could use some eggs this morning", she said, glancing over her shoulder and seeing that he was awake, "but I made you steak and mashed potatoes too, in case you are the stubborn sort who wants the same meal every day. I fried the mashed potatoes, though."

Michael could see clouds through the window behind her, moving quickly in both directions, with nature's fireworks lighting a shadow puppet show in the sky between them. The light from each heat lightning strike showed her beautiful figure through the thin robe, and her smile seemed to light the room as though she were an angel, come to rescue him from the lingering darkness outside. In fact, her smile seemed to shine more light on the room than the window could ever offer. Michael just smiled.

She set up a small tray in front of him that was just big enough to hold the two breakfasts, and Michael greedily cleaned his plate while watching her eat. She made it seem dainty, and yet finished the same size serving she had given him at almost precisely the same time.

Michael found himself again looking at the trophies and the deer antlers, His curiosity must have showed.

"My daddy's fault", she said with a small smile. "He died recently, but all my life right up until almost the day he passed, he persuaded me to compete and took me deer hunting, mostly bow and arrow. I preferred the cross-bow, but was pretty good with a compound bow, too. It was never really my thing but it made him happy. I still practice with the cross-bow sometimes, and it reminds me of the times we shared."

"Never would have expected that, seeing you", Michael said.

"Life's full of surprises. So, anyway, what makes you so certain the cat burglar is also the killer?", she asked, continuing their conversation from the night before.

Michael explained to her again, step by step, what he had found and what he knew to be true of cat burglars in general. When he had finished she nodded her head thoughtfully and stared off into space quietly for several minutes.

152

Finally she said, "We've got to get your rental car hidden better, in case someone at the rental place sees the news and recognizes you, unlikely as that may be. Where you hid it is too obviously hidden, so if anyone comes down my driveway or flies over it, they will know something is up.

We'll put it behind the trailer on a concrete pad I had installed. Even if someone comes up to the house and knocks on the door they won't see it. And, if it is seen, It will appear to be in plain sight rather than hidden, even though in truth it would only be visible from the water or overhead, and from either of those it will simply look like it belongs there. You can use my car for the time being. I am off work for the next two days anyway."

Michael carefully backed the car out of its palm encrusted hiding place and onto her approach road. She then guided him to back into a space on the other side of the mobile home where it was, as she had promised, both ready for immediate access should he need to use it to exit in a hurry and yet fully hidden by the mobile home from prying eyes on all visibly accessible sides.

The light rain had stopped and the heavy winds had gone away into the deep waters. The sky was clear now except for a single bright star blazing in the morning sky. Still, a faint smell of dampness and ozone hung in the air.

She dressed herself in a tank top and white shorts, sunglasses and a large sun hat. They went into town together, where Michael handed over a few twenties and waited patiently in the car while she shopped.

She surprised him again by being a rather efficient shopper with a good eye for detail. She returned to the car much more quickly than Michael had expected her to, and her purchases, though perfectly sized for him, identified him as someone else. She had purchased the loudest and most visible Hawaiian shirt the store had to offer, expensive sunglasses, tan shorts and white boat shoes. She even bought a large older camera from the pawn shop next door, so his look was complete.

Michael looked like an idiot, which meant he looked like a first time tourist. Michael was now invisible. No one would give him a second look except the kids selling maps, and even they would probably be busy staring at the hot tourist lady in the tank top.

Michael had to admit that Nicki had a real talent for this sort of thing. For the first time in days he felt totally safe. He secretly wished she had bought a laser measuring tape, also, but he had not told her of his plans for later that night, so it was his fault and not hers. Michael decided to keep quiet about it.

They drove to the library where Michael continued his research, trying to find out more about the fire at the first address and more about the whereabouts of its former resident, as well as more about the possible fences in the area.

Michael found it was anything but easy to find exactly what he was looking for. He confirmed the owner's name was Stickney, which he had known all along, and learned that Stickney was not present when the fire occurred but that his wife was, and was now deceased.

The cause of the fire was believed to be a lit cigarette while smoking in bed. It was not considered suspicious in nature.

There had been two previous occurrences at the address in which the local fire department had arrived while it was still smoldering, and in both cases the wife had fallen asleep while smoking.

But there was no follow-up to the story, and the husband was barely mentioned, giving Michael no clue as to where to locate him.

The library is a good place to think, however, and Michael did a lot of thinking about the irony of his being in both burglarized areas in the same approximate time as the killer.

There had to be more to it than mere coincidence. There had to be a tie between the two. Unfortunately, the best solution would be if Jim Fentworth would just throw another party and Michael could get himself invited, but the person best suited to help him find that tie was now dead because of it.

Michael was beginning to feel like he might soon be dead also if something did not click. He could not hide forever, and hiding for long periods is not what Michael did best.

Michael could tell Nicki was becoming very bored in the library. In the beginning she had been very helpful, but as the leads started to diminish, he could feel her boredom increase. She was being very patient and helpful with someone she barely knew, and Michael was grateful for that, but wondered when her boredom might turn her opinions or actions around.

Paranoia is sort of a sideline with being a thief. It is what keeps him from making faulty assumptions about partnerships and on his toes in selecting fences. It is what made Michael work every step out many times in advance before a typical job. But right now it was making him afraid of Nicki. At least he hoped it was paranoia, and not simply fact.

It would be so easy for her to point Michael out in this large, quiet place. Any noise would attract nearly everyone's attention.

Michael began to look around. Most of the newspaper area was filled with old timers, some looking well off and others looking as if they were looking at tonight's bed when they looked at the newspaper.

But there were lots of college kids in the computer book and law book areas, and unlike what someone might have expected to see in an earlier time, these were not wimps. They looked like they worked out regularly.

A single middle-aged guard stood near the main door, ignoring most of the people around him except when asked a direct question. The guard, too, looked bored and was armed with only a Tonfa for a night stick.

Taken individually, none seemed a genuine threat to Michael, but collectively all they needed to do was slow him down long enough for the Librarian to call the police, and he believed they could probably do that. The fear was growing. Michael could feel it in every part of his body, crawling along every nerve path.

Then Michael felt two hands on his, and saw two beautiful mixed green and gold and hazel eyes staring into his, and heard Nicki's gentle whisper.

"We gotta go, sugar. We need to go NOW. OK?"

Michael nodded his head, put the sunglasses back on and they quietly left. When they got back into the little red Volkswagen, she asked "What the HELL was happening to you in there?"

It was then that Michael realized he had been having a panic attack. Michael was always a control freak. He took great pride in controlling every aspect of his life very carefully, and suddenly for the first time, he was not in control. He was a puppet for some unknown puppeteer who may barely even know Michael existed. And it made him afraid. Not cautious or alert. It made him afraid. And for the first time in his life he had experienced a panic attack.

"If you hadn't pulled me out of there…", Michael began.

"I know", she replied. "You should have seen your face. That was NOT the you I have seen for the past couple of days. You've got to get a grip, guy. I did not get into this to help someone like that. I got into it to help you. So stick with me, ok? No more of that guy?"

Michael nodded his head. "I promise. I will be ok now. I think I just had to get that out of me in order to get past it."

She looked deeply into his eyes for several seconds before replying. "I believe you" she said quietly. "What's our next step?"

Something inside him noted that she had said 'our' next step. It felt warm and good and Michael felt safe again.

"Well, we seem to be up against a wall. My only other possible suspect, Stickney, doesn't seem to have attracted any attention since his house burned down, killing his wife. I thought perhaps this search might show us where he might have gone, but found nothing. So that is sort of a dead end.

156

But I did notice that one of the fences was charged with misdemeanor possession of stolen property at about the same time as Stickney was questioned, so there may be a link there worth checking out. There also has to be a tie between the Levine killing and the killing of Fentworth and Linda, but they are all dead so they can't tell us what it is. Another dead end."

Michael paused a moment to think, then continued.

"The police have already tossed Fentworth's house, but as big as the house was, it would be easy for them to miss something, particularly with the video already pointing to a likely suspect. If Fentworth videotaped all his parties, that might give us a lead on the tie between the two. If not, all we have is Ramos, and he probably already saw my picture in the paper, so I am reluctant to visit him again. I think the next step is for me has to be to re-check Fentworth's house for anything the police might have missed."

They began the short trip to her mobile home. As they drove, Michael asked, "What is your last name, by the way? I think you only told me your first name."

"Fontaine", she smiled. "I thought I told you. Anyway, you can see that Nicki Fontaine sounds much more like me than Nichole Fontaine, can't you?"

Michael agreed it did seem to somehow fit her better. Inside, a part of Michael knew with guilt that the only reason he had asked her was because he barely remembered Linda's, and it was tormenting him. Michael was quiet the remainder of the trip.

Once they arrived, Nicki insisted that Michael come in and get a proper meal before going out again. Remembering how tasty breakfast had been, Michael could hardly decline or argue. He caught a short nap on the couch while she prepared it, and surprisingly, slept peacefully.

This meal, once she had awakened him for the second time that day, was eaten on the meal table in the kitchenette. Not only was it delicious and filling, but it included a dessert she had prepared earlier and which still tasted fresh. She had a talent for cooking. A big part of Michael wanted to just stay there and not go hunting for a killer. After all, he was a thief, not a cop. Michael wanted to enjoy life again, not be constantly afraid.

But Michael knew what he had to do, so shortly after the meal he laid down on the couch and took another brief nap.

Chapter 26

At a little before one am he awoke and left the double-wide. He got behind the wheel of Nicki's car and drove to Fentworth's. Michael parked two blocks away and sat there watching for any signs of movement up the block, including in parked cars.

A couple of hours later Michael drove the car around the block and parked a block and a half away in the other direction and watched again. If he saw any signs of movement, such as a foot accidentally hitting the brake pedal or someone hanging out in the street near it, Michael could be fairly sure it was under surveillance and he would have to postpone it and adjust his plans.

At one point, an SUV went up the block and pulled into one of the other driveways. Michael was ready to bolt until a young mother opened all the doors and unloaded her children and groceries. He could see well enough to know there was no place for anyone to be hiding in the vehicle. Michael wondered why she was returning at such an hour, but decided it was probably nothing to be concerned about.

Finally Michael was fairly sure it was safe and he moved his vehicle closer to Fentworth's home, and slowly approached it, being as nonchalant as he could. He was pleasantly surprised the outer gate was still wide open.

 Michael's heart was racing, but he concentrated on thoughts of the recent meal and stayed outwardly calm. Ignoring the yellow police tape, Michael knocked loudly on the door. When no one, outside or inside, responded, he felt fairly certain the area was not being monitored.

True, it could have been watched from a neighbor's house, even the SUV mom's, but he had to draw the line somewhere on his cautious behavior. And the houses were fairly distant. It was nothing like a

New York street where the buildings ran together, and lent themselves to being used for surveillance.

Michael quickly picked the locks, though the deadbolt picked easier than its cheap counterpart in the knob. Michael suspected that even the right key probably worked roughly in the knob lock. Glancing around quickly, he entered the home and shut the door. Michael locked both locks with their inside turn buttons even though he had left the deadbolt cylinder partly turned as usual to slow down anyone with a key, and had once again inserted a piece of a toothpick in the keyway.

Michael's first stop was the bedroom. At least at first look, there was no sign of anything of interest there. The small rack of videos was empty. Without a doubt its contents had found their way to the police station, and possibly already to the evidence room. But the rack was smaller than Michael would have expected. Unless Fentworth was re-using them or not keeping a copy for himself, which seemed unlikely, there must be more somewhere else in the large house.

Michael searched room to room, finding cameras in many of the ceilings that were wired back to an attic video lab, which currently seemed to contain no videos. He found another small empty video rack, but once again, the area showed no sign of videos and the rack was small. Chances are good the cops probably cleaned out whatever might have been there.

The house was still well-cooled despite the fact the police had been out of the building for over a day in the hot Florida Sun with the air conditioning turned off. Other than the brief early morning rain today, there had been little respite from the temperatures, so the room had to be well built and well insulated. Otherwise, tapes would deteriorate or DVD's and CD's would eventually warp.

In almost every building, room and area Michael found more cameras and still no sign of the videos, so he began looking for anything that seemed out of place. But Fentworth's lack of taste made even that a formidable obstacle. Everything was out of place.

At one point the distant lights of a passing car outside the house lit up the inside in prisms of twisted luminescence and Michael instinctively dived under a desk and practiced calmly holding his breath.

But it had gone by without slowing down so Michael eventually came out of hiding and resumed the search.

The house was huge, with many bedrooms and two libraries, a pool and the boat house, so just the first preliminary look had taken hours. The second look was a little quicker but still was quite time-consuming. As Michael looked over the pool toward the open beach behind the boat house, he could see the first light of daybreak beginning on the distant horizon. His time on the site would soon need to come to a halt whether he found anything or not. He had pushed all the limits way beyond what any intelligent thief would even consider and Michael still had nothing.

Michael started taking inside and outside rough measurements using measured footsteps in the two libraries, and was disappointed to find that the measurements lined up closely enough to rule out any hidden doors or closets in the libraries. The same was true in the large commercial kitchen and the luxuriously appointed dining hall. He had hoped that somehow the large china cabinets might be hiding an entry but there was no way that was true.

Slowly Michael worked from room to room using his measured footsteps as a crude ruler, and wishing he had spoken up and asked Nicki to obtain a laser measuring device. It would have been so much simpler, and considerably faster. Why hadn't he, he wondered. Michael was rapidly becoming more discouraged as he went. Finally he was back to his original starting place, Fentworth's master bedroom. Half-heartedly Michael stepped through the measurements and was totally shocked to find the discrepancy he had been looking for.

But before Michael could fine tune its location and discover how to access it, he heard a sound at the front door and Michael made a bee line through the house to a secondary exit he had identified. As he reached his car and began to drive off, Michael realized he had merely heard the morning newspaper delivery. Michael watched as the delivery person exited the gate and continued from house to house. Still, the sun was making beautiful paintings in the sky over the ocean which told Michael his own time was up for this trip.

Two blocks down Michael stopped the delivery person and asked if she had a spare paper, for which he then overpaid. Much to his pleasure there was no news related to the murders or burglaries.

Michael smiled widely as he drove back to Nicki's trailer and was pleasantly surprised to find breakfast in the making when he got there. She was wearing the thin robe again, and in the pinks and oranges of the morning sky looked almost naked. The sight was not unpleasant.

"Find anything?", she asked.

"I think I found his hiding place, but I had to leave before I could find out if there was anything helpful in it. I'll have to go back another night."

"Anything else?"

"Nothing that can't wait until I taste the food you're making."

Over breakfast Michael told her everything he had discovered on the night's sojourn. Michael helped her clean the dishes to minimize the work of the small dishwasher next to the sink, and then caught a nap while she took her morning shower. The smell of her bath soap and shampoo wafted through the air with an almost hypnotic appeal, and his dreams used them to brighten their mood. When Michael awoke, he could not remember any of the dreams but he had a smile on his face.

Chapter 27

At precisely 7 am in Sunset Cove's station house, Chief Lawson began the daily morning briefing. Once a week, the entire department was asked to attend rather than just the oncoming shift. Today was that day. Scapoletti, Wolf and Camponi were off duty, but still sat in. Sue Bennet had brought the donuts from the local Dunkin Donuts, and had gone to the extra effort and expense to also pick up coffee from there in two large containers. The guys eagerly filled their cups before sitting, enjoying the unexpected reprieve from the usual station coffee.

"Okay, people", the Chief began, "We have three murders and a host of burglaries. For a small tourist town like ours, that is a death knell. If we don't clean it up soon, the City Council might vote to turn everything over to the County or the State. So give me some progress. Mickey, you first."

"Not much good news there, Chief", Mickey Clements stated. "I interviewed a Margaret Hoover and several others near the latest hit by the kids, and I mention Hoover because she was the only one who really had anything to offer, although even that does not help us much.

As usual, the three kids she describes don't match any previous descriptions, and seemed like 'nice kids'. They were polite and she cannot believe they had anything to do with the burglaries. She insists it must just be a coincidence.

Also, Ed and I picked up a guy using Levine's credit card, and have him cold on dealing drugs and identity theft, but so far it looks unlikely he is linked directly to any of the burglaries, and probably is not the murderer."

"Yeah, one MORE coincidence", Tommy Williamson muttered.

"You want to talk, you can go next", the Chief said.

Tommy sat up straighter in the chair and began.

"I talked to the offices at all the local schools. Nobody was absent at ALL for the day of the latest kiddie burglars hit. I followed up on every hit they had made, comparing absentee records, and there were very few to begin with and no patterns. So I got nothing new to report. I'm sorry."

"Don't be sorry", the Chief said, "If we keep following up on the details, sooner or later we will find a pattern. Larry and Don?"

"Don and I took two different paths on this one, so I'll let Don tell you about his separately. We talked in depth with Ted Whiting and we think we see a pattern of sorts in the pawn shops. The pattern is that there is NO pattern. Every traceable item we found was brought in by someone different. We checked on most of them and it looks like of the ones we COULD trace, most of them were military guys home on leave, and were simply approached by kids who asked them to help them out because their 'mom was sick and they needed grocery money'. The others, about two thirds, are probably vagrants. A couple of them we know for certain are, because Saint Petersburg deputies ran them in for minor violations before. The kids probably bought their services for a buck or two. So I think this will also be a dead end.

"There is one ray of sunshine, though. According to Mickey's list, part of what they got from this last hit were some really rare coins. Ted has asked the coin collector stores and pawn shops to call him if they show up, so we might at least catch one while it is fresh in the guy's memory, and maybe before they can leave the area."

Larry Evanston finished and looked to Don Falcone, the rookie who was Larry's partner. Don pulled up a stack of papers and began to talk.

"I looked into the distance between here and the pawn shops. Most of the stuff stolen is small enough to be carried without attracting much attention, so I could not rule out any method of getting it there. I checked the bus companies, the taxi records, you name it. There were no long trips by cab anywhere near the distance, and the bus drivers had no passengers who rode any great distance that they could recall. I specifically asked the drivers about kids, and they said now and then a kid rides, but never for very far, so no help there either."

The chief nodded to Don and turned to Kevin Wolf. Kevin, a member of the Lenape tribe up in Pennsylvania and a former Pennsylvania state trooper, was usually a great resource. "What have you got on the condo scene?", the Chief asked Kevin, who stood to give his report, unlike those before him. As usual, his uniform was crisp, his black hair tightly combed, and his demeanor professional.

"Well, we got a real break on the latest burglary. A tourist girl caught the guy in full frontal jumping off the ledge of one of the condos at about the time we think it was hit. Might or might not be the same guy who killed the girl there, but almost definitely our burglar.

Unfortunately, because she went to the television news first, the guy probably already knows that we know roughly what he looks like, so it is likely he will try to hide for a while.

Unless, of course, he is a druggie in which case, he won't be able to. Right now, that is my biggest hope.

But I think we will have it solved before long either way. I asked Saint Pete to see what their IT guys could do to improve the video. I am checking with all the hotels, motels and rooming houses to see if he is an outsider. And if he is a local, somebody in town must know him and will probably turn him in before too long, hoping to get their own five minutes of fame on TV."

Kevin finished talking and sat back down.

"So we might close that one soon", the Chief stated. "That's ONE. Let's hope he admits to the killings too, when we get him."

The Chief looked to Ed Camponi.

"You're up", he stated. "What do we have on the double murder?"

"Good news, there, Chief", Camponi began, nodding toward Kevin. "The guy in the girl's TV video looks a LOT like a match to the video we found in the bedroom. At least to me, it looks like the boyfriend and the condo burglar are probably the same person. And that means once Saint Pete finishes, we will have a clear picture to show people while we are searching. I charged the girl with obstruction anyway, though, for taking it to the media instead of us. She cost us a full day we could have had to catch him, and made it more difficult"

"Excellent. The court will probably throw it out, but maybe the word will get out to not do that sort of thing. At any rate, I'd really like to be able to close all three this week and get Council off my back at least a little. This sounds like that could now be a possibility. Scapoletti, anything?"

As Kevin Wolf had, Paul Scapoletti stood to speak, but he was not as professional looking when he did. His wrinkled shirt was out of his trousers and over the belt slightly, showing off his large waistline. He was taller than the other officers, but his weight made him seem shorter. His bald head glistened in the overhead lights. And as the Chief had expected, his report was not overly impressive either.

"Gave out 35 tickets to tourists at the bridge yesterday", he began, "so the city coffers are a little better off. Nothing much else."

Finally, the Chief turned to Sue Bennet.

"Sue, thanks for picking up the donuts today."

"AND the coffee.", Larry shouted, followed by murmurs of assent from all the others except Scapoletti. Sue blushed a little.

"Anything on the dispatch end of things?", the Chief continued.

"Couple of things.", Sue answered. "Officer Wolf asked me to look into similar killings to the Levine killing, and we found a few. Following up with the departments involved yielded a coincidence that might be worth noting. Seems that her boyfriend Jose Ramos was the focus of a drug related surveillance in the Fort Lauderdale area, where he had flown that day. That was really the only thing of interest I was able to turn up."

"So it is possible that killing could instead be drug related", Chief Lawson commented. "Interesting."

"On a separate topic we received a BOLO from FDLE on someone hitting banks along the coastline", Sue continued. "They are somehow ripping off the night deposit drop boxes. Doesn't seem anyone has any clue who or how, but they are asking every department to keep an extra close eye on the night deposit boxes whenever possible. They hit eight banks so far. None very close to our area yet, though."

When Sue seemed to have nothing further to say, the Chief addressed the small crowd. "Okay, people, another day. Like they used to say on TV, 'Be safe out there.' Get to it."

The meeting broke up. Sue noticed with a certain amount of glee that there was only one donut left and no coffee. She knew that the happier the guys were, the easier her job would be.

But ten minutes later, her glee turned sour when a jogger phoned to report finding a bag of antique coins on the banks of the St. John river. Sue thanked him for his honesty, asked him to wait for the officers to arrive, and radioed Larry and Don with the bad news. Larry broke protocol by voicing his emotional response over the radio in no uncertain terms.

Chapter 28

The killer was furious. He did not want to get caught, so at first he had been a little pleased when the news claimed it to be the result of an interrupted burglary. He had even been a little pleased when a video of another burglar leaving the condos caught the eye of the news.

It was non-specific enough that it was just a good smokescreen for him to hide behind. But now some individual son-of-a-bitch was getting the credit for the kills at the Fentworth place.

That just wasn't right. Fentworth and his old lady were a part of HIM now. That guy had no business taking credit for their deaths.

Worse yet, there were similarities between the guy in the video and the guy the police were looking for. It might be the same guy stealing both his recent kills.

A part of him knew that he should be grateful because it meant he could go on killing in the same area a little longer without anyone suspecting him. But the truth was, he was so smart that they had not EVER suspected him. So this wasn't a help to him. It was an insult.

And NOBODY should insult him and get away with it. His first kill had been about that. She had insulted him, called him a loser, and was going to turn him in. He thought back to that night for a moment and briefly felt pleased by the memory.

But this was an even bigger insult. "That lousy smart-ass burglar has to pay for this" he thought. "Nobody gets away with insulting me like that."

But how would he find the guy? He thought about it, and the only thing he could come up with was to put out the word to the fences he knew and ask them to watch for anybody trying to turn over large amounts of gold. He had plenty of it for himself, and could use that as a bargaining chip to get the fences to cooperate. He knew a dozen within a short distance, and the guy had to be using one of them if he was hitting the same spots. He would make each a very profitable offer.

Yes, that guy would pay. It might not be right away, but he would pay. His anger began to simmer rather than rage. He could wait, but he would be satisfied. He would see to that no matter what it took.

The killer went to his closet and opened its door, revealing a recently acquired suitcase which he knew contained a large number of blocks of cocaine. Opening the suitcase, he removed one small plastic bag, cut it open and laid out three small lines on the nightstand next to his bed. Using a hollow coffee straw, he took each in. Now he felt ready.

He reflected that one of these days he should probably try to find a buyer for some of it, but he really was in no hurry to dispose of it. He wasn't on anyone's radar, so there was no reason to rush.

He quickly showered and pulled on his clothing. For tonight, he had chosen a thin black polo shirt and a pair of black stretch denim trousers, along with black socks and dark boat shoes.

He quietly grouped the tools of his trade into various pockets for quick retrieval, with the garrote in his back left pocket and his knife in the right. Habits like this reduced the risks and made his movements more precise.

As he left the cheap motel room, he again stopped briefly by the pool to read the papers left by the day's visitors. Tonight, the guy's picture was no longer in the news, but there were still articles relating to the burglaries and killings. It still angered him that some fool was becoming famous taking credit for killings that he had himself committed. That anger had not abated in the least. He had saved the pictures from the news, of course, but it was of no one he recognized.

"The guy has to pay", he thought to himself once again, "but not tonight. Tonight is about rebuilding me, restoring the part of me that he stole."

169

As he walked, he thought once again about his wife who had threatened to turn him in and called him a loser.

"Who's the loser, now", he thought to himself once again, smiling as he remembered her neck being crushed and then cut, the first cut of many.

She was the only one he had burned. He had burned her body because she could be traced directly back to him. But he found that while it had not disappointed him to watch her burn, it had added very little to the experience. Nevertheless, he thought once more how she had looked with the flames dancing on her fatty body, and smiled widely.

He had sliced her with his knife in anger, even long after she was already dead, and the pattern of cuts had given him the idea of burning the body to dispose of it and hide the killing. He inserted wicks, removed from candles, into the slices of her fat body. He lit each of the wicks with a lighter, and then lit a cigarette near the body.

Soon the flames were dancing joyously, celebrating her death and his freedom. He hadn't even needed an accelerant. Her body fat had helped spread the fire, and the wooden structure, filled with many highly flammable items, was secluded enough that it had drawn no attention before it burned down completely. There were no homes very close by and people in the area often lit bonfires in their lawns to burn off yard waste or trees they had cut down. No one had suspected anything. The fire department had listed it as "not suspicious in nature", and it had hidden the slashes and the strangulation quite well.

That kill had been about freedom, but every kill since had been about wealth and youth. He had amassed a small fortune, most of it hidden away. When he needed it, he would know precisely where every bit of it was. But in the meantime, he simply appreciated knowing it existed. It was a warm knowledge, warm like the blood he would soon release from his victims.

But he always had an emergency stash of several tens of thousands in cash in a gym bag, in case he needed to leave the area quickly. He kept it in the trunk of his beat-up older car, where no one would expect to find it or anything else of any real value.

 He finally arrived at the bar. The front doors had not yet been locked and the sign was still on, but he knew that would only be the case for a few more minutes. Because of the late hour and the lack of a band, there had been no cover charge at this bar tonight. That meant one less person to potentially remember him, which he took as a good sign.

He entered the main barroom, and chose a table near the rest rooms where he was certain he could see most of the patrons. The killer ordered a drink, which he nursed as he watched the couple at the table across from his side of the bar. Their money and egocentric behavior were obvious signs of an easy life valuing nothing. It made him furious thinking about it, but he kept his face calm.

He would have preferred to know them better before moving ahead, but they had moved up the list a little more quickly than he had originally planned. Still, his hunger for success was almost overwhelming. He needed to finish a couple tonight, which meant doing it without the usual careful planning. He had watched them a few days, but less than he was comfortable with. Still, watching viable victims in their last night of life always made him feel a little happy.

In fact, watching them actually made him so happy he almost missed when the last call came and the young couple unexpectedly started for the door. He had expected them to linger a bit longer.

When he had first spotted the couple, their accent had told him it was unlikely they were locals, and he had hoped they would not be driving, because he hated following in his car which was a piece of garbage and stood out like the lamp posts on the streets in this part of town. Fortunately for him they were staying nearby, and tonight, they left the bar and started walking in the opposite direction of the parking area.

He followed on foot a safe distance behind. He wanted to be close enough to see where they went in case they varied their routine, but not so close that they would spot him or that they would anger him more by what they said. As expected, they turned into one of the Residence Suite hotels. That had initially been a little bit of a disappointment for him, because it meant he might have had a much tougher time breaking in.

The better hotels such as this were on a key card and had a 'Charlie-bar' lock on the patio doors. Of course, the electronic lock had a hidden core and he knew where it was, but he also knew from past experience that particular hotel chain used a type of core which was much harder to pick than standard locks.

He had run into one of them in the next county to the South recently, and barely gotten it picked when he heard the elevator ding announcing an arrival. He had almost been caught that time, and all because the core was hard to pick.

But It had turned out Fate was on his side on that night, and it was his intended victims in the elevator. Knowing there were no cameras in that particular hotel, he had instead immediately used the tire thumper on both the husband and wife before they finished getting out of the elevator. He then used their key card to enter their room, dragged them inside, enjoyed himself and finally stole their identity, cash and jewelry.

But in tonight's case, a ruse had allowed him to get a key card. Days earlier he had waited till the middle of the night, stripped down to just a tee shirt and shorts, and approached the night clerk with a story of becoming locked out when he went for ice. The clerk happily assisted him by creating an additional key card for the room. He had then swiped it but not entered the room. Now, several days later, the card would be long forgotten from the clerk's memory.

Of course, it still was in the system memory and it still would work, and he could soon be in, quickly and quietly. He knew that getting into this room on this night was his destiny. He was pleased to note that the suite they had entered was away from the view from the elevators and in tonight's hotel, there were no cameras in the hallway, only in the elevator.

But he was even more pleased when he heard, through the door, the sound of them removing the aluminum bar and sliding the patio door open. It was on the second floor, so it would be easy to reach. Now there would not even need to be an extra key card swipe recorded to raise questions. He would leave the extra card in the room unused.

He went back down the stairs to the ground floor and crossed the street. Fifteen minutes later, the couple's room lights went out. An hour after that he rolled a trash dumpster ten feet from its original location, climbed on top and pulled himself up on their balcony, entering through the open patio door.

He could feel the anger rising like bile in his throat. They had everything and deserved nothing. He deserved everything and had nothing. He came from a wealthy family just two generations back, but his father had been discredited and they had lived in poverty most of his life. Then he married too young and had to steal stuff to support the wife, who did nothing but moan and complain, and point to people like these. But to top it all off, several years later, when she finally learned where their extra income came from, she was insulting as hell and was going to turn him in.

Once again, he remembered what she had looked like as she died and the killer relaxed a little.

Entering the suite he made his way to the bedroom, where he used his tire thumper on the young man, bound his wrists and ankles, and positioned him. Then he began to work on the young lady. He bound her wrists so she could not scratch him at any point, strangled her, then raped her. He cut her several times with the knife, flipped her over and felt her soft round ass against him as he entered her anally again and again, thrusting with all his force. He flipped her back over, stabbed her till his arm got tired and then slit her throat, all while muttering "Bitch." repeatedly.

The final thrust was straight into her heart through her back. He was a little disappointed the male had not been conscious at all, to suffer watching her get what she deserved.

As almost an afterthought, the killer inserted the long thin blade beneath the man's rib cage, angled up so as to stop the guy's heart forever.

He put a fresh pair of latex gloves on and began collecting anything of value in an undamaged pillowcase. He flushed his condom down the bathroom toilet, with an extra flush to be certain it went down. Then he carefully scanned the area before leaving, and he left by the main entry door. He exited using the stairwell instead of the elevator in order to avoid the cameras.

Chapter 29

The call had come from the manager of the Residence Suite hotel, after one of the maids had hysterically reported her findings to him.

Officer Kevin Wolf pulled up at the Residence Suite hotel and paused to look around for a moment before going in. His keen eyes noted a dumpster that seemed out of place, being where the odors from it would waft into the rooms. He was pleased to note there were as yet no news vans or reporters visible on the premises. He recalled his displeasure at the previous scene he had attended in the Playa del Sol condominiums.

Dispatch had said the room used a second floor entrance, so he rode the elevator to the second floor and began watching room numbers. But before he had gone very far, the obviously distraught manager came running down the hall toward him, shouting "Back here."

Kevin followed the man to the room, and the manager immediately began talking rapidly.

"They booked for a month with full maid service. Then we found them dead this morning. They've only been here a little over a week. They had maid service every morning and a turn down every evening. They were not there for the turn-down last night, but they were dead in there this morning."

"Who discovered the bodies?", Kevin asked.

"The floor maid, Maria Fuentes. She's been with us for over a dozen years and is very reliable."

"Where is she right now?", Kevin continued his questioning.

"She's in the maid's lounge. She was vomiting and crying. Some of the other maids are trying to calm her down."

"Did you talk to her at all?"

"Yes. She was hard to understand because she was crying so much, but she basically said that she went into the bedroom when no one answered her knock, figuring they had gotten an early start at the beach and might want clean sheets when they return. We change them every three days, you see, and this would have been their third change. She often found them to be early risers and gone when she knocked so she thought nothing of it. But when she got to the bedroom door, she saw them, and lost it. You can see that is where she first vomited."

Kevin found it a bit difficult to write down everything being said because the manager was rambling so rapidly, but felt sure he was getting it down correctly even so. This would have been a good time for one of the portable recorders some of the officers used. He made a mental note to pick one up the next day he had off work.

"OK", Kevin said, "Wait here while I take a look and some preliminary photos."

Kevin took the small camera from his belt and took shots of the outer room, then the bathroom, where the maid had obviously gone after her initial vomiting session, and finally, the approach to the bedroom itself.

He could hardly believe what he was seeing. Except for the presence of a second body, the scene was almost exactly identical to what he had seen at the Levine killing. Being careful where he stepped, he entered the room and took a closer look, only to confirm that he had been entirely correct. This time, however, no one had stepped in any of the blood, so the maid must not have come past the bedroom door.

He then took some shots of the two bodies, paying particular attention to the male victim. Kevin observed the male, quite unlike the female, showed no signs of torture, but had a head wound, chicken ties on his wrists and ankles, a gag of cloth from what appeared to be the female victim's panties filling his mouth, and what appeared to Kevin to be a single knife wound under the rib cage at an upward angle. His throat had also been cut, but there was very little bleeding from it, so he personally suspected it was made after the victim was already dead, probably as a check to be certain he was dead.

Kevin carefully stepped back out of the room, and went to the patio door, which was wide open. He examined it for any signs of an entry attack, but found none immediately visible.

He realized that did not mean none were there, of course, but that if they were it would be the forensics guys who found them.

Stepping out onto the balcony and looking down, he observed that the dumpster he had noted was out of place was immediately below the patio, providing a reasonable easy method of access.

He made a mental note to ask the crime scene guys to carefully dust the balcony and dumpster. They would not like that, and would like him telling them to do it even less, but he knew they would comply.

Re-entering the suite, Kevin clicked on his radio and called for the Medical Examiner and Crime Scene. Sue was on duty and promised to call both immediately. He knew she would.

Leading the manager back out into the hallway, Kevin instructed him carefully as to the next steps.

"We are going to need to keep this room off limits to everyone until the Medical Examiner and Crime Scene technicians complete their work", he began. "Can you remove all keycard access from the main desk on this model of lock, or does it lack that capability?"

"Yes, we can do it. We simply set the permissions to not permit card access until a later time and date."

"Can you then re-set it when the team gets here, or is it all too difficult?", Kevin asked.

"Sure, that's really no problem,", the manager responded. "With the model we had on here last year it would not have been possible, but we did an upgrade last Summer."

"Excellent", Kevin responded. "Do so immediately then." He pulled the door shut, placed several strips of yellow crime scene tape across to warn people to stay out, then turned back to the manager. "Let's go talk to the maid", Kevin said.

The two took the elevator to the ground floor. Before they entered it, however, he noticed the hallway camera outside it.

"Do these cameras cover the hallway, also?", Kevin asked.

"No, just the elevator lobby on each floor. Guests would not like it very much if it watched the hallways. Some even complain about the lobby cameras.", the manager answered.

I will need footage on the second floor camera from last night to this morning", Kevin instructed.

"No problem", the manager answered, "I will have my IT guy pull it for you."

They rode down to the ground floor and walked to the rear of the building where the maids' lounge was located. The manager knocked, then opened to door and shouted, "Manager and a guest coming in."

They waited a count of ten and then proceeded to enter. Three maids were attempting to comfort an obviously distraught slightly overweight fourth maid.

"I never saw nothing like that before", she immediately said to the manager, a defensive tremor in her voice. "I didn't mean to get sick in the room. I really didn't."

Kevin found it a little disturbing that she seemed afraid of losing her job over something like that. He had never been insecure and found those who were a bit disconcerting.

Gently he spoke to the woman, trying to calm her down. "I'm sure management is not upset at you for it. Right?" he asked, indicating his attention was to the manager and looking for support.

"That's absolutely correct. Maria, you have nothing to worry about. The hotel is not upset with your actions.", the manager responded.

Kevin could see the woman's shoulders relax and her breathing come easier almost immediately.

"Did you notice anything other than the victims that seemed out of place or unusual to you?", he asked.

"The missus, she always left a lot of jewelry out. I know because I was always afraid she say I stole something, and I never would. But I see today none there.", Maria answered.

"Anything else?", Kevin asked.

"No, sir.", Maria answered.

"Here is my card, in case you think of anything else.", Kevin said, handing her his card.

"For now that is all I need."

He nodded to the manager, and the two left. "You will take care of the lockout on that suite?", Kevin asked.

"Yes. Immediately.", the manager responded.

"I will let the Medical Examiner and Crime Scene know they need to contact you when they get on scene", Kevin stated.

But as it turned out, neither step was necessary. As they entered the lobby, they were met by the Medical Examiner, who was followed by a distance of maybe twenty feet by the Crime Scene technicians.

Kevin returned to his patrol car and began doing the paperwork on the case using the vehicle's built-in laptop.

Chapter 30

Michael spent most of the next day at Nicki's table, re-reading his notes taken from the library newspapers. Nicki had taken her car to pick up her paycheck at the diner and then do some shopping.

Toward evening, she returned and they had a quiet but enjoyable meal she had brought home pre-made from the food market. It wasn't as good as a home-cooked dinner might have been but it was quite good nonetheless.

"You do any good with your notes today?", she asked.

"Not really. I can't shake the feeling that the guy whose home burned down is my best lead, but I have no clue how to find him."

"So what's your next plan?"

"As soon as it gets a little later, I'm going to drive up to where I stashed the stuff from the last visit I made to the condos, and tomorrow I start talking to fences. I have put it off as long as I could, but it is all I have now."

"You going to be all right? You scared me in the library, you know."

"Yeah, I'm sorry about that, but I'm okay."

"You're positive?"

"Positive."

Nicki did not seem very convinced. A few minutes later she made a decision, and followed up on it without letting Michael know.

An hour later it was late enough that most of the fisherman would be back in, but still light enough to find his way at the grove, so he told her he would be back in about an hour, and started toward the grove in her car which he hoped despite its color would be less noticeable there than his newer rental. Also he really wanted the small bit of extra leg room.

At about the same time Michael began his drive, a few miles away, Billy and Bobby Cooper pulled the small flatboat into the grove of Palm trees and tied it to the base of a lone tall tree. It had not been a particularly good day.

They had been out since 4 am and Billy's bald head was redder than it had been in weeks because he forgot to bring his hat today. Worse yet, they had only managed to catch one mullet and two sea bass, barely enough for a good dinner and some jerky, and not enough to leave anything to sell for beer money, which was beginning to get low.

Loading the small flat boat seemed like more work than it was worth right then. They threw the cooler into the back of Billy's pickup truck and drove up on the long road toward town to Smiley's Bar at the crossroads a mile away.

They would return for their boat later, once their thirst was quenched and they were feeling a little better.

When they entered, Jerry, the night bartender, winced and looked to the corner. Seeing Emory Cooper's small frame there, Jerry felt a moment of relief, and went to wait on the burly brothers. They ordered their usual - a Bud and a shot of Old Crow each.

They quickly downed them and ordered two more in as many minutes. Jerry kept watching Emory, hoping soon he would walk over, but Emory seemed not to have even noticed his cousins' presence.

Fortunately, Bobby was fully absorbed watching the news on the television, where a video taken on a celphone was playing under the banner reading "Enhanced video of thief leaving scene of burglaries and recent murder".

But finally the moment Jerry had dreaded came. Billy turned to Jon Williams, who was quietly sipping a Blue Moon ale, and said, "What're YOU lookin' at, Jon?"

"Nothing, honest, Billy", Jon answered.

"You sayin' I'm nothing?"

"I wasn't looking at you, Billy. Honest I wasn't"

"You sayin' yer too good to pay any attention to me?"

"No, Billy, honest. I don't want any trouble. Please"

Jon's eyes were wide and his voice trembled. His eyeglasses were slipping down his nose from the sweat coming off his brow. Jon sold auto insurance at the mall. He was not accustomed to anybody like Billy confronting him. People at work were always nice to him, hoping to get a better deal.

Billy, on the other hand, was obviously invigorated by the confrontation. His eyes shown like hot coals in the dim light of the bar. It was plain to everyone in the bar that he was enjoying the fear expressed by the smaller chubby man next to him. His hands clenched and he tightened his arm muscles preparatory to the first strike. His hunger for the moment of impact was nearly palpable.

Jerry moved closer to the large breaker bar under the bar, but made no attempt to pick it up. He felt his own hands begin to shake a little. The whole room was quiet except for a small whisper of soft soles on the dusty floor.

Then Emory touched Billy's shoulder and in a voice too low for anyone but Billy to hear, muttered a short sentence. Billy's face went white and he turned back to his empty drink glasses. He turned one slowly in his hands, paused a moment, put it down and as Jerry breathed a sigh of relief, both the brothers got off their stools and walked out the door.

As he had many times in the past, Jerry wondered what Emory had said to his cousin. The Cooper brothers were a nearly unstoppable and cruel force if Emory did not intervene.

Jerry had once hit Bobby across the cheek with the three foot breaker bar, which had been created for, and was intended for use by, truck mechanics, and hauled the wounded body out to the ditch.

But before the ambulance could arrive, Bobby had returned to the bar and put three patrons in the hospital. And that was on a day without Billy at his side, unlike today.

Yet all it ever seemed to take to send both the brothers packing was a few quiet words from Emory.

Each of the brothers would make almost three of Emory, and although he was very strong from shoeing horses for a living up near Ocala, he was otherwise not very impressive looking. His face was nearly invisible in the thick short beard and loose curly hair, leaving only two grey eyes to identify that there was even a person there. But unimpressive as he may have seemed to the rest of the world, the brothers treated him like a Kryptonite bomb. Jerry suspected he would never understand it.

In the past, he had contemplated calling the cops on the brothers, but had been afraid to. In the first place, the bar is in the middle of nowhere, in the unincorporated portion of the county, so there were no city police a minute or two away. If he was lucky, there might be a county sheriff's deputy within ten or twenty minutes. More likely, it would be a half an hour before a lone FDLE State trooper would show up. And he would not be likely to be much of a match for the two cruel and crazy brothers.

But scarier still was the second part of the equation. Once the brothers realized it was he who had called the cops, Jerry would never be safe again. Smiley did not pay well enough to take risks like that, so Jerry never called.

He just hoped Emory would magically appear when he was needed. And much of the time, he did, because Emory spent a lot of his time there. But sometimes Emory wasn't there, and Jerry was left feeling like a coward and a fool.

Fortunately, today was not one of those days. He stood at the door watching the pickup truck head back down the highway toward the Fisherman's Cove docking area.

As the brothers returned to the grove, they spotted a small imported car nearly hidden at the edge, and a lone individual digging at the base of one of the palm trees. It was just light enough to make out his face from the distance. He did not seem aware of them or their truck.

"Hey, that looks like HIM.", Bobby shouted in the cab of the truck.

"Who him?"

"Him, the guy from the video on TV."

"What the hell you talkin' about?"

"On TV. The other day, some kid caught a video on her phone of the burglar leaving the same condos where that murder happened. At first they didn't have a good picture from it, but now they got a nice close-up of his face and everything, and that's him."

"That's him?"

"That's him. And he got a lot of stuff from his hits. Thousands and thousands."

"You're full of shit."

"Am not, asswipe."

"Come on, you're shitting me."

"I'm not, Billy. I SWEAR it. That's the guy they showed on TV."

"No effin' shit."

"No shit, and besides, who would be digging out here unless they were hiding something or digging it up?. We gonna be effin' RICH."

"Let's get him."

The wind had picked up, and the palm trees swayed noisily against the crashing sounds of an angry tide. Michael hoped there was no storm coming, but he hadn't turned the television or radio on that day, so he couldn't be sure, although it was not storm season. This would not be a great place to be in a storm, and as it got darker, maneuvering through the brush without getting bit by something potentially nasty would make it tougher.

But there had been no afternoon thunderstorm, which was more likely than any other type of storm at this time of year in Florida, so Michael was fairly confident there would be no storm and he would be long gone before it got too dark to safely find his way through the grove. He continued digging up the gains from his latest visit to the condos.

When it was fully exposed, Michael dropped the shovel and bent down to pick up the bag he had wrapped it in. He never heard anyone approach. In fact, the next sound he heard was his shovel as it hit the back of his head. He never felt the hands remove the car keys from his pocket.

Chapter 31

Michael's whole head hurt, and his wrists ached. The pain in his face was sharper than the pain in the back of his head. Slowly he realized he wasn't dead. He tried to say "Not dead." but what he heard was barely audible if at all and sounded more like "Nnndd". He was not even certain he had heard it. Certainly no one else nearby would have.

He gradually awoke to the smell of urine and feces, if you can call it waking up. Michael could barely open his eyes through the pain, and when he did, very little was visible through their squinting view. His head felt like a thousand drummers were marching on the back of it.

He was naked and his arms were painfully fastened behind the chair he was sitting on.

But it was the stench that was most noticeable. Michael thought it must be animal related. Nothing human would let such an odor collect, he thought, and the only exception he could think of was an old outhouse, which would be much smaller, and even that would have less concentrated of an odor.

Soon Michael began to detect a strong aroma of sweat added to the mixture he was smelling.

He heard someone say, "That fucking guy gonna' sleep forever?"

"You know Mama rolls over in her grave every time you say that word.", another voice answered.

"OK, but I'm getting' effin' tired of waiting. Hey. Wait, Billy, I think he's awake."

"Bout damn time. He shoulda' woke up hours ago. Effin' pussy."

"Get him to tell us where the rest is, Billy."

"Oh, he'll tell us. Yes, he will."

Michael heard a sharp cracking sound, and a maniacal laugh, followed by the other voice echoing the laugh. Then a beefy hand slapped his face, hard and sudden, with no warning.

"Time to talk, pussy. Tell us where the rest of the stuff is."

"Stuff?", Michael muttered, his mind barely sorting the words he was hearing.

"The shit you stole in all them burglaries, asshole. Where is it?"

"There's no stuff", Michael muttered again through dry, cracked lips that he could barely move.

The big hand slapped him again.

"Don't EVEN lie to me, asshole. I'll effin' kill you if you don't tell me."

A little more alert now, Michael said, "What was under the tree is all there is."

"Bullshit." and the next slap came almost instantaneously, followed by a second slap and then a closed fist punch. Michael felt blood running down his cheek where the huge knuckles had dug into his flesh.

"Tell me where it is."

"Look. I only did one job here and that is all I got."

Nicki watched the scene unfolding inside the barn through a wide space in the old wooden slats that made up its walls.

She had waited patiently for a while after Michael left, but when it began to be later than she had expected, she used her laptop to track the GPS tracker she had put into her car while Michael napped after his incident in the library.

She had ridden her scooter, periodically checking the map on her laptop, and found herself at this secluded barn.

But she now felt somewhat useless watching as Michael was being tortured. It really seemed they were going to kill him, but what could she do?

Then she realized they had hidden her car on the far side of the barn, and she became somewhat hopeful. If her memory was correct...

Michael could see better now and he watched the angry eyes below the red bald head. At first he was glad to finally see his attacker, because he could look forward to catching up with him some day.

But then he realized the implications. Either the guy was really stupid, or was not planning on Michael getting out of this alive, or both.

Michael decided to hope for stupid, and the guy really did not look like the brightest bulb in the lamp, so he felt justified having that hope.

"Okay, then. We gonna' have some fun. 'Cuz you WILL talk, asshole."

Michael heard the cracking sound again, just as a pail of filthy water splashed in his face and covered the front of his body. At that point he knew what the sound was before he even saw the battery and jumper cables, and he knew the guy was not just stupid. This was likely to be Michael's last day on Earth.

The pain was unbelievable and Michael's whole body tensed in a huge and painful spasm. He felt his attention slipping away.

"Damn, Billy, I think you kilt him."

"Nah, he's just out of it. Effin' pussy. I hit him again, I bet he wakes up."

Michael felt the unbearable pain again and began to scream at the top of his lungs begging them to stop.

"He still ain't moving, Billy."

"He will. Just gotta' keep hitting him till he does."

The pain came again, and Michael screamed again, long and hard.

"I think he's beginning to come to, again, Billy. I think I heard him whisper something."

The pain came again. Michael was screaming and crying and begging. A tiny part of him realized they could not hear him, but he kept screaming anyway.

"Yeah, I heard it that time, too."

Fists began to punch Michael 's stomach and face and slowly he began to see the face of the man again. His chest felt like there was an elephant sitting on it.

"Tell me where the rest of the stuff is", the guy shouted.

"That's all there is. That's all there is. That's all ..."

Before Michael could finish the sentence again, he saw the jumper cables coming toward him, and knew the next jolt could kill him, but then Michael saw the angry eyes go to confused instead.

Michael was confused too, seeing an arrow facing him below the guy's chin. In his dazed state, Michael wondered where the guy got it and why.

In almost slow motion Michael saw his assailant drop to the wet floor and his body jump repeatedly as the cables landed, and hit him again and again. For a brief moment, Michael thought about what it would have felt like if the guy had continued to do that to him instead.

Michael heard a thumping sound and watched as the assailant's partner followed the first body down, landing on top of Michael's assailant, the bolt of a short arrow protruding from his eye socket. Soon that guy began to jump also and a burning meat smell drowned out the stench of the feces and urine.

Then Nicki was undoing the straps that held Michael, using a sharp hunting knife, and helped him back into his clothes. The bag Michael had buried and dug up was open and its contents had been spread across a makeshift table comprised of two hand-made wooden horses and an old door. Without so much as a word, Nicki quickly gathered them up and tossed them back into the bag, which she put into the trunk of her car. Only then did Nicki speak.

"Are you going to be okay, or do we need to take you to an emergency room?"

"I'll be okay", Michael lied, "but what was THAT? And where did you come from?"

"Your little trip to LaLa land yesterday had me worried, so I put a GPS tracking device in the engine compartment of my car before letting you drive again. When you didn't show back up after a couple of hours, I looked it up on the laptop computer, and tracked it to this barn on my scooter. Who are these guys?"

"Never saw them before. They came at me when I was digging up the stash, and the next thing I knew I was here. I have no idea how the car got here."

"They must have brought it here to hide it or to strip it for saleable parts. I'm just glad I got here in time. I'm quite sure they were going to kill you."

"But you killed them. Are YOU okay?"

"Remember that my daddy used to take me deer hunting? That's why I still had a hunting crossbow in the trunk of my car. I rode my scooter here and when I saw what was happening, I got my Tenpoint 180-lb crossbow and deer bolts out of the car. I honestly feel less guilty killing things like them than I did a deer."

"Cold."

"Not really. I didn't like having to do it.", Nicki said defensively.

"But it had to be done", Michael said, nodding his head slightly.

"And now that it has, I don't feel particularly bad about having done it."

"Because it had to be done."

"You complaining?"

"No", Michael replied, "Not at all. You sure are good with that crossbow."

"Nope. I was aiming for the heart in both cases. Guess I over-estimated how much drop the arrows would have in the distance. Just got lucky that I hit the one guy's spine and the other's brain through the eye socket."

"Lucky?"

"Lucky."

"I wasn't feeling very lucky myself, until you showed up."

"I kind of hope it stays like that", she smiled.

Was he imagining it or was she actually hitting on him in a barn full of animal stench and death? Michael decided to let the question wait for another time and place. This place was worse than disgusting, even without the two fried bodies.

"What are we going to do with them?", Michael asked, feeling like it should be him who knew the answer, but knowing he didn't.

"I think we should burn the place down. Guys like that, maybe nobody misses them provided it doesn't start a brush fire. It seems like there is a pretty wide clearing around the place, and it rained recently, so I don't think that is likely."

She removed the deer bolts from the bodies, rinsed them in a cattle trough along one wall, and put them back in their holder and returned them to the trunk of her car. It would be daylight soon, so they both knew they needed to get on the road before long. Michael was in no shape to be driving during morning traffic.

Looking around, they found a couple of large containers of tractor fuel, which they used to spread a pattern around the interior of the barn and all over the bodies and the chair where he had been sitting. She half carried him until they were clear.

Michael then made a makeshift Molotov cocktail using an empty Old Crow bottle and a rag and a small amount of the fuel, and threw it into the area, igniting it in a frenzy of heat and flame, and they each drove away, Nicki on her scooter and Michael following in her car. If anyone investigated, the fire would most certainly be ruled suspicious but there should be nothing to link either of them to the area or the event.

Michael followed her scooter carefully, not being familiar with the roads that had led him there, and soon they were back on the main road heading toward her home. Michael was in a lot of pain, more than he would even admit to himself, but he managed to survive the drive.

There were almost no moving cars on the road at that wee hour, which was good because his driving was by no means the best it had ever been. The pain caused him to swerve quite often and he was terrified a police car might spot them, but fortunately, none did.

Chapter 32

Michael slept badly that night. He had recurring nightmares of being on fire and of being attacked by huge monsters with arrows projecting from their face and neck. In his dream he was tied into a knot and the fires were all around him but the monsters kept attacking.

Michael awoke when Nicki re-entered her home carrying bags of food and medicines. He had not heard her leave, so it was a little disorienting at first.

"I have a friend who is a pharmacist with her own small compounding pharmacy", she stated, "and she helped me with pain medicine, a paste to put on the burns, and dressings."

She spread those items on the table and began putting most of the food she had brought into the refrigerator and cupboards, leaving only the breakfast items on the table next to the medicines.

"Over here", she said, holding a chair next to the table.

Michael sat at the seat she held and she began treating his wounds. Every touch hurt but afterward each felt improved, just a little bit. When she finished, she handed him a pill and a small bottle of water.

"Oxycodone", she said, "My friend Felicia shouldn't have given me them because this state makes it highly controlled, but she owes me a really big favor and I called it in."

Michael swallowed the pill without comment. It did not matter to him how she got it. He welcomed the possible relief.

"Now the bad medicine", she said, and handed him the morning newspaper.

There, above the fold, were two photos - one of the young tourist who was being charged with obstruction by the police for selling her video to the newspapers instead of taking it to them, and next to it, the subject of the video, a clear shot of Michael's face.

Michael was now likely to be the most recognizable burglar in the state of Florida, although it technically only stated he was a 'person of interest' in the investigation.

He had not seen anyone when he left the condos the other day, but obviously, this young tourist had seen and photographed him.

How long, he wondered, before the Police recognized it as the same picture they had worked with on in the double murder case? He did not realize he had missed the coverage on television a day earlier or that it had actually led to his torture and that the police were already concentrating heavily on the search for him.

"This is NOT good", Michael said, stating the obvious for no particular reason.

"No", she replied.

"I guess that kills my idea of hunting down a fence to try to find the guy with the burned down house."

"I could do that for you", she said, "but first, I have to tell you something."

"No", I said, "I don't want to get you involved."

"I am involved. Are you forgetting the guys in that barn?"

"Any MORE involved."

"Well, that's what I have to talk to you about. I'm already more involved."

"That's sweet, and I'm flattered you care, but this is on me."

"And THAT is 'sweet', even if it is a little egotistical, but I am not talking about caring about you."

"Then what?"

"Suppose, just for a minute, that maybe the burglar who hit the condo where the girl was killed was NOT the murderer."

"I already know he's not, because that was me. But SOMEBODY hit it again after me and killed her."

"No."

"What do you mean, no?"

"I mean, maybe a second burglar did hit the place after you did but is NOT the murderer."

"What? Why would I think that? It makes no sense. It's just WAY too coincidental."

"Maybe it is. But illogical things happen every day."

"So what are you saying? That I should give up hunting for the guy whose home burned down and who I believe hit the place after I did because he MIGHT be innocent and it might just be coincidental?"

"No, because I don't know if he had anything to do with it at all, so maybe he did and maybe he didn't. But maybe he was not the burglar who immediately followed you."

"Why would you say that? Are you just trying to discourage me from keeping the hunt going?"

"No."

"Then what?"

"I'm trying to get up the nerve to tell you that the burglar who hit the condo after you was me."

Time stopped. There was no noise in the universe. Even the clouds out the window seemed to freeze in place.

Finally, Michael stammered "What the hell?"

"That's why I was not afraid to help you. It was a really strange coincidence that I hit the place right after you did, and an even bigger coincidence that we met and were attracted to each other, but it happened."

"What the hell." Michael repeated stupidly, and sat staring at her.

Chapter 33

Michael sat, staring at Nicki and yet staring into a void simultaneously. He felt very lost and very confused.

"Nicki, I think you had better start from the beginning", he said after a few moments.

"I'm a burglar. Perhaps not quite as skilled as you, but quite highly skilled. My first adult boyfriend was a locksmith and I helped in his shop until we broke up. I learned a lot.

After that, I found I was broke, and working as a waitress in a diner is NOT the path to riches, let me tell you. So I began to hit a few places, nothing very big, but enough to support myself.

I've always window shopped for nice jewelry, so I have learned what good stuff looks like as opposed to attractive junk, which helped me a lot."

Michael just sat there wordlessly as she continued.

"I happened to hit the condo at the Playa del Sol because I saw a guy with a lot of flash cash and whose girlfriend had plenty of jewelry that looked expensive. I had never seen you and had no way of knowing you had also hit the place until you told me the other day.

"I must have picked the lock right after you left, as nearly as I can figure, because I took as much as I could easily carry that was of value, so there would have been less left than you described seeing. There was nobody there when I hit the place."

"You took almost everything of value?", I asked, picking up on the possible discrepancy.

"No, but I took a lot. There was a large gold medallion and some other heavy looking gold pieces that just smacked of being too identifiable, so I left them. And there was some other stuff that all together would have been too heavy for me to carry discreetly. But I didn't leave as much as you described. In fact, I took some pieces matching what you said you saw."

"And the drugs?"

"No, I admit I had no interest in them. And I found a LOT of them. There was a brick of coke on the table, open, but I also found a stash of about thirty more bricks, about twenty in a suitcase under the bed and in the rest lying in a stack in one of the closets."

Michael thought about it a couple of seconds, then asked, "You picked the lock?"

"Yes, why?"

"The main door lock?"

"I said yes. Why?"

"Because I went back and talked to the boyfriend and checked a few things out. SOMEBODY jimmied the patio door lock. So there was a third entry, for sure."

"And maybe it was occupied when they hit and they did not like not finding as much of value as they had expected."

"Maybe. And you said you left a large medallion, which her boyfriend specifically mentioned to me had been stolen."

"So we're back to checking on the other thief by consulting with fences. And because I have been doing business in the area, I have a certain credibility with them already."

"Okay, point made."

"And with your face on TV, you cannot appear in public very much. A fence might just turn you in to get good karma with the cops."

"True that. That was why I had been putting it off."

"And also, I have a pretty good hunch which one I would use for such things, and it is one of the same ones you marked on your list as the most likely candidates. So it's settled", she said with a small smile and an air of finality. She seemed to enjoy getting in the last word.

It took Nicki about 45 minutes to get to central St. Petersburg, and park near the store she was looking for.

Eddie Augustine ran a small electronics repair shop in St. Petersburg. He repaired laptops, lamps, DVD players, pretty much anything you brought in to him. He also paid top dollar for stolen items which he sent to his cousin in Brooklyn, who was his business partner. Because everything was sold far from where it was stolen, the risks were greatly decreased and the profits were infinitely larger. And because it was a business shipping to another business, it went through a trucking company where it was not subject to the sort of searches done at the post office or UPS.

Eddie surveyed the items Nicki had brought in, and gave her a price. It was a lot, though lower than it should have probably otherwise have been, but Nicki was not there to get rich today. She also understood that the notoriety of the heists would make the pieces less desirable to most fences in the area, which Augustine would capitalize on.

"I'll take half that if you do me a favor", she said.

"Half? Must be a big favor."

"Not really. Someone else is operating in my territory, and I want to work out a deal with him so we don't hit the same places or follow each other up or accidentally do anything to get the other caught. I figure you probably know who it is."

"And you would give up half to find out?"

"I will."

"How do I know you haven't already been caught and this is just a police ruse?"

"You know me better than that. Would I give up the best fence in central Florida for a slight break on my sentencing? And more importantly, would I believe the police if they offered a bigger break?"

"Good point. Tell you what. I won't give you much but his nickname, but I WILL contact him and give him YOUR info. That way it is you taking the risks, not me, and not him unless he follows it up."

"OK. I have a prepaid burner phone I bought at Wal-Mart. Here is my number."

Nicki wrote the number on the back of one of Eddie's business cards from the counter and handed it to him. He looked at it, and nodded.

"Fair enough.", he stated, and reaching into a bag behind the counter, he continued "Here is your half of what I quoted. And his nickname is Stick."

Eddie took a wad of bills from the handful he had removed from the bag, peeled off enough hundreds and twenties to make up the correct amount and handed it to her. She put it in her own pocket and walked out. He admired her ass as she did.

"Be a shame if anything happened to that", he muttered to himself. He then picked up his own cellphone, which was also a burner phone, and dialed a number of yet another burner phone.

"Wal-Mart is the real one benefitting from all this", he muttered to himself as he waited for the other phone to be answered.

"You know who this is", he began, "You asked me to watch for certain types of items and let you know if they showed up."

Stickney answered "Yes."

"And you promised to let me handle what you got in your last hit in exchange?"

"I did."

"You understand what will happen if you cross me?"

"I do."

"Okay. Here is the number of the person who brought it in. Better yet, they want to talk to you, too. Want to work out a deal. You now owe me and I will expect to see the merchandise within 24 hours."

"Done."

Eddie gave Stickney the number and hung up, removed the SIMM card from the phone and put another in its place. The old SIMM card went into a metal bucket he kept for old paperwork and used wrapping paper, which he then lit with a lighter in the shape of a large matchstick. He watched it burn till the fire went out then checked to make sure it had been destroyed. It had.

"Not a bad day's work", Eddie said aloud in the empty shop, and smiled widely.

Michael smiled when Nicki came in the door to her double-wide trailer home, where he was sitting on the cheap couch doing a Sudoku puzzle from the newspaper. He was still in a lot of pain but just seeing her seemed to take some of it away. Her news took away even more of it.

"Guy's nickname is 'Stick'", she said, "and he should call me before long."

"Stick - so we were probably right. The guy with the burned out trailer was named Stickney."

"So it sounds like the same guy. Let's hope he turns out to be the killer instead of just ANOTHER burglar who hit the place, and we find a way to prove it."

"Sure does, but what did you mean 'he'll call you'?"

"I gave him my burner phone's number to arrange a meet. Said it was to make an agreement for both our mutual interests."

"Burner phone is good. But we will need to meet him somewhere, or at least get him somewhere, from which we can tail him."

"I know some places that will work", she said.

"Good", he replied, "because I wouldn't have."

"Home court advantage", she said, smiling, "Let's change those dressings."

And she did. When she was finished the pain had again diminished greatly. Michael guessed the old dressings had been binding in the burned flesh even with the white cream spread on it. But the new bandages seemed to not be doing that, at least so far.

As she had worked, Michael could do little except watch her. Her beautiful hazel eyes sometimes took on an almost golden tint, and at other times a green, both of which complemented her auburn hair. She was one of the most strikingly beautiful women he had ever been that close to. And to think she was also a skilled burglar. Wow.

She wasn't a bad home nurse, either.

But then the phone rang.

"Well, unless that's the diner, that didn't take long. Nobody else has this number", she said as she accepted the call.

Chapter 34

Nicki had set it up for a meeting in the parking lot of an abandoned ice cream shop. The shop's original owners had thought being in central Florida on the West coast and selling ice cream was a surefire way to make money. But they did not factor in the damage that a couple of TV news fillers about bugs in the small building could do. In under six months they had shut down for good, and no other food business was likely to move in.

But what made this ideal for Nicki and Michael was that there was a strip mall across the street, with plenty of traffic and a large parking lot, and with a line of sight view of the parking lot at the ice cream shop. Nicki waited on her scooter at the ice cream shop and Michael watched from her car at the strip mall.

The plan was for her to talk to the guy and negotiate to help prevent crossovers like had happened at the Playa del Sol condos. Then she would take off, while he tailed the guy. Michael had shaken enough tails himself over the years to have a pretty good idea of what does and does not work when tailing someone.

Michael had a pair of binoculars Nicki had used when deer hunting. They were excellent and were designed not to reflect light off the lens that a deer would spot. So Stickney would not know Michael was watching.

Nicki was wearing all black. She had a pair of black slacks, tall black boots and a black T-shirt, on top of which she wore a black leather jacket. Her helmet remained unused on a hook on the scooter, but it was also black, as was the scooter. If not for the Silver trim buttons on the jacket she might have been difficult to spot. Michael assumed this was her outfit for when she was on a job.

The scooter was a 600cc Yamaha with an automatic transmission. It would easily do 80 mph in a hurry if needed, was highly maneuverable, and could quickly be parked in a hidden location almost anywhere.

Hopefully, Stickney would be lulled into a state of over-confidence by this presentation. She looked the part and it should put him at ease.

Michael munched on a bag of pre-made buttered popcorn, and sipped bottled water while she waited and he watched. It was tasty, though he would have usually preferred white cheddar flavored for his pre-made popcorn. But Michael did not want sticky hands in case he had to work later.

There was a lot of traffic in and out of his parking lot, and lots of others sitting in cars waiting for their friends or family to finish shopping, so Michael was essentially invisible. On the off chance that Stickney decided to follow her and she could not shake him, they had a rendezvous point picked out a couple miles away. It was the lot of a Super-K box store so there would be plenty of people around, enough that she would be in no danger and Michael should not have to let the guy know that Michael was tailing him tailing her. There was no reason to think it would be necessary, but if this guy was the killer, it did not make sense to take chances unnecessarily.

Michael finished the large bag of popcorn and two bottles of water and felt stuffed, but there was still no sign of the guy. Then he saw her reach in her pocket and bring her hand up to her ear. He assumed she had received a phone call.

Shortly after that, she started her scooter and left the lot. Michael waited thirty seconds to see if anyone was following her, then drove to the Super-K. She was waiting when he got there.

"He phoned to cancel", she said as Michael approached her. "Said a problem from his day job had come up and he could not make it. Asked to reschedule for tomorrow night."

"Shit", he muttered.

"Yup. Another day to wait. Wonder if he will show then or do a couple more stalls to make sure I'm on the level?"

"You think that's what he is doing?"

"Wouldn't you? If someone you didn't know tried to set up a meet?"

"Yeah, I guess I would. Well, nothing we can do about it. The ball's in his court for now."

"That's the way I see it. Wanna' grab some pizza on the way back?"

"Sure. I assume you know a place?"

"Yes. Down by the water. New York style slices and a stuffed pizza to die for."

"Sounds great. Lead the way."

From the outside the place, which bore the name of a recognizably infamous organized crime family, did not look like a pizza joint. It looked like a high class restaurant or club. Inside, it looked more like a bar with a LOT of tables and waitresses in short white skirts and low cut blue blouses. Sinatra music was piped through the halls at a low enough level to permit easy conversation, while loud enough to be identifiable and to empower discreet conversation as well. Not at all what he would have expected for a pizza place, but Michael wasn't complaining.

Michael was complaining even less when he tasted the pizza. He had planned on only having a slice, being a little full of popcorn, but that thought went away instantly.

It truly was excellent. A lot of people say New York has the best pizza, but that had not generally been his experience. Most places he had tried there were just good, not great. He preferred a place called My Pi or a place called Rias, both of which were in Chicago, not New York. The worst pizza, on the other hand, was from a shop just outside Pittsburgh, Pennsylvania. The dough there had the texture of burnt toast.

But this place made up for all of it. It really was the best pizza he had ever tasted, and the crust was just right. Not quite a cracker crust like you get at Pizza Hut, nor a flat dough like Domino's and Papa John's.

It had just the perfect consistency to bring out the flavor of the pizza sauce and cheeses and toppings. And the oven was at the perfect temperature, so there were no burnt spots or bubbles as you sometimes get at other pizza places. Michael liked the flavor of Caesar Caesar, for example, but it almost always had large crust bubbles from uneven heat. This place did not, and the slices were huge.

Michael nursed a Blue Moon ale with his pizza and felt the evening was far from wasted. He watched as Nicki greedily downed several slices. He was surprised. His experience with women who had a figure like hers was that they barely take in any food, as though the odor of the food alone would add inches to their waistline. It was nice to see a woman who could enjoy her meal.

She had a beer with hers as well, but she went with a Sam Adams winter ale. In addition to the great pizza, he was surprised at the variety of beers on tap or in bottles or cans. A sign proclaimed over 150 brands available.

As they were leaving, Michael learned how the place got its name. He could see into the office from the cash register area, and there sat 'Little Tony', the youngest member of the New York family known by the same name as the restaurant. Michael hurried toward the door. There was no reason for Little Tony to know who Michael was but he preferred to keep it that way, especially with the possibility of Johnny the Dentist DiCenzo wanting him dead. Michael guessed this was Little Tony's winter home. Or maybe he lived here year round. None of Michael 's business, and he did not particularly want to know.

Michael followed Nicki's scooter back to the double wide trailer home and they went inside. She gave him a sweet kiss, thanked him for a great evening, and went into her bedroom. Michael laid down on the couch and thought good thoughts until he fell asleep.

Chapter 35

Stickney watched as the black scooter left the ice cream shop. From his vantage point in the strip mall parking lot, he had a clear line of sight as its rider paced back and forth waiting for him. But he knew that the female figure, while it matched the female voice that had set up the meeting, did not match the burglar from the video on television, and he felt sure that that burglar was the same one she was pretending to be. And he was absolutely certain that no stupid woman could really be a burglar. There was not a doubt in his mind. What kind of fool did she take him for? So he waited.

Finally he called the number he had obtained from the fence, and begged off the meeting, asking to set it up later. He then watched as she left and noted she had not used her phone to call anyone else. He gave the black-clad woman he was watching almost a full minute's lead, but not so long that he would not be able to catch up to her and follow her.

And he was just about to follow her when a small car cut in front of him and did exactly that. At first he wondered if it might be the cops. But then another car's headlights lit up that driver's face. It was the one from the newspapers and television and he knew he had been right for sure. They were working together, trying to make a fool of him. And they would pay for that. They would pay dearly. He smiled, thinking of what he could see happening soon.

He gave them a slight headstart, then followed. Sometimes he would pass the car and follow the scooter. Other times he would follow the car. He watched as they went into some sort of what seemed to be a fancy club and spent an hour, and he was waiting when they came out. He watched as they closely followed each other to a remote patch of land outside of town and they went into a double-wide mobile home. He watched as first the living room and kitchen lights came on, then the bedroom, and then the living room and kitchen darkened, and finally, as the bedroom itself darkened.

He could see them in his mind, making love and laughing about him, and his anger grew. But he knew he had to wait.

Waiting took its toll and he felt his eyelids getting heavy, so he took out some of the coke he had stolen from the condo a few days ago, laid out three lines on the dashboard and used a plastic coffee stirrer to inhale each line, one after the other. The rush almost set his mind on fire. It made the waiting seem like nothing. Hours flew like seconds yet seconds seemed like hours.

When the clock on his dashboard showed 3:30 am, the killer exited his car and withdrew his tools from the trunk. He put the hunting knife and its sheath onto his belt, pulled on the latex gloves, and grabbed the tire thumper and looped its strap around his left hand. A handful of long plastic cable ties went into his front pocket. He picked up the small pry bar with his right hand and started for the trailer.

He was extremely pleased the couple had not locked the deadbolt, proving once more to him the extent of their stupidity. The door popped open easily when he pried the latch back. It was noiseless. He could almost taste what he was about to do.

He quickly and quietly strode through the black darkness toward the bedroom. He grabbed the tire thumper to silence the male.

But when he got there, in the moonlight from the bedroom window he saw only the woman. Where had the guy gone? And how had he missed it when he left? He quietly backed out of the bedroom and checked the bathroom next to it, but it was empty.

Obviously the guy had somehow escaped. He would have to find out from the woman how and where he had gone. It would delay his pleasure, but it would be fun at the same time. The more questions he had for her, the more delicious pain she would endure.

He returned to the bedroom and lay the tire thumper onto the bed. Carefully he pulled first one of the woman's arms and then the other toward him, so as to not wake her yet, then bound them at the wrist with the cable ties.

'BITCH', he whispered to himself, "You're about to tell me everything."

He took the knife in his right hand and slowly cut a line down between her shoulder blades. The woman awoke screaming and he smiled.

Chapter 36

Michael didn't know what woke him up. He could feel a pressure in his bladder from the pizza and beer, and at first thought that must be it.

Then he heard a scream from the bedroom.

"Nicki must be having a nightmare about the barn", Michael thought. He arose and plodded toward the bedroom to console her.

Then she screamed again and he ran the last twenty steps. When he got there he saw a gaunt man with a knife attacking her. Michael had only a split second to process the scene and realize the man must be Stickney before the man turned and came at him. Michael could tell Nicki was bound somehow and had been cut. He could not tell how badly.

The thin man swung the knife in an arc near Michael's midsection, but Michael pulled back in time to cause it to slice only empty air. Stickney then thrust it toward Michael's solar plexus and Michael twisted to let the thrust cause Stickney to overextend as it whizzed past him, missing his stomach by fractions of an inch. Michael backhanded Stickney with his left fist, then brought his elbow down on Stickney's arm. Stickney dropped the knife, and its sharp blade embedded itself in the soft tile floor of the trailer. Stickney bent forward, planning to retrieve it.

Michael followed up with a kick to the chin with his right leg as Stickney twisted back.

Stickney fell to the bed. Michael now knew he had him, and he closed in to finish it.

Then Michael's head seemed to explode and his eyes could barely see. Slowly he realized Stickney had another weapon, a bat of some sort, that had been lying on the bed, and when Michael drove him backward, he had landed in a perfect placement to grab it and use it against him. Michael was seeing double yet it seemed he was also seeing only half the view, the other half in blackness.

Michael kicked out again, catching Stickney in the groin. He had not planned it. He had just kicked and that was where it landed.

Stickney bent over and retched slightly, then jabbed the bat into Michael's stomach. Stickney drove it in so deeply that he lost his grip on it.

Michael doubled over and Stickney ran to the door of the trailer and left. Michael heard the car start almost immediately and heard gravel and sand fly as Stickney left.

Michael remained crouched on the floor there, bleeding from the head, half blinded and dazed. If Stickney had stayed Michael knew he would have been helpless. Evidently Stickney had not known it though. Michael's stomach felt like there was a bulldozer inside, crushing it, and every burn and bruise he had suffered earlier was on fire. All he could think about was Nicki, but he could not see her or hear her. He wondered if she were dead. Something in him tried to cry but could not. The pain was too much to concentrate enough to produce tears. Michael tried to shout to her, but his brain could not form words or produce sounds.

He tried to think about what to do next, about what he should be doing now, but Michael could not think at all. All he could do was stare into the night and feel the pain. He could not move. Gradually everything went dark.

When he could see again, Michael had no idea how long he had lain like that. It felt like days had passed. But daylight had not yet lit up the room, or if it had he was not able to see it. He could not say which.

But slowly the pain seemed to increase in his arms and legs, while at the same time they became capable of movement. Slowly that movement extended to his hip and back. Then he could move his head slowly. Michael could hear a fountain, and the darkness gradually turned to red.

Then the double vision became single vision and he could almost focus.

Still he lay there, though. He could not shape a plan of what to do. Michael could only observe what was happening as though he was outside it taking notes. but it did not feel like being outside taking notes. The pain kept increasing.

Then he shook his head and watched as tiny red bubbles flew around, like water being shaken off a wet dog. Somehow a part of him knew that was his blood flying around the room, and that had been the fountain he heard earlier, but it did not seem important. Only the pain seemed important.

Gradually Michael managed to get himself to a sitting position. He didn't know how. He did not plan it, and could not recall how it was done. But it was.

It felt important to move his legs, to get them beneath him. Michael tried but it made no sense to him. Why would legs go beneath him? Why was he trying to move them? He had no clue but it seemed important somehow.

Finally Michael found himself standing and swaying like a thin blade of tall grass in a windstorm. and it felt like he was truly in the middle of a storm. It felt like he was being buffeted in all directions. Just standing in one place took many steps backward and forward and left to right to accomplish.

Then Michael saw Nicki. He could see blood on various parts of her body and soaking her pillowcase. And he knew she was dead. And he knew it was his fault, as had been Linda's and for all he knew maybe even Rebeccah's. Michael did not want to believe she was dead, but he knew it.

Because he did not want to believe it, Michael told himself he could see small movements, but he knew it was a sensory illusion. She was dead and his mind did not want to admit he had gotten her killed.

Michael even began to imagine he could hear her moan slightly. But it was all in his head. She was dead, and he was not able to deal with it.

Michael reached out and touched her dead body, and she said, "Michael?" but it was just his mind working overtime. He would probably continue to see and hear her for years. He loved the sound of her voice, even muffled by blood and pillows. He thought of how he had loved her laughter the first night in the diner. He thought about her saving his life in the barn, only to die in her bed a couple nights later because he failed to save her in return.

A part of him watched as she strained against the cable ties that bound her wrists. Then he wondered why he imagined that. Yet it continued and became more frantic.

"Michael?", she screamed at him. It confused him.

And then he realized that it was not his imagination.

Michael bent over, nearly falling on his face in doing so, and grabbed the hunting knife protruding from the floor and cut the plastic ties. She rolled over.

"I passed out". she said. "What happened? Who was that guy and where is he?"

Michael couldn't answer. His eyes were more or less working, though through a red screen of some sort, and his hands and legs were somewhat operable but it still took too much energy he did not have to form words. He just looked at her. She was alive. That was enough for now.

Michael dropped the knife.

"Where is he?", she screamed at him again.

Michael tried to answer, but when he did, the red turned to black, then everything turned to black. His last observation of it was a thumping sound.

Chapter 37

The next thing Michael remembered was waking in Nicki's bed. The sheets were clean and his head was surrounded by a huge bandage. He felt like an actor playing the Mummy.

His burns had all been tended to again. Nicki stood over him. She had bandages on her arms and the side of her neck. and a small bandage on the top right of her head.

"What happened?", he managed to ask.

"I'll tell you if you tell me", Nicki said.

"Hunh?", he asked wittily.

"After you freed me, you passed out from your head wound", she said. "You were breathing okay, so I took the time to stop my own bleeding and then tended to yours. Something made a pretty good amount of damage to your head, and head wounds bleed a lot, I guess. I stopped your bleeding and bandaged you. But I wasn't sure you were going to come out of it okay."

"Okay", he said.

"So ARE you okay?", she asked. "Do you know where you are?"

"Bed", he said.

"Okay, but are you aware of what is going on around you, or do we need to take you to a hospital? I didn't want to do that unless we have no choice, because they'd notify the police and you would go down for the murders."

"Aware", he said.

"Are you?", she asked again.

"Yes. Aware", he replied.

You're not talking much", she said.

"Hurts. Hard to." he said.

"But you understand what we are saying?"

"Understand. Yes."

The next thing he remembered was waking in Nicki's bed. The sheets were clean and his head was surrounded by a huge bandage. He felt like an actor playing the Mummy.

It had a familiar feel to it.

There was someone with Nicki. She was gorgeous. That was true no matter which woman the pronoun referred to. The other woman had blonde hair and blue eyes and a smile that seemed to have always been there. There were no frown lines or other marks to detract from the smile and it enveloped her whole being. She was built a lot like Nicki.

"This is my friend, Felicia", Nicki said when she saw he was awake. "She's had some medical training."

"I worked as a nurse to earn my way through pharmacy school", Felicia stated matter-of-factly.

"Felicia", he said.

Felicia took a small flashlight and moved it in front of his eyes, first one, then the other, and then back and forth.

She took out an otoscope and looked in his ears, nose and throat.

She took his temperature, then his blood pressure and pulse.

"Urine next", he tried to ask, but it came out flat, more like a statement.

Felicia laughed. "It would be if I had a lab", she said, "but I don't."

She turned to Nicki.

"I think he will be okay, but it may take a few days for him to get all the puzzle pieces back in order. If it weren't for the situation, I would say he should still go to a hospital. But to be honest, he will probably do as well just resting anywhere."

"I appreciate this", Nicki said. "More than you know. I really owe you now - big time."

"No, you were there when I needed you. You took care of my kids while I worked as a nurse and went to school. Without your help I would have had to stay with that bum and let him hit me whenever he felt badly about himself. At the worst, we're even. Give him one of these every eight hours until they run out, and keep his dressings clean."

"Thanks again."

"Are you sure you don't want the two of you to move in with me for a few more days until you are both somewhat back on your feet and up to speed?"

"No. I think I sort of know who the guy is and what he wants. And more importantly, I think I know his limitations. A while back I bought a pick resistant deadbolt, good window locks, and a wireless alarm system. After I called you, I put them in. So I now have sensors hidden at every approach to the place and a secure entrance. He won't be able to sneak up on us again, and I went by Daddy's place and borrowed some of his weapons from his widow."

How IS your step-mother?", Felicia asked.

"Still two years younger than me, same as she ever was", Nicki stated drily.

Felicia chuckled, then they talked a little about Felicia's children and their school, and finally gave each other a warm hug and parted ways, with Felicia taking her medical bag back to her four by four and leaving.

The next thing Michael remembered was waking in Nicki's bed. The sheets were clean and his head was surrounded by a huge bandage. He felt like an actor playing the Mummy.

It had a familiar feel to it.

"How do you feel?", Nicki asked.

"Not too bad, considering", he stated.

"Multiple words, all in a row", Nicki said, smiling, "I'm impressed."

"So am I", he said. "I guess we got Stickney's attention."

"More than that", she said. "We have his murder weapons."

She pointed to a short baseball bat and a hunting knife on the nightstand next to the bed.

"Good and bad", he said. "Means we can now be found in possession of the murder weapon on top of all the other evidence against me."

"But it will have his prints on it", she said excitedly.

"Nope. He was wearing gloves. And my prints will be on the knife. That's what I used to cut you loose."

"Shit."

"Shit indeed", Michael replied.

"Never saw a short bat like that before", Michael said.

"Tire thumper", she explained, "Truckers use them to be sure all their tires are pressurized. Hardwood with a solid metal core."

"Sure does a job on your head, too", he stated. "My brain still feels more like scrambled eggs."

"He did a number on you. That's for sure. But it's nothing compared to what I guess he had in store for me."

"Yeah."

"Good thing you came in when you did."

"I barely made it in time. And I wasn't very effective when I did get there."

"But you did make it in time, and I am alive because of it."

"No, you're alive because he did not realize how badly he had injured me. I don't think Stickney ever had to actually fight someone before."

"Or because you are good", she said.

"Not that good", Michael replied. "I've had some training, and I did everything my training told me to do, but Stickney still really beat me because I failed to realize he might have more than one weapon. Stickney just got scared and did not realize he had won. Otherwise he could have stayed and finished what he started."

"And we would both be dead."

"I thought you were", Michael said, choking back a tear, "When I saw you lying there, unconscious in your own blood, I really thought I had lost you."

"Would you miss me?", she asked jokingly.

"Don't even kid about it.", Michael said. "It was terrible."

"Well, it is over now, and we're here", she said. "We survived."

"Just barely."

"Barely means we are still here. So we survived. That is what matters."

"That and getting the son-of- a-bitch"

"First I ever heard you cuss or even really get angry."

"First I really had a good reason to."

"Well, we will get him, but for now, we just have to take it easy and heal. We need to both be a lot stronger the next time we cross paths with him."

Chapter 38

Kevin Wolf pulled his cruiser up to the back door of McDonald's and knocked a familiar 3-2-1 knock. The manager opened the door for him, and he stepped in, closing the door behind him.

"Be right with you", the manager, Kurt Thompson, said, "Just one more line to balance."

"No hurry", Wolf answered.

He stood at the window looking out and remembering the Spaghetti Palace that used to be across the street. He chuckled to himself, recalling the night Officer Camponi had burned it down.

Camponi had been cruising behind it in the wee hours of the morning, a little before daylight, with the windows of the cruiser open, and heard a sound. Thinking it might be a burglary in progress, Camponi jammed the cruiser into reverse and sped back to the area of the sound in reverse gear. To his eternal embarrassment, he had hit a power pole, bursting his gas tank, and the electrical power wire had snapped. When it fell, it sparked and gas leaking from the tank of the cruiser had caught fire next to the dumpster. In seconds, the fire spread to the dumpster and then to the Spaghetti Palace.

Most buildings in the area, especially commercial buildings, were of block construction but the Spaghetti Palace was all wooden. Before the Fire department could arrive, it had burned to the ground.

Camponi had been the laughing stock of the city for several years afterward, and still took an occasional ribbing for it. If he had not been the brother-in-law of one of the Councilmen, he probably would have lost his job that night. He almost did anyway, when the Council had to vote to appropriate funds to pay the damages because the city was self-insured. Camponi's wife took it all very hard and divorced him, a messy and nearly bloody proceedings, taking everything of value that he owned, and then moved out of the state.

Now the area was still just an open lot. When the McDonald's was crowded, people often parked there instead.

The manager finished his bookkeeping and picked up the deposit bag. He then walked over to the counter and picked up a large box that was sitting on top of it.

"There's plenty of burgers, fries, and coffee in here. It was left over after we closed tonight. Take it back to the station for anyone who wants it, okay?"

"Sounds great, Kurt", Kevin answered, "The guys will appreciate it - especially the coffee. Ours is the WORST."

The manager smiled.

They went out the back door and into the cruiser. Kevin opened the passenger door for the manager, rather than making him sit in the perp seat. The box of food and coffee gave the cruiser a fresh odor that Kevin appreciated.

They carefully drove to the bank. But as they turned the corner a block away, Kevin spotted an unusual sight. Two men were opening a fishing net at the bank's night deposit box area, normally used for businesses to drop their bank bags each night. Kevin stopped his cruiser and backed up so it would be nearly invisible from the bank but he could still see the events occurring there.

"What's going on, Kevin? Why're you backing up?", the manager asked.

"Not sure. There's something going on over there. I want to see what before we go there."

"Cool", the manager stated excitedly. "Police drama." He smiled widely.

Kevin ignored him and continued to watch the pair at the bank. They opened the night depository door and dropped the fishing net into it. They fumbled around for a minute or two, then closed the door and left. Once they were gone, Officer Wolf drove the cruiser up to the drop.

"Open the door, but don't make your drop yet", Kevin ordered.

"Okay."

Kevin watched as the manager turned his key and the door pivoted open. Once the door was open, Kevin examined it. At first it looked normal. But on closer examination he spotted two hooks in the corner of the hinge area, and could make out the beginnings of the net attached to them.

"You're not making a deposit tonight, Kurt", he said.

"What? I have to", he replied.

"No. If you do, it will be stolen. I will give you a receipt for it and put it into the evidence locker at the station."

"I don't understand."

Kevin pointed to the two hooks and explained it to him.

"Those guys put a net into the box to catch the deposits above the baffles. Later they will come back and steal any deposits that were made."

"No shit. How'd you figure that out?", the manager asked.

"Combination of excellent police work and a native American background", Kevin joked.

"Wow", the manager said, truly impressed.

They drove to the station, and Kevin had Jim Sullivan call the Chief at home. Kevin explained things to the Chief and got the combination for the safe in the Chief's office. Instead of putting the deposit bag into the evidence locker, accessible by every officer in the small group, they deposited it into the Chief's safe which prior to Kevin learning it tonight had been accessible only by the Chief.

Kevin then gave Kurt Thompson a receipt for the bag and drove him back to the restaurant where he got into his own car and went home.

Kevin then went back to the area of the bank and located a spot where he could hide the car and still see the bank. He then sat and waited. His patience was amazing, though he did dip into the box for more than one coffee while he was waiting.

Shortly before six am, Kevin spotted the pair returning to the bank. He radioed in for backup.

"And tell everybody 3X", he ordered. "Lights as needed but no sirens."

Sullivan acknowledged it and shortly three other patrol cruisers formed a circle in the blocks around the bank, communicating on the tech channel.

When the pair had retrieved the proceeds from their net and stored the net and contents in the truck, the cruisers closed in and Kevin arrested them.

It went smoothly with no complications whatsoever.

After the pair were booked and in cells, Kevin brought the box in to the office area and Jim called all the cruisers in. While they finished their paperwork, everyone enjoyed the burgers, fries and coffee.

At precisely 7 am Chief Lawson began the morning briefing, as he did each morning.

"We'll start with Kevin today. Kevin caught the guys who have been hitting the bank night deposit boxes all up and down the coast", the Chief said.

As usual, Kevin stood to give his report. He detailed exactly how he had spotted them and each step of the process up to the final booking and their placement in a cell.

The Chief added. "Until this morning, no one knew how the thefts were occurring. Now we know they opened an account, got a key, and dropped the net in. Excellent work, Kevin. Ok, how about the rest of our cases?"

To the Chief's chagrin, nothing else had made any real progress. Most of the attendees had only patrol duties and little or nothing to report. Larry's report was the closest to being a positive one.

"We thought we had a break in the case when they stole some rare coins. Ted Whiting had every pawn shop and coin store in the area on the alert. But the other day we got a call. A small bag with them in was found by one of the local residents on the bank of the St. John River. They must have realized it was traceable and dumped it. Fortunately for us and the owner, the guy who found it realized what it must be and called us. Lab in St. Pete finally got back to us and says we got some kids' fingerprints from the bag. Bad news is that right now we have nothing to compare them to."

"Almost nine months they have been doing this and all we have is a set of prints we can compare if we ever catch them", the chief complained. Larry said nothing in response.

The only other slightly positive report came from Paul Scapoletti, who as usual had ticketed a large number of tourists for speeding. Scapoletti was a bully, and had a thing about Northerners. His hiding place behind the billboard at the base of the bridge from the mainland gave him an opportunity to clock everyone coming over and see which ones had out of state plates.

It seemed unbelievable to the Chief that they could have a clear photo of the suspect in one string of burglaries and several murders and not have any progress. Worse yet, the child-assisted burglaries were going into their ninth month and still no progress there, either. He had begun to wonder if the City Council was right about his department until Kevin solved the bank thefts. At least now they had one win under their belt.

When the meeting was over, everyone, including Sue Bennet, thanked Kevin for the McDonald's coffee.

Chapter 39

Stickney had returned to his motel room to inspect his wounds. He discovered he probably had a few broken or bruised ribs, but little else that was very serious, though he would be in pain for a while. He rested for a while, then he returned to a spot just off the side of the road from which he could observe the doublewide without being spotted, even by any visitors to the home.

He sat in his beat up old car with the motor idling and heat on during the nights and the windows rolled down during the day. Saturday merged into Sunday and Sunday into Monday.

He was becoming frustrated that there were still no signs of anyone leaving the double-wide trailer.

He had spotted the tiny alarm sensors at the corners of the home through his binoculars on the first look, so he knew that going in undetected was unlikely. But he also knew they were probably calling off work at whatever they do for a day job and nursing their wounds.

Finally he decided his time could be better spent taking care of Eddie Augustine. Eddie was a loose end. He knew the link between the woman and himself, and might turn him in when the body surfaced after he finished with her.

Stickney had promised him the gold and jewelry from the Fentworth hit. If he failed to turn up fairly soon, Augustine might either put out a hit on him or give his info to the cops.

"No sense taking chances", Stickney said aloud in the empty car.

Picking up the burner phone he was using for contact with Eddie, the killer phoned him.

"You ready for a meet?", Stickney asked.

"You ready with the stuff?", Eddie answered.

"Yeah", he replied, "say an hour?"

"Works for me", Eddie answered, and they both clicked off.

Eddie paced the showroom a little. This was a tough call. If this guy is a killer, Eddie wanted no part of doing business with him. Yet the goods that were taken were a strong encouragement to do so a little longer, anyway. He continued to pace for nearly ten minutes before deciding.

As he paced, Eddie found himself realigning various items on the shelves, turning price tags to be more visible, and the myriad of other tiny jobs that need to be done regularly. He almost reached for the broom to sweep up when he finally realized he was just killing time. And that time was getting shorter while he did. The skinny guy with the dead eyes would be there soon.

Eddie pressed the numbers on the burner phone.

"Pawn Shop Detail", Ted Whiting answered.

Stickney regretted the loss of the tire thumper. There was no place locally he could pick up another one, because this was not a big trucking area. Tourists don't buy very many tire thumpers for some reason. That would make what he had to do tougher.

But he had the Taser unit that he kept as an emergency backup weapon in the glove box, so he was not without some degree of protection. And the eight inch hunting knife that was also in the glove box brought him almost up to normal speed. Also, both would be easier to hide during daylight as he approached than the tire thumper would have been.

He smiled, looking at the knife.

"It's a shame you ain't got a lady friend", he said to Augustine, although there was no one, including Augustine, to hear it.

At a traffic light, Stickney paused and inspected the contents of the navy duffle bag he was carrying. He thought about it a little, but the light changed before he could really even decide.

"What if something goes wrong and I have to leave in a hurry?", he thought to himself. "Don't want to risk leaving everything behind."

He pulled the car into a small lot, and opened the trunk, using the release button on the side of the driver's seat. He then placed about half the items from the duffle bag into the trunk, lying loosely, next to the duffle bags of emergency cash already there. He was careful to choose things unlikely to easily roll around and make noise. Then he threw a blanket on top, just to be safe.

Stickney arrived at Augustine's shop a little after nine am. He looked around to see if there were any signs of trouble. Everything looked normal, so he grabbed the grey duffle bag and started in. With half its original contents missing, it was not as balanced a carry as it had been when he put it in the car in the first place, following the Fentworth job.

Adjusting for its shifting contents Stickney almost dropped the Taser unit. Fortunately for him, it was before he was in the shop, so Augustine did not notice.

"Is that it?", Eddie asked.

"See for yourself", Stickney answered, handing him the heavy grey duffel bag.

Eddie bent over the bag and untied the end of it. As he did, Stickney brought out the Taser from behind his back and prepared to zap him. But Eddie caught the movement out of the corner of his eye and slapped Stickney's hand away.

The Taser skidded across the floor. Both men watched it for a brief moment. Then Stickney grabbed one of the larger gold items and slammed it against Eddie's head. Eddie staggered backward against a display cabinet, smashing it. Shards of glass pierced his skin.

But before he even felt it, Stickney had the hunting knife out and had slit Eddie's throat. It didn't cut through the tough muscle, but it hit the main artery in the side of the throat, and blood spread around the room as if it were being sprayed from a wide angle lawn hose fitting. Eddie sank to the floor and Stickney moved in to continue to stab him.

In a last desperate attempt to save himself, Eddie grabbed a shard of glass and shoved it into his assailant's abdomen. He ripped it to the right and his last sight in life was his attacker's guts beginning to pour out.

Stickney pushed his innards in and grabbed a tablecloth from one of the display tables, which he used to hold everything in place as he ran for the door. But before he could exit it, he saw the patrol cars pulling up. He did not know it, but Ted Whiting had been in a small minivan a half block up and photographed him as he entered. He had then called for backup and it had arrived.

Before they could exit the patrol cars, Stickney was already running out the back. He rounded the corner and saw that he had a clear path to his car. The cops were on the other side of it facing the shop. He ran to the car as quietly as he could, feeling as if each footstep echoed through the alleys and against the buildings.

Fortunately for him, the car started right away, and he reversed it and was gone, just at the moment the police entered the shop.

Chapter 40

It was two in the afternoon, and the Florida Sun was directly overhead. Even with the air conditioner cranking, the humidity inside the cruiser was almost unbearable.

Scapoletti watched with envy as a convertible crossed the bridge and flew by him. It was a young couple. She had long blonde hair and it blew in the breeze. He was wearing a slouch hat and sunglasses.

Scapoletti was hopeful. The kid looked like a tourist. But when they passed his hiding spot behind the billboard welcoming everyone to Sunset Cove, he saw they had Florida tags.

It was a real disappointment. He would have enjoyed watching the blonde's face as he demeaned the driver. But Florida tags mean Florida contacts, and he was not going to put his cushy job on the line over one convertible.

Scapoletti went back to the graphic novel he was reading. It was a classic in the 'Sin City' series. He enjoyed that series very much. He didn't know why, and didn't care. It gave him something to do between speeders.

The other guys wasted their time driving all over town and doing nothing to make the town coffers profitable. Not him. Day in and day out he sat here, in HIS spot, in the shade of the billboard, watching for tourists to speed as they entered the town. Before they could notice the drop in the speed limit, he would have nailed them.

And because they were from out of town, a court date ten days later almost guaranteed a 'No Contest' and paying the fines. City Council loved him, and he knew it, no matter how the other guys on the force taunted him, or whether Council members ever said it. It was him carrying their butts, not the other way around.

Camponi had once cost the city a small fortune by burning down the Spaghetti Palace. And how about the night Mickey tore up the transmission on his cruiser chasing a UFO behind the school, that turned out to be the Goodyear blimp?

No, the other guys were a liability for the city, but he, and only he, was making them money. So why hadn't they promoted him, he wondered.

And why does the Chief seem to prefer to deal with Larry, Kevin and even Don rather than him? Just stupid, that's all he could figure. Too stupid to know where the real value was in the department.

This had been a good week. Just yesterday alone he had done 16 tickets. That was almost two thousand in fines and costs. And yesterday had been his slowest day of the month.

He went back to the graphic novel. He wished it had more color. Make it easier to see in the shadows in the car. But it also might take away from the story, he thought, and that would not be good, because the story was pretty good.

He glanced up and watched as a small-framed boy came out of the side street on the other side of the road, and crossed to his side. The kid had not noticed him there. If he had, he might not have stuck out his thumb and tried to hitch a ride back into the downtown area. But he had, and this was an opportunity for Scapoletti to make another big contribution to the city.

Scapoletti would teach the kid that breaking the law by hitchhiking was not a good plan. He would show him what it felt like to be on the wrong side of the law.

The city council should give him a medal for what he was about to do. Scare this kid straight today and the city won't have bigger problems with him later when he becomes a teenager. Fear is a good thing. It keeps kids like this in line, now and in the future.

Slowly he got out of his cruiser and stretched to his full height. He pulled on his 'Smokey the Bear' hat and put on his mirrored sunglasses and started for the kid. When the kid spotted him, it looked like he would run.

"Don't try it, kid", Scapoletti shouted. "I will beat the crap out of you if you make me run after you."

The kid stopped, turned back toward him and stood there watching him approach.

Scapoletti said nothing. He could see the fears running through the kid's mind and he knew nothing he said right now could scare him worse than his silence did. He continued to look down through his mirrored sunglasses and crossed his arms in front of him.

Suddenly the kid began to cry, big alligator tears that ran down his face.

"It wasn't my idea", he shouted. "Timmy made me do it. He said we'd starve if we didn't."

"What the hell was this kid talking about?", Scapoletti wondered. "How does someone make you hitchhike and how does doing it keep you from starving? Stupid kid must be nuts. Or on drugs", he thought, but still he just stood there looking down at the kid.

"My mom only comes home when dad's boat is in town", the kid continued, "and the fridge was empty, like it always is except when he's here."

Scapoletti was getting really confused. This kid made no sense whatsoever. "Definitely drugs I bet", he thought to himself, but still he just stood there looking down.

"And Timmy said as long as we followed his map of who goes where and when we wouldn't get caught."

Scapoletti spoke.

"How old are you, kid?", he asked.

"Ten", the boy replied.

"Started drugs way too young ", Scapoletti thought. "but he's old enough to know better."

"You should know better." Scapoletti stated.

"Timmy said as long as we stopped after each break-in and went back to school, no one would be able to find us", he said, as if it somehow answered Scapoletti's question.

"Break-in", Scapoletti said, puzzled.

"And I always did. I did. I just didn't feel like walking today."

Suddenly it dawned on Scapoletti what was going on.

"So you just finished a break-in?", Scapoletti asked.

"Yes, but Joey and Bill took the stuff to the drop-off, so I had to go back to school alone."

"And you decided to hitchhike back?"

"I wanted to get back fast so no one would know I was gone", the boy answered, his voice dropping off toward the end.

"Where's the drop-off?", Scapoletti asked.

"At the crossover tunnel under Main Street by the St. John River", the boy answered.

"What's your name, kid?"

"Eddie Post", the kid answered.

"Get in the back of the car, Eddie". Scapoletti ordered. "You're under arrest."

Once the kid was in the backseat, Scapoletti drove to Main Street and turned toward the St. John.

Just short of it, he saw two kids on a side street walking toward it, carrying a large blue duffle bag.

"Is that Joey and Bill?", Scapoletti asked.

"Yuh", the kid answered, his voice making it sound like he was pouting.

Scapoletti pulled the cruiser onto the side street, and turned on the lights and siren. The boys started to turn and run, dropping the large duffle bag they were carrying.

Scapoletti used the megaphone built into the cruiser.

"Stop where you are, or you could get shot", he threatened, knowing full well that there was no way he would get away with shooting within the town's city limits, much less shooting at unarmed kids.

But the boys didn't know that and they stopped and raised their hands high above their heads, like the arrested do on TV.

He got them into the cruiser, closed the doors and retrieved the bag they had been carrying. Inside were many valuable items as well as a handgun and a rifle.

"Whew", Scapoletti thought. "Good thing they didn't grab that instead of running."

He headed back toward the station house. He radioed in to tell Sullivan to let the Chief know he had caught the three kids that were breaking in for the past nine months.

Chapter 41

Chief Lawson stood at the observation window and watched as the three boys were booked, then led into the interrogation area. They could not be questioned without contacting their parents, which was a shame. The most likely scenario was that one of the parents of one of the kids was in on it, and was the Fagin.

He wondered momentarily at the fact that all three of the boys were white with dark hair, but Mrs. Hoover's statement clearly described a "black child" and a "tow-headed blond". Then he recalled that according to Scapoletti, who was admittedly not the brightest bulb in the string, the first boy had said Timmy talked him into it. So there were other kids involved, almost for certain.

Scapoletti started to split up the boys, one per room, but Lawson interrupted the process.

"Put them all in #3", the Chief ordered.

"All together?", Scapoletti asked, confused by the break from procedure.

"All together", replied the Chief, and Scapoletti complied reluctantly.

After the boys were in the room and the door locked, Scapoletti exited the room and approached the Chief.

"What gives?", Scapoletti asked.

"Now that they're in custody, they have rights. As minors, we cannot question them without a parent or adult representative present. What you got so far is admissible because it is a spontaneous confession.

But now that they've been charged, we have to wait to question them until either a parent, or at least someone from Child Protective Services out of Saint Petersburg, arrives."

"That's why they gotta' be separated, Chief", Scapoletti responded. "Otherwise they'll talk together and get their stories straight. We'll be lucky to see CPS within a day if the parents aren't around."

"Exactly."

"Exactly?"

"Exactly. While they talk together to get their story straight, we'll be listening and that IS admissible."

"Got it", Scapoletti said, nodding.

And that was exactly what happened. The boys began arguing and laying blame, and discussing what had and had not been told to the police. Most of the time was spent blaming Eddie Post, but at the same time, they asked if he had said anything about this or that. Within an hour, Chief Lawson had a pretty clear picture of the situation.

If what he understood was correct, there was no adult Fagin. The kid named Timmy Baxter was the ringleader, and had laid out the whole process in a notebook while in school.

All the kids involved were the children of shrimpers, who went out for a couple months at a time on the shrimp boats. When they were in port, the family lived as though they were rich. But when they left, often the mothers took whatever money remained and left the kids to fend for themselves.

Timmy had come up with the plan to help them do exactly that, and kept all the details in a notebook.

Chief Lawson had Sue Bennet come in early and sit outside the observation window taking notes, while he went to the Courthouse and secured warrants for the homes of the three boys and Timmy Baxter.

He gave one warrant to each of the patrol cars, while Scapoletti worked on the initial arrest report paperwork.

He gave Larry the Baxter family warrant. Larry was methodical. He would locate the notebook, and with it, the case would most likely be completely solved and provable.

Larry and Don rode together to the address listed for the Baxter child. The cruiser could not have been more silent, with both engaged in the thought of kids, without ANY adult help, pulling off all of what they had fought to solve for so long. Kids baffling their best attempts, with the media blazing down their shoulders for ineffectiveness in solving the burglaries. How much worse was that media attention about to get?

Larry pulled the cruiser into an angled parking space about two doors down from the Baxter address, and he and Don walked over to the address. It was a small residential apartment building, two stories tall, a wooden structure badly in need of a new paint job, but otherwise decent looking.

They had obtained a warrant, but not been able to find anyone to supply them with a key. The owner of record resided in a Northern state, and the address was not officially listed as an apartment building, so no onsite or local management could be found.

Larry planned to kick the door in with a mule kick. He chuckled, thinking about how on TV the cops often break down the door with a shoulder or front kick - both of which are likely to break bones and cause a lot of pain. The mule kick, on the other hand, used some of the strongest muscles and bones in the human body and had the advantage of applying the force almost directly where it is needed to apply pressure to the locking bolt area.

But when they arrived at the door they needed through, it was out-swinging, and could not have been kicked in. Larry was perplexed, but Don simply reached into his wallet and pulled out two small spring steel tools. He had the door unlocked in a matter of seconds.

"Where'd you learn to do that?", Larry asked, impressed by what he had just seen.

"You took a Gunsmithing course for your hobby, right? Well, I took a Locksmithing course. I thought I would become a Locksmith if I ever became unemployed. It's my emergency parachute."

"Well, just for the record, rookie, you're doing fine. You won't be needing your parachute anytime soon."

"That's easy to say, but look at how City Council is treating us. We could all be looking for a new way to earn an income any day."

"Yeah, I guess you're right. Well, I have my Gunsmithing to fall back on, though that's not why I studied it."

"But it's nice to know you have a fall-back, right?"

"Now that I think more about it, yes, it is."

Don swung the door open, and they got their first look inside the apartment. It was filthy, from a housekeeping point of view. There were food wrappers piled around a full garbage can in the kitchen area, and spilled drink stains on the floors and carpet in various areas.

They entered, pulled on gloves, and Don opened the refrigerator. It was empty. Not so much as a sign it had ever had food in it remained. It even had the musty odor of long-term lack of usage.

The main bedroom had crumpled bed sheets, but the room had a light layer of dust on everything. It was obvious it had not been recently used by anyone.

The boy's bedroom had sheets so worn they were hanging in strings at various areas, but not a single toy was anywhere to be found in the room. There were a handful of books lying around, and clothes spread out on the floor as if airing out

Larry opened some of the books and noted that a few had library stamps inside, while others bore selling price labels from local stores. He wondered if they had been stolen, considering why he and Don were there.

But amazingly, the dining room table, clear for the most part, bore a notebook and some scrap sheets of paper with calculations on them, lying in plain sight. The notebook was the intended object of their search. They looked around a bit more, then Larry bagged the notebook and scrap sheets in an evidence bag.

As they closed and re-locked the door, Larry commented to Don "Pretty sad place, huh?"

Don just nodded. They started back to the office.

The chief smiled to himself. City council would be pleased when the case was officially solved, but who knew it would be the plodding do-nothing Scapoletti who would solve it? He was reminded of an old joke: "Almost half the world is below average." Scapoletti seemed to lack more than a quarter the brain power and enthusiasm of Larry or Don, and less than ten percent of the professionalism of Kevin Wolf. Yet it was he, and not them, who would be credited with solving the case, after all their careful work.

But maybe it would propel Scapoletti into a position with another department somewhere, and that would not be a bad thing overall, though city Council would miss the revenue he brought in if he left.

"Which is worse?", the Chief silently mused, "Having him or not having him?"

A short while later, the cars had all returned. Interestingly, none was accompanied by a parent. None had been found. In every house and apartment, the place had been empty of occupants except the children. The ringleader Timmy, they learned, was seven years old. The oldest was eleven.

Further, a search of the premises showed every cupboard and refrigerator was empty of usable food. The closest was a six month old half bottle of milk at Eddie's parent's home. Every house and apartment was full of garbage, though - food wrappers from fast food restaurants and convenience stores, and empty cans of soft drinks.

Larry handed the notebook and scrap sheets to Chief Lawson and went to his desk to do the paperwork on serving the warrant and entering and searching the property.

The Chief took the notebook into his office, sat in his ergonomically designed, well-padded swivel chair, and began to read.

Chapter 42

What Chief Lawson read fascinated him. Apparently, there were twelve boys involved in the burglary ring. Timmy had numbered them 1 to 12, and associated each name with its number on a chart on the first page of the notebook.

He had then written out all the possible groups of three on the second, third and fourth page of the notebook, in ten rows of ten numbers each on the first and second page, and the remaining 21 numbers in two rows of ten and one final combination in the third column on that page, accounting for all 221 possible combinations of twelve boys.

To the right of each of those numbers was another number. These numbers were arranged sequentially, from 1 to 221.

The fifth page of the notebook had a crude map of Sunset Cove, on which had also been written those numbers from 1 to 221.

And finally, for that section, there was a calendar, onto which the numbers from 1 to 221 had been seemingly randomly placed, with six numbers per date.

Timmy had provided careful instructions on the following page. Each boy was to find his number from 1-12. Each day he would see if the numbers for that day included his number and when. Each of the six for that day represented an hour during the day.

No one was to leave school during the first or last hour of the school day, when the Office people were most aware of what was going on.

If the child's group appeared first for that date, he and the other two affected by it would leave after the first hour, and begin scouring the area assigned on the map for empty homes.

If they found a good one, they broke in as Timmy had taught them to do, and stole the types of things Timmy had listed on the first page of the second section of the notebook.

If they had a successful hit, they would put the items which would fit into their backpacks, and share the carrying of a large gym bag for items that did not fit.

They would take these items to the drop point, an abandoned tunnel under Main Street, near the St John River. They would then return to school.

If the hour was nearly up and they had not had a successful hit, they would still return to the school. No one was to miss more than an hour of any school day.

The same pattern would continue for each of the next six hours, and the groups assigned for it.

Once a week, usually on Saturday, they would travel to Saint Petersburg to cash in their merchandise at the pawn shops.

They would each carry what they could in their back packs and would travel according to the instructions in section three of the notebook, which delineated who took which method of travel how far and in what order.

They used a combination of short taxi rides, short bus rides and walking to cover the distance to Saint. Pete.

Once they arrived there, they would look first for servicemen home on shore leave. The boys would approach them (or vagrants, if they could not find a serviceman) and tell them a sad story about their mom being pregnant and not being able to work, and being too sick to go to the store for food even if she had the money.

So they were trying to sell stuff from their home to get food. But, the boys said, the pawn shop owners were mean to kids and would not buy from them, so the boys offered half the proceeds to anyone who would pawn the merchandise for them.

Servicemen were great, because usually they would not accept their share of the proceeds from the pawn shop, insisting the boys instead spend it for food and medicine.

Once a month the larger items would be carried in little red wagons all the way to Saint Petersburg as well. Timmy had arranged drop-off points similar to the abandoned tunnel in each area, so whoever was on walking duty for a given area took transportation to it, picked up the wagon and walked it to the next drop-off. That way, no one got too tired of walking and made a mistake of any kind to call attention to themselves.

The final section of the notebook was an account log, outlining the merchandise, what it had brought in, and how it was distributed among the twelve boys. In spite of the fact Timmy had carefully done all the planning, he still fulfilled his duties. He was person 1 on the list, and took only an equal share to each of the others.

"At seven years old.", the Chief said aloud, impressed.

John Lawson pushed the notebook away and shook his head. He then took his head in his hands and closed his eyes. He was amazed at what he had read. For children, this would seem an impossible undertaking. And why had they done it? Because the system had failed them.

John was familiar with the pattern. Their mothers had become pregnant so the wealthy shrimpers would marry them. And they were rewarded with riches when the boats came in every few months.

But when the boats were out, they drank and did drugs and ignored the kids. They did not share the wealth with them, and they did not care for them. They did not buy them food or clothing except when the boats were due in.

How could you blame the poor kids for turning to a life of crime? No doubt someone in Child Protective Services in Saint Pete had some idea of the problem. But that was a goodly distance from Sunset Cove and CPS had its hands full in Saint Pete already. So the kids were ignored.

Lawson did not want to arrest them. Juvenile Hall or the Training Camps would just teach them to be mean on top of being smart. Society would not gain any benefit from that.

But on the other hand, looking at the numbers in the final section of the notebook, he had little chance of convincing anyone else of that.

And the newspapers and TV had already been having a field day with it. How would THEY react to this outcome? No doubt some would call for maximum punishment and others would blame the City. It would be a media feeding frenzy.

And in a media feeding frenzy, City Council probably would not be looking to reward the department. It would be punished for having taking so long to stop the burglaries and for allowing it become such a severe problem. The department would probably be dismantled, and the city's protection turned over to the County or FDLE.

He shook his head again. Jack Stadtler from FDLE was a great guy, and dependable as all get out, but he would be alone in protecting the city if FDLE took over. Lawson thought about everything he had given up for the good of the city and the thought of one man trying to replace his entire team made him shudder.

Then he called Kevin Wolf into his office.

"Kevin. do you think once we pick up the rest of the kids we can keep this under our hats for a couple of days?"

"Sir?"

"I don't think these kids' parents are going to miss them. And I don't think they need to be rushed into the system. I want a chance to think about how to handle it for the best of all concerned."

"I am not certain I follow your logic, sir", Kevin answered honestly.

The Chief explained it to him, right down to the idea of Jack Stadtler being the only one assigned to care for the town, and that in addition to the areas he was already covering. Kevin nodded his head at the appropriate times to show he was following.

"I do not know how long we can pull it off, Chief, but I know the men will support you and try to keep it quiet."

"Ok, the first thing we need to do is send officers to pick up the other nine kids at the school before they realize we have these three.", the Chief stated. He then reached into his pocket, withdrew his wallet and took out two credit cards.

"Once they are in custody, get pizzas, burgers, fries, coffee and milk shakes enough for everybody out there, and for all the kids."

"Not to argue, Chief, but would not Quiznos or Subway be better for the kids?"

"It might. Tell you what. Get plenty of their sandwiches too. I want everyone to eat well for the next day or so. What isn't eaten right away can go into the refrigerator in the break room. Okay?"

Kevin nodded his assent.

"I will take the school with Larry, and will send Mickey to the Pizza places, Tommy to McDonald's and Don to Quiznos, if that is okay."

The Chief took a final credit card out of his wallet and handed it to Kevin.

"Make it so", he stated.

As Kevin left, the Chief wondered if this would possibly be the last time the group would all be intact. He dreaded facing City Council, and as he consulted his desk calendar, he realized they were scheduled for a meeting next Tuesday evening. A frown formed on his usually stoic face.

Chapter 43

It was the middle of the afternoon and the Florida sun beat down on the trees and bushes exposing every leaf and insect.

"Fargo", Michael said.

"Hunh?", Nicki asked.

"Reminds me of the line in the television version of Fargo where the killer mentions that the human eye can see more shades of green than any other color, and the deputy later explains it is because we were designed to spot predators against the background of the jungle."

"Ha. See any?"

"No, I don't. This might be a good time to stock up on supplies if we are going to continue to camp out here in your home a couple more days."

"Good idea", Nicki said, "I can see Felicia and update our medical supplies, too. Some are getting pretty low. Are you sure there's no one out there?"

"As sure as I can be. Your alarm sensors would pick him up if he came close, and scanning the scenery out there, I see nothing but green."

"OK. Give me a minute to change my clothes and put on makeup, ok?"

"A minute?"

"Well, maybe a couple of minutes."

Michael laughed. It hurt a little to do it, but at the same time it felt good.

It took her almost exactly eight minutes, which amazed him to no end. From his experience that simple set of steps took most of the women he knew about an hour. His appreciation of Nicki was growing the more he learned about her. She certainly was not like anyone else he had ever spent any time with.

For a brief moment, his thoughts went to Linda Beecher, who was also quite unique, but in a totally different way. What an interesting universe this is that can create such creatures. But inside Michael knew that while Linda had been a fantastically entertaining person with a unique outlook, Nicki was much more. She was, in every sense, very real. She faced the world around her, and remained unchanged. She had lived through some truly Hellish experiences, and still had a bright outlook, yet in a very realistic way, not like a Pollyanna hiding her fears in unjustified optimism.

When she was ready, they left. She paused a moment to set the alarm, then closed the door and locked the bottom lock and the deadbolt.

Stickney was in a lot of pain, and was bleeding fairly heavily. He felt like he was running a fever, but the air conditioner in the car had stopped working for some reason, so he could not be sure it was not just the weather.

With no place else to go, he planned on going back to the trailer home and forcing the woman to treat his wounds before killing her. He figured a tire iron should take care of the guy, and this time the guy would not take him by surprise.

Stickney had not yet formed a plan in his head when he saw the couple on the front steps of the home. He did not know if they were going in or out but an idea quickly formed in his head.

Stickney stepped on the gas and aimed the old car directly at them.

Michael heard the sound of an engine roaring and tires slipping on the gravel and soft sand. He did not even completely realize what was going on, but he somehow pushed Nicki away from the door and jumped.

The car hit Michael's leg just below the knee, but missed the rest of him. He was pinned in place and could not immediately see if Nicki made it.

The car had struck Nicki's door and destroyed most of the door and frame area. The hood and trunk of the car both popped open from the force of the contact. Stickney pulled on the door handle to get out and finish the job on Michael, but the handle would not turn. He tried a few more times and then began to crawl out through the window.

Stickney was almost out when he saw Nicki. She raised the tire iron from his trunk and brought it down on the top of his head. She raised it again and brought it down on the back of his neck. It made a sickening crunching sound. She hit his head again. Then she dropped the tire iron, and ran toward Michael.

"Well, it looks like you saved me again", Michael said.

Nicki moved some of the rubble from the damaged entryway, and freed Michael's leg enough to allow him to free himself from beneath the bumper of Stickney's car. The pain was immeasurable.

Michael tried desperately to stand but could only get one knee to move. She helped him up and looked at his damaged other leg, which was at a rather odd angle.

"I think it's broke.", Michael said.

"No Duh", she commented, sneering at him a little. "Do you think?"

"Well, right now I'm not thinking very much, but we'll have some serious thinking to do pretty soon."

She glanced at Stickney's body lying half in and half out of the car window. Then she looked at her home.

"Yes, we will."

She tried the door and it simply fell the rest of the way into the home.

"Let's get you inside and I'll call Felicia. I think this is a bit much for me to fix."

Together they managed to get him inside and onto the couch. It wasn't easy, and it increased his pain level with every step, but they got there.

She picked up the phone.

"Felicia, it's Nicki. I have a real problem, and I don't know if you can help or not this time."

She paused a moment.

"Well, that is easy to say from where you are right now. But I am standing in the middle of a real mess. That guy came back and attacked us again. He's dead now, and I think Mike has a broken leg, maybe worse. If you don't want any part of it, I'll understand."

She listened again.

"Okay, I'll be here."

She logged off the phone and returned it to her purse.

Looking at Michael, she said, "Felicia's coming, be about an hour or so. Can you hold on?"

"How about something for the pain?", Michael said.

She went to the cabinet, got the last of the remaining medicine and a tall bottle of water from the refrigerator. Michael drank it down greedily, washing the pills down with it.

He sat, staring at the digital clock on the television, watching the minutes go by, trying not to feel the intense pain. The pain meds weren't doing much to alleviate the pain. Maybe the clock would.

Chapter 44

Most of an hour had passed and still Felicia had not appeared. Michael's attitude was beginning to show through as the pain built up. It was painful for Nicki to watch as he continued to deteriorate. She tried hard to focus on little jobs around the house that needed done, but really did not seem to make any progress on even the smallest of them.

Michael's face was about the only undamaged part of his body right now, but the face was showing what the rest of his body was experiencing. His brow appeared to be knotted so tightly he could probably have held a ship in the docks, or at least that was how it seemed to her.

Finally she needed to get away, if only a little bit and for a little while. She carefully stepped around the door on the floor and holding onto what little was left of the railing, jumped down the few feet to the ground. Once she was down she could see one end of the former stairs formed a small pyramid.

She pulled and dragged it over to be under the now wide open area where the doorway used to be, and flipped it so that it formed a sort of makeshift stair-case again. It was not overly steady, but it was usable. She dragged short pieces of boards to provide additional support under it, until she felt confident it was safe to use to get in and out of what had been her home.

She tried not to look at Stickney while she was doing all this, but failed several times, and each time it took her breath away and forced her to stare frozen in place for several long seconds.

His head was no longer overly discernible as to ever having been one. It was a pulpy, bloody mess, and it took all her willpower not to retch and fall down screaming.

This was very different from the cruel brothers earlier. It had been up close and she recognized him as some semblance of human, and the results were much more vile to look at. She had no doubt she would see him in her nightmares for years to come.

She tried to rationalize it. He was, after all, trying to kill not only Michael but her as well, and likely would have if he was not stopped permanently. That made him worse than the brothers in the barn. So why did it not feel that way?

She tried to focus on other matters. Michael, she knew, really needed to go to a hospital this time. But if he did, the police would catch up with him. but if he did not, he would likely die. Which was really worse?

She thought about it a while and decided it was Michael's decision, assuming he was coherent enough to make it. But what if he were not? He definitely had some serious bone breakage and probably lots of internal bleeding and tearing. What if he blacked out from it and she had to decide?

Then she got another look at Stickney and all the thoughts, decisions and rationale left her brain entirely as once again she sat and stared, and felt the panic rising.

Slowly she turned and climbed the make-shift stairs she had built. She had no way of knowing that the Universe was about to take some of the decisions away from her.

Chapter 45

Sue Bennet watched the Chief's office from the dispatch room.

Chief Lawson picked up the phone and dialed the 146th number on the list he had received from her. She could tell he was more than tired of this, but was not going to quit until he had contacted all 198 banks in the multi-county area. When it was answered he asked, as he had for each of the others, for the senior manager or President.

She admired the man. She had been in the department long enough to know that most other Chiefs would simply have arrested the guys for what they had them on and dropped it. For a moment she wondered why he had not.

"And what is the other thing all about?", she wondered.

"This is Chief Lawson, at Sunset Cove PD", he began after a brief pause. "We have arrested two men in regard to a string of bank burglaries involving drop boxes. I'm trying to locate any banks where night deposit receipts are missing, that might not yet have reported it to the FBI."

He listened to the response.

"You did, hunh?" Can you give me any idea how much you estimate?"

He listened again.

"Well, we will add it to our list and see what we can do about it. Our goal is to get back as much from them as they took and haven't gotten rid of, and get it back where it belongs as soon as possible."

He listened to the phone again for a short while. Obviously the person at the other end was pleased to hear that, and was expressing it.

"While I have you on the phone, can I bother you with another matter, a personal one?"

Once again, a brief pause ensued.

"My aunt is suffering from Dementia", the Chief then continued. "And she has developed a rather disturbing pattern. She was in the mail order business, and it was keeping her alert. But now she is making bank accounts all over the place, then taking out some of the funds and hiding them all over the place, and then forgetting where she has accounts and where she put the money."

A pause.

"Her name? This is where it gets REALLY problematic. She has been married several times, and she evidently has ID's in all her names for some reason. So I don't even have a clue what names the accounts are in. I need to catch up with her and try to straighten it all out. Have you run into anyone with a pattern of behavior that might match her?"

Another pause, and the Chief began to smile.

"She has? She what? THIS Friday?" he asked, in succession. "I will be there", he said, and asked for the specific address of the branch, which he wrote down.

Sue was happy to see him smile. Whatever it was all about, he obviously had finally got an answer he liked.

He hung up the phone and it rang as he did.

"Chief Lawson", he answered. "Oh, hello, Ted?"

"You what?"

"What do you mean by almost?"

"Well, we already have a pretty good idea what he looks like."

"No?", give me the details."

He wrote something down, quite a few somethings, Sue noted.

"Send it over. And thanks, Ted."

He hung up the phone and sat with his head in his hands for about two full minutes.

Sue's curiosity got the best of her. she walked into his office.

"What was that all about?", she asked.

"That was Ted Whiting, over at St. Pete pawn shop detail", the Chief began. "Says they almost caught our killer."

"Almost?"

"Guy got away, but not before adding another victim. Head wound and severe stabbing, same as the others. No female victim involved this time, apparently, unless he took her with him, which would be an escalation for him. But they got a good photo of him. He's going to FAX it over."

"Don't we already know what he looks like?", Sue asked.

"Evidently not", the Chief answered. "He says it is a different guy, but they got some of the identifiable items we listed from the Fentworth killings, and the MO on this killing is similar enough to be pretty certain it is him. Guess we have another burglar we were unaware of, and the guy we were looking for is just another burglar. One MORE case for us to go in front of Council with as unsolved."

"Well, at least you got the kiddie bandits. That's one solved, right? That's a little progress."

He explained his fears about that to her. She frowned.

"So because there is no adult involved and the kids were only trying to survive, you think Council will take it out on us?" she asked, even though that was almost to a word what he had just explained.

"I do", he replied. "But I am working on a solution. And the good thing is, Ted is pretty sure our killer is injured. Notify the hospital and the two clinics in case he turns up here instead of in St. Pete. OK?"

"Okay." she responded, and went back to the dispatch area to do it.

"And, Sue?", the Chief called. "Ask Kevin to bring Ramos in for an ID when we get the photo. I want him to see both pictures."

About an hour later, Sue watched as Kevin brought in the boyfriend from the first killing. He had been in before, so she recognized him. Curious, she went to the observation room to watch the interview.

"Do either of these guys look familiar?", Kevin asked.

"Yes. Both of them. The skinny guy on the left must live in my neighborhood, because I have seen him at clubs in the area and at my building a couple of times before the murder. Haven't seen him recently, though. The other guy is… let me think. I have his card here somewhere."

He dug through his wallet and retrieved the business card.

"Sam Brown of Citywide Detectives, from over in St. Pete", he continued. "He's working for the insurance company."

"A private eye, hunh?", Kevin stated.

"Yeah, he stopped by right after the murder."

"You're sure it was after and not before?"

"Yeah, I never saw him before that."

"That explains a lot. But you have seen the thin guy, too. If you had to guess, where do you think I might find him?"

"No clue, sir." Ramos answered, "Like I say I saw him around but nowhere in particular. Clubs, and sometimes near my condo."

"Okay, let me see if the Chief has any more questions, then I will drive you back to the condo."

Sue went back to the dispatch area before anyone caught her spying. Kevin went in and talked to the Chief.

"Private eye snooping around and gets photographed leaving the premises. What a clown. He's lucky we didn't find him earlier. He might be doing life in Tallahassee", the Chief commented.

"Guy must be shitting bricks with his face all over TV. Want me to call him and let him know he's no longer our suspect?"

"No. He should have come forward and made our job easier when it came out. Let him sweat a while. He can find out when the rest of the world does, after the case is closed."

Kevin chuckled. "That will teach him, all right."

"Okay, take Ramos home. Remind him we will need him when it comes time for court."

"One more thing, though, Chief. I think he may be high on Coke or something. And remember? Fort Lauderdale said their drug squad had him under surveillance."

"That's not good, but we don't want to impugn his testimony, so until after the trial, keep that under your hat. And then we will keep an eye on him. He lives pretty well. It's likely he's dealing. Once this is over, we can deal with it if he is."

"Will do, Chief", Kevin said, leaving the room and returning to Ramos.

They left, and Sue went back to the Sudoku book she was working on.

Chapter 46

Once she got inside, Nicki found she finally could stand the quiet no longer.

"You mind if I put the TV on?", she asked.

"Why not?", Michael replied, "Won't affect how long it is until she gets here."

Nicki turned on the television. A rerun of Friends was playing, not exactly her favorite show. She preferred dramas with strong female leads. But she left it on, figuring the laugh track might keep Michael's mind off the pain and the clock.

"We interrupt the program previously scheduled for this time, to bring an alert from the County Sheriff's office. Police ask you to be on the lookout for this man, currently wanted in relation to a string of murders in the area. Channel ten had earlier shown another man to be a person of interest, but they have identified him as a local private detective and are no longer seeking him. Repeating, Police are asking you to be on the lookout for this man. If you see him, do not approach him. He is believed to be armed and dangerous. He may be injured, but do not, repeat do not, attempt to help him. This man is believed to be armed and extremely dangerous."

Stickney's face loomed at them from the 52 inch flat LCD screen.

Michael began to laugh uncontrollably. It hurt so badly when he did, but he could do nothing about it. He could not stop laughing.

"You're hysterical, Mike.", Nicki shouted. "Get a grip. You're going to hurt yourself worse."

"Don't you see? It's over. Not only is he dead, but I am cleared. They think I am Sam Brown. Ramos must have identified me. It's over."

"Well, not quite over. We still have his body sticking out of the car out front and the damage to my home, and we have the murder weapons."

"Yes, but we can handle all that. I know we can. It's over."

He continued to laugh. Nicki looked worried but said nothing.

It took Felicia a total of 52 minutes to arrive at the trailer. She cautiously stepped over the demolished door and frame parts and entered.

"Girl, when you said he was dead, I had no idea how much you meant it.", she exclaimed.

"Yeah. He aimed his car at us and then was getting out to finish the job he started the other night. I stopped him with his own tire iron."

"Did you see all that other stuff in his trunk?", Felicia asked.

"I didn't really look", Nicki answered. "I didn't have much free time on my hands."

"Well, there's a lot of gold and jewelry in the trunk", Felicia volunteered.

"Really? How strange", Nicki answered, keeping in mind that Felicia did not know Nicki was also a burglar.

How's your guy doing?"

"I think he's in shock a little", Nicki said. "He keeps laughing. We saw on TV the cops know it was not him but the other guy, and that is a relief, but not so big a relief that he should be laughing like that."

"You're probably right. I will do what I can, but I think he might need a hospital from the angle on that leg and his behavior."

Felicia examined Michael, took his vitals, gave him a shot of pain medicine she had brought along, and fashioned a restraint to keep pressure off his leg.

When she had done that, she stated, "That's about as much as I am qualified to do. Can you get him to a hospital? You said earlier you couldn't because the police thought he was the killer. But if they know now that he's not, he should be okay for the hospital, right?"

"Yes."

"You want me to drive you?"

"No, I don't want to get you officially involved. I can drive him."

"Okay. I wouldn't wait too long. I think he really needs help this time."

"I will, and thanks again."

"Like I said on the phone, I owe you more than I can EVER repay. I'm just glad to be able to give back a little."

The ladies hugged and Felicia left.

Nicki looked at Michael.

"Will you be okay a little while?", she asked.

"Yeah", he mumbled, obviously dulled by the shot Felicia had given him.

"All right. I will be right back."

She went out to Stickney's car, careful not to step in any of the blood this time.

She looked in the trunk and was amazed at the pile of gold and jewelry spread out there.

She pulled a pair of gloves out of her small purse and put them on. She then began going through the pieces, selecting ones of higher value but lesser identifiability. When she came to the gym bag full of cash, she was truly amazed.

She took a minute to place it in the trunk of her own car, confident the police would have no reason to search it. It was parked a good distance from the house and a tiny red car hardly looks menacing.

She then rearranged what was left to look like a normal pattern of how the contents might be expected to be lying in the trunk after an accident, and put the items she had selected into the trunk of her scooter.

She went back into her home and grabbed the tire thumper and knife, wiped the knife onto Stickney's shirt to remove any prints left by Michael, and tossed them into the back seat of Stickney's car.

She then drove her scooter about a mile up the road to an abandoned school bus stop. Using a branch, she dug a small hole behind the dilapidated structure and planted the items there. She covered them and returned to the trailer.

Once inside, she checked on Michael. He seemed okay, starting to show some pain again, but still okay.

She pulled the phone from her purse and dialed the police department.

"You've got to help me", she stated breathlessly, "I just killed someone who was trying to kill both me and a Private Eye who was protecting me. And the private eye is hurt, pretty bad. He will need an ambulance. But the other guy is dead. Ohmigod. I killed him. He was trying to kill me but I killed him instead. Ohmigod."

The dispatcher, a gravelly voiced old man, told her to stay calm, that a patrol car and an ambulance would be there shortly. He kept her on the line for the time it took for the patrol car to arrive on the scene. It was Larry Evanston.

"This guy attacked me the other night. He hit me with a tire thumper and cut me with a knife and I think he was going to rape me. But this Private Eye was on his trail and saved me. The guy got away, but we were both hurt. Today was the first we felt strong enough to go to the police station and fill out a complaint. But he must have been waiting outside somewhere, and when we stepped out, he tried to kill us with his car."

She paused a moment to catch her breath.

"He hurt Sam Brown, but not before Sam managed to push me clear, saving me again"

She shook her head as if trying to shake off the memory.

"I saw the tire iron in his trunk and when he was getting out of the car, I hit him with it. I was so scared I just kept hitting him. I don't know how many times. I couldn't stop. I was afraid if I did, he would get me again."

"Okay, within the next couple of days, we will need to get you and the detective to make a statement. But right now, I think we can just get you to the hospital and get you checked out", Larry advised.

"Thank you, Detective", Nicki said.

"Not a detective. Just an officer. And always proud to serve and protect. You should have called us earlier, though."

He smiled.

She knew he was flirting a little with her, but that was fine. If it helped him believe her story, so much the better. It was fairly close to the truth anyway. Just a few items left out that might muddy the water.

The ambulance arrived and they put Michael on a stretcher. They allowed Nicki to accompany 'Sam Brown' in the same ambulance. One of the attendants examined her cuts and bruises as they drove.

Chapter 47

Michael awoke in the hospital bed and was confused. He saw Nicki sitting in the chair next to the bed, holding his hand, but her eyes were closed and she breathed the soft murmur of sleep. He looked around the room. His leg was suspended, with a heavy cast on it, and there were bandages over large portions of his body.

An IV bottle drained slowly into his veins, and electronic sensors were pasted on his body with wires leading to a piece of monitoring equipment. There was a small push button next to his free hand that he discovered gave him a pleasant lessening of pain when pushed.

Michael tried to remember why he was there and how he got there. At first he could not, but then it all came rushing back to him, right up to the moment when the EMT gave him a shot of something and everything went black.

He must have shifted or something because Nicki jerked awake, gripping his hand tighter.

"You're awake", she said.

"I think that is obvious", Michael said, trying to grin. He was not sure he achieved it. The face felt a little funny.

"Officer Evanston is outside. He has been waiting a couple of hours to talk to you. Are you okay?"

"I'm not okay. I hurt all over. But I can talk. What does he know?"

"That Stickney tried to kill us and you are a Private Investigator and saved me once but today he hit you with the car trying to kill us again. He would have killed us both, but I somehow managed to kill him first."

"Okay, send him in", Michael said, trying to sound confident.

Nicki went to the door and opened it.

"Officer Evanston? I think he is waking up now", she stated.

The officer who entered the room was tall and had wide shoulders. He carried himself with the air of a military man, but had a free attitude showing through that made Michael wonder if he actually had been.

"I'd like to just get a brief statement from you if I could", the officer began.

"Sure. Not much to it. I was asked to look into the burglary and killing at the Playa del Sol condominiums. When I did, I picked up a possible trail that led me to try to follow Stickney. But after his second hit at the condos, he must have spotted me. He almost shook me, but I caught up with him just as he was beginning his attack on this young lady. We fought, and he actually won, but I guess he did not realize it, because he ran off. Nicki here nursed us both back to health for a few days and then we started in to town to report the incident. But he was waiting for us. He did all this to me, but I pushed Nicki out of the way, and that allowed her to stop him."

"Why didn't you phone it in immediately? Anyone else would have."

"Anyone else was not the number one suspect being looked at by the police. I had to think it through and decide if it was worth the risk or if I should just try to pick up his trail again. She persuaded me to take the chance of contacting you once the news reported you had the right suspect, but I wanted to do it in person."

"Not the best move. You should have called us immediately. Who knows what else he could, and in fact DID, do while you were healing."

"And what he could do to us in another attack, also", Michael responded. "I sure learned my lesson the hard way, but it could have been worse. This lady saved my life."

Evanston looked at Nicki and Michael could see the appraisal in Evanston's eyes.

"Yes", he stated, "She seems like an amazing woman."

"Is there anything else, Officer?", Michael asked. "I'd like to hit the painkiller switch and get some more sleep."

"No, I think I have what I need", Larry answered. He closed his notebook and left the room.

Michael smiled at Nicki, then hit the painkiller switch several times and dozed off.

Chapter 48

Friday morning Chief John Lawson drove to Marion County and found the bank he was looking for. He thought briefly about how much more difficult it would have been before GPS units. Marion County, and especially the Ocala area, was very complex, with nothing really going North and South or East and West, even though they were often marked as such or as Southwest, etc.

As soon as the bank opened, he went in and introduced himself to the President. It was a small local chain of banks, and the President was very helpful. Of course, thinking he might get back some or all of what had turned up missing in the night deposits gave him a reason to be accommodating. He had been running internal audits and questioning his own people until the Chief's call.

He and the chief talked a little about the fishing net and how the thefts had been accomplished.

About twenty minutes after opening, an elderly lady entered the bank, and the assistant to the President notified the President she was there to pick up her money.

"Looks like your aunt is here", he said to the Chief. "I will get her money for you."

"No, just leave it in the account for now", the Chief answered. "How much was she asking for again?"

"One hundred ninety five thousand. I 'm glad you're leaving it here, but I wish I had known that a week ago. I don't like having that much cash around, even though it is a small part of her account."

"Yeah, I am surprised by the amount, but I should have said something. Sorry", the Chief answered. "Is she out there?"

"Sitting in the waiting area."

"Thanks."

Chief Lawson shook the man's hand and left the office, walking to the elderly lady sitting in the waiting area.

"You need to come with me", he said.

"To get my money?", she asked.

"Yes", he lied. "I made arrangements to keep it in an armored car around the corner."

"That's unusual isn't it?"

"Well, it IS a lot of money, ma'am."

"All right."

She followed him out of the bank and to his unmarked cruiser. It was unusual, but Lawson was confident it shouldn't set off any alarm bells in her brain. She should accept unusual reactions. What she was doing was not very common, either.

"THIS?", she asked, obviously confused by the car's difference from her expectations.

"I figured we would drive to the money and back to your car, so you don't have to carry it. We kept it a little ways from the bank so no one would see you carrying such a large amount of cash", he explained.

"Oh."

She got in the passenger seat, and he drove to the Super K- Mart a block away.

When they got there, he showed her his badge.

"Game's up", he said.

"Why, I have no idea what you are talking about. I thought you were taking me to my money", she said innocently.

"You can drop the ruse. I tracked you all over the State of Florida. I know what you have been up to."

"You must be mistaken, young man. I admit I get a little confused sometimes, but I'm old. You have to expect that. I am certainly no criminal."

"Nice try", he responded, "but I have you on enough Federal counts to ensure you'll never see the light of day again. Your age won't hide that many occurrences."

She looked him in the eye, and began to dispute the idea. But she saw in his eyes that he was not bluffing.

"Well, it was fun while it lasted", she said.

"FUN?", he exclaimed.

"Yes, fun, young man. It started as a way of surviving. My Henry was a good man, but he was in a cash business, and lied on his taxes. As a result, when he died before he could retire, what he had paid into Social Security wasn't enough for me to live on. But after the first time, I discovered it was a thrill. It was like starting a whole new life where I could have anything I wanted and had something to do all the time. I could have lived on just that one time, but I enjoyed having someplace to go, people to talk to."

"How much did you get?, the Chief asked.

"Millions", she replied, "and I discovered that most bank managers would find a way to bury it, so the FBI was never called. "Millions of dollars and no risk. At least until today.

"And I guess even jail won't be that bad, at my age."

Chief Lawson thought about it.

"Maybe I can keep you out of jail. Do you still have access to the money?", he asked.

"Yes. But I have no idea how much I got from where, so don't ask me to return it. Or are you asking for a bribe? If you are, that would work for me."

"Wouldn't work for me, though. I couldn't live with myself if I took one."

"Oh", she replied, her face clearly showing her disappointment.

"How do you feel about kids?"

"I love them. But my Henry always worked so hard we never got around to raising a family. But what an unusual question."

"What were you going to do with the money?"

"I really was just sort of collecting it. I have it all in an account in Jacksonville, and in safety deposit boxes there and in Saint Augustine. I figured when I died, the government would seize it, and they would figure a way to spend it all quickly, I'm sure."

"You took a large sum from the bank in my town. I'll need that back. That's the first step in my plan. Is that okay with you?"

"Of course. I have no need of it. I just don't remember where I got the rest."

"All right. You're going to become a very popular lady. You're going to provide for a lawyer and a trust fund and college fund for a dozen children, and build a community center where all kids can go after school and get a nice warm nutritious meal, and sit and do homework or play or read. And you will be in charge of running it. You do the hiring, manage the volunteers, and interact with the children of the community. How would you feel about that?"

"Are you serious? I mean, that sounds great, but I don't know anything about the business of running a Community Center."

"That's where the hiring comes in. You hire consultants and a financial manager, and you provide the funding out of what you have

in the bank. Every day you will have somewhere to go, people to interact with, and the respect of the community."

"And I don't go to jail?"

"Let's face it. The bank managers have mostly already either paid the price for their carelessness, or covered it up. No one wants this to come to light. People would be trying it all over the country before long if it got out. And sending you to jail would not only bring it out, but mean the government gets to mis-spend the money. Frankly, I think my City Council will be more appreciative of benefitting from it in the form of a place to keep our kids out of trouble. Do we have a deal?"

"We sure do."

"One thing, though. The first time I find out there is even a question of anything illegal going on, You WILL go to jail, and I will frame you if I have to in order to make it happen, and you'll be in there for the rest of your life. Are we clear?"

"Absolutely clear, sir. Frankly, this sounds like a dream come true. I won't mess it up."

"I believe you. But I mean it, nonetheless."

Chapter 49

Kevin entered the Chief's office with a grim look on his face.

"Looks like we have some new information, Chief."

"You're not going to spoil my mood now that I'm beginning to think I can survive Council, are you?"

"No. Actually, it might even help a little."

"So what do you have?"

"Two things, and they seem to fit together, Chief", Kevin answered. "First, the techs going over Stickney's car found a lot of coke in it too, as well as some of the items on the list of missing things from the Ramos murder and burglary, and some items recognizable from videos found in in Fentworth's place. They also found a motel card and checking the room there turned up blocks of wrapped cocaine as well as more stolen jewelry from around the State. Nowhere near what was apparently stolen, but enough to be certain he was the one who did it. It positively links him to several other murders."

"Okay, so that pretty much proves our conclusion that he committed both those murders and killed Augustine in a dispute over the value of the stolen items. Pretty much closes those two cases and some of our burglaries."

"Yes, but we might also have a motive in the Levine killing at least. Our watch on Ramos has proven something else. You were right. He is not only a user, but is also dealing the coke. We have him on video making several large deliveries, and we managed to get an undercover out of Saint Pete to do a buy as well."

"That's excellent, but how does it tie in with the murderer?"

"The lab says the coke found in Stickney's car is an exact match to the coke the undercover bought from Ramos. Looks like Stickney thought

Ramos had cheated him somehow and murdered Ramos' girlfriend to teach him a lesson. Probably planned on killing Ramos, too, but Ramos was out of the county making a buy at the time he showed up to kill them."

"Excellent. A nice bow tying the whole thing together. So why so grim?"

"I don't like that we missed all this the first time."

"Well, get a warrant and get Ramos in custody before tomorrow night's Council meeting, and I think we will look just fine."

"All right, Sir", Kevin answered and left.

Two hours later, he returned, smiling.

"They must have worked together, too", he said. "In the freezer of his refrigerator, we found diamonds in a crushed ice container. Almost missed them, but when we were checking for coke, we found a lot of cash in the freezer. While we were retrieving it, one diamond fell from the ice box to the floor."

"That's the icing on the cake", Chief Lawson stated.

"It gets even better than that, Chief."

"How so?"

"Don Falcone went back to the Fentworth place, and poked around some more. He found a hidden room full of videos burned to disc. He only watched a couple so far, but chose them by their dates. We have video of Ramos providing coke to Fentworth, and we have the grisly video of Fentworth and the Beecher girl being murdered by Stickney. Sews up the package as tightly as you could possibly ask for."

"Nice. Remind me to find a way to reward you guys."

"Now if only we could find a solution to the kiddie ring", Kevin complained.

"I have that solved, too, Officer Wolf. I found a generous and wealthy matron who is going to start a community center to provide food and shelter and a safe place for the kids of the city. Local restaurants have volunteered to provide food at a discount to the center, so the kids can eat good food free. And the matron is also going to provide legal counsel to represent the child burglars, as well as providing a fund for them to live on and to get a proper education later on if they stay on the straight and narrow. I think City Council will be happy as all get out. I don't think we will hear another word about disbanding the department for a long, long time."

"That is great", Kevin said, his face beaming.

"And if I know Council, I suspect they'll find a legal way to add the diamonds to the city coffers before long also."

"I am certain they will, sir."

"Spread the word throughout the department that I am VERY pleased with everyone for the fine police work this past couple weeks. You all outdid my expectations."

Kevin smiled again.

"I will, sir", he said, and left the office.

Chapter 50

Michael was excited almost beyond words. He looked into Nicki's eyes, and could not decide if they were grey, hazel, blue, green or gold. What an unusual woman in every way.

Michael felt like the luckiest guy in the world, even after everything they had gone through. She had agreed to stay with him for a month in his home in Pennsylvania while repairs were being made to her double-wide. Michael couldn't stop smiling.

They had retrieved the buried items from Stickney's car and boxed them up and sent them to his address in Pennsylvania with appropriate accompanying wrapping paper and so forth to keep any shipping X-rays from being likely to draw attention to the box.

The cash from the gym bag had been vacuumed off (in case any of the coke had spilled on it, although it looked clean), stacked neatly, and put into a USPS Priority flat rate box with 'BOOKS' written in marker on one edge. It, too, was sent to 'Brian Stonewell' at his home in Pennsylvania. They had decided against spending any of it in Florida.

And now, because of his leg brace and crutch, they were getting priority boarding on the Southwest Air plane to Philadelphia, where the Gypsy had agreed to pick them up. Nicki had some funds hidden away from her night job as a burglar before they met, and they used a tiny part of it to fly first class. The flight was excellent. The seats were soft and spacious, the drinks kept flowing, and they even had a passably edible lunch.

When they arrived at his home, he rewarded the Gypsy with some of the proceeds from the package waiting there for him, and thanked the Gypsy, who had left quite happy with the transaction, feeling that both sides were balanced.

Michael knew from experience that balance is important to the Gypsies. If one side or the other gets an advantage, it does not bode well for either side, and they will do what is necessary to restore the balance. But it was obvious this transaction met his expectations precisely.

Michael showed Nicki around the house. She marveled at some of the art on the walls and admired the furniture. And he showed her the bedrooms. When we got to his, she looked him straight in the eye.

"You have some healing to do. But when you are healed enough, I plan to spend more than a few nights in this room. Is that okay?"

Of course it was. Michael was beginning to believe he had found a path that might allow him to one day raise a family as his Grandfather had.

The next day, Nicki rode with him on the bus to New York City. He believed her when she said she could drive in the big Apple, but having done so for many years himself, he also knew it is not as easy as it might seem at first. With his leg in restraints Michael wanted no sudden stops and starts. Besides, the bus made talking easier.

When they got to his mid-town office, she asked for a map of the city and the subway system, and they agreed she could wander the city at will doing the tourist bit. Michael would have preferred to go with her, but the crutches would have spoiled a lot of the sights she wanted to see.

After she left, he phoned Shemuel.

"I'm back, and you agreed to do some buying at my store", Michael said into the phone.

"Yes. I can be there in an hour", Shemuel stated.

True to his word, fifty nine minutes later Shemuel walked through the door, accompanied by his sons. Once again, he dispatched them to the hall to stand guard.

Michael brought out the box he had shipped to himself. Shemuel admired the contents, holding some up to the light, measuring others with his finger joints and by their weight in his hands.

"This is very much", Shemuel said. "Much more than I can give you today. Will you trust me to get you the rest within a week?"

"You trusted me through a really tough time", Michael said. "If you hadn't, the killer would've gone free and I would be dead. So if you can trust me, it stands to reason I should trust you."

"I think we will do a lot of business together", Shemuel stated. "Like your Grandfather and my own Father."

"That would please me a lot", Michael said, "but can you tell me now what this was really all about?"

Shemuel thought about it for several moments. Michael suspected a negative answer was coming.

"I have not even told my own children", Shemuel began, "but I will tell you. You have earned the right. You brought my daughter's killer to true justice."

It was really Nicki that had done that, but Michael saw no reason to correct him.

"Between the canvas of the painting and the leather backing that protects it, there is a silken cloth, wrapping a few hundred pages of what is known as the Aleppo Codex. Have you ever heard of the Aleppo Codex?"

"I have not", Michael answered.

"According to the stories of my people, early in the sixth century, a group of sages led by the Ben-Asher family in Tiberias, on the Sea of Galilee, undertook the task of creating a formal and final assembly of all 24 original holy books. They used what is known as codex technology, a method that made it possible to record information on both sides of a page, in book form, as a cheaper alternative to scrolls. This was the first definitive Tanakh, or Hebrew Bible."

"Wow. That has to be valuable."

"Indeed. Almost beyond the ability to place a value. But on Nov. 30, 1947, the morning after the U.N. General Assembly voted in favor of the establishment of a Jewish state, a mob stormed the Jewish quarter of Aleppo, attacking the Jews and demolishing their businesses and setting fire to the synagogues. The Codex was believed lost."

"We can't be talking about IT, can we?"

"No. But when it was later recovered there were some sections missing. Legend has it that anyone stealing the book is cursed, but there have been many attempts to do so. At some point someone decided to preserve it by separating it until the tribes are fully united. What is in the silken wrap is one of those separated portions."

"I can see its historical value. But why not put it all together now?"

"Some pieces are being returned. Recently, a portion of the Book of Exodus, which relates how, after the Nile turned to blood, Aaron stretched forth his staff, causing a plague of frogs to descend on Egypt, was added to the parts on display.

"So why not this part? Why take such risks to hide and protect it?"

"Because in the past greedy men have sought to steal parts of it and not to preserve them. Twenty Million dollars was offered for a part half this size in 1953 by a private collector. It is vital that the codex, and all its parts, be treated as the holy work it is. Only when the time is right can the pieces be safely united."

"I have to say, that is an amazing story."

"And you are a part of the legend, now, because you have restored one part to its caretaker."

"Hunh. Didn't feel much like I was being a legend. But maybe the curse explains some of what happened in Florida, do you think?"

"Stranger stories abound of what has happened to thieves who stole it in the past. I do not judge which stories are true. I only know that a man would have to be very foolish and greedy to steal such a holy work, and such greed and foolishness rarely works out well."

Of course, Michael didn't really believe in curses. On the other hand, like the monkey trap, some diversions can be deadly.

Shemuel left and at the appointed hour, Nicki returned. The two of them went to dinner at a nice restaurant Michael knew which was properly overpriced, where people nonetheless did not dress for the occasion, and which had exquisite food. Over a nice meal and a few rather well aged scotches, they talked.

They talked about the future. They talked about their dreams. They talked about each other. Michael suspected, and hoped, they would be talking for a long time about many things.

The adventure continues . . .

Follow the continuing adventures of Michael O'Shea and Nicki Fontaine at:

http://donrizzo. com/

Stay in touch with Don Rizzo via Facebook:

https://www.facebook.com/profile.php?id=100008491869430

DonRizzo@donrizzo. com

If you liked Death at Sunset, please post a review at Amazon, and let your friends know about the Sunset series.